Mistletoe and Magnolias

by

Leigh Raffaele

Blue Collar Hero

Mistletoe and Magnolias

Cover Art by *Teddi Black*

The Wild Rose Press, Inc.
PO Box 708
Adams Basin, NY 14410-0708
Visit us at www.thewildrosepress.com

Publishing History
First Edition, 2025
Trade Paperback Print ISBN 978-1-5092-6367-7
Digital ISBN 978-1-5092-6368-4

Blue Collar Hero
Published in the United States of America

Dedication

Dave—my husband, and anchor when things get tough
or challenging, you're always there for me.

My children—Robin, Adam, Anthony, and Colleen—
my biggest cheerleaders.

And, my son, David—who fiercely loves his wife and
daughters, and can accomplish anything and
everything…the perfect model for the character, Adam,
my series hero.

Acknowledgements

Thank you to:

JoAnn Fascenelli—whose encouragement, suggestions, and excitement for my writing is a treasured gift.

Captain John Kaufman, Ret.—whose legal advice on crime and incarceration helped bring depth to the story.

Rosemarie Hoover—my 'agent' whose support aids my career in ways I never imagined.

Elise Holck, Owner Calico Country Flowers—your guidance on the inner workings of owning a flower shop brought The Laurel Wreath to life…hope my depiction is correct.

Beth-Ann Kerber, Lena Pinto, and Miriam Allenson—more than the best critique partners…my lifelong friends!

Chapter 1

One thing Adam Carlson learned in his thirty-four years…anything could happen in Cedar Ridge and probably would.

But this?

He rocked his head from side to side, easing the tension from his neck, but relief didn't come. And it wouldn't.

The words he heard played with his mind. The town Adam called home for over a decade stood poised to become the laughingstock of northwestern New Jersey over Stanley Palmer's insane proposal. He focused on the funeral director standing before him and his fellow municipal council members presenting some lamebrain idea to attract more tourists to their village. The Phase One Revitalization they initiated two years ago delivered too many strangers. The suffocating effects of all the tourists descending on their small, rural village ruined the residents' peaceful existence.

Now this?

****

Laurel Eldridge rushed into the large meeting room at the Cedar Ridge Municipal Building, catching the breath that left her lungs, her heart thrumming her chest.

"You're late." Jeanine pushed a whisp of curly blonde hair from her face and extended an agenda and proposal.

Laurel plopped into the adjacent seat next to her friend. "I just closed the flower shop." Her words escaped in a winded huff. The high energy in the room vibrated the emergency council meeting with the large number of people in attendance increasing her curiosity.

With a quick glance at the agenda, she then focused on the members of the village council already seated on the dais at the front of the room.

Darn...she jerked her head in the opposite direction, her pulse quickening at the sight of the youngest councilman.

Adam Carlson.

Always distracting her.

Laurel tore her thoughts from the sight of the long curl of black hair ruggedly cascading over his right forehead boosting his casual style. But that casualness masked his take-charge, get-it-done trait—somewhat appealing on one hand, but also bordering on control freak. Definitely *not* appealing. Laurel peeked again at his infectious smile now molded into a scowl.

"The meeting started a half hour ago," Jeanine whispered.

Laurel returned her attention to the reason for the meeting.

"I know." She fidgeted with her shoes, her feet sore from standing all day. "The flowers for the Gleason wedding took longer than I thought." She glanced at the village funeral director. "What going on with Stanley? Why is Ron from the planning board here, too?"

Jeanine lifted a shoulder and pointed her chin toward the row of seats in the front. "Stanley has some crazy paranormal stuff to ramp up the village revitalization project."

"Para…what?" Laurel snorted and then lowered her voice. "That's ridiculous, especially coming from Stanley." *What made him think the afterlife could save the village's struggling economy?*

"That's what I thought," Jeanine whispered again.

"This is Cedar Ridge." Laurel waved her hand. "Anything's possible."

****

Ghosts?

Yep. Adam heard right.

"Rutledge Manor would provide a destination venue for different groups and events to visit Cedar Ridge." Stanley Palmer puffed his chest. The more he spoke, the more he revved the enthusiastic crowd. "Revolutionary War buffs, ghost chasers, romance readers, séances, war re-enactments; you name it. The manor has the story to entice them all!"

Adam rolled his eyes, then squeezed them tight. The village didn't need nut-job tourists communicating with spirits. This insanity needed to stop before it took hold. But Stanley was a pretty convincing guy, knowing the exact thing to say to people at the right time. Adam didn't want to take chances the town's funeral director would convince the council and planning board chair that he would provide a pot of gold for the village coffers.

"First off," Adam raised a hand to address the attendees. "Rumors the manor is haunted have got to stop. Everyone knows the manor is *not* haunted." He targeted his attention on Stanley. "Weren't you going to keep Rutledge Manor to relocate your funeral home? Why the sudden change?"

Stanley tugged at his collar and wriggled his neck. "To be honest, it's too costly. The funeral home will stay put. And…business has been slow." He raised a hand as the crowd groaned. "Don't get me wrong; that's a good thing. We don't want to lose our friends too soon. Renovating the old manor will take a lot of money," he continued. "But with the *decrease* of our dearly departed, it's not advantageous for me to switch locations. Turning the manor into a tourist attraction would create jobs we desperately need; provide revenue to our businesses. It'll help my bottom line."

"I see your point." Adam sat back in his seat and drummed his fingers on the countertop. A positive cash flow meant staying in business. Without it—in Stanley's terms—business owners dig their own graves. And that's the last thing Adam wanted for his landscape business. "You can't guarantee all those groups will come. What makes you think you can drum up interest?"

"Since the manor is a historical landmark, I've been contacted by the *Historic Network* cable channel to do a short segment. They want to see if they can get interest before signing onto a long-term contract for a series."

"A series!" Adam blurted and straightened his back into an attention position. *Man, this was worse than I thought.* The segment alone would entice hordes of people to town. A series would ruin the village's peaceful existence. Shaking his head while tapping his fingers on the counter, he conjured ways to stop this runaway train.

Spending his entire childhood yearning for a place to settle down had been in his nightly prayers—to be in a real home where he, Mom, and sister, Karen, would be safe. Cedar Ridge had been just the place with its small-town charm and welcoming people. Here, the residents accepted the Carlsons, even though they were aware of his father's sordid past. That's why Adam decided to run for the council and promised to slow the growth, keeping Cedar Ridge the same safe, peaceful place that had healed his family. But wait…"If the manor is a historical landmark, doesn't that mean stringent renovations?"

Stanley lowered his head and paused. Within a few seconds, he raised his eyes. "Yes, that's correct. That's another reason I decided to turn it into a museum. The renovation restrictions cost a pretty penny. Bringing in visitors will help defray the costs."

"Museum?" Mayor Winston Farley leaned forward.

"Yes. The story behind Rutledge Manor is legendary." Stanley aimed his gaze to the dais. "We all know it, but the rest of the world doesn't. A museum tells the story. We can employ a lot of people— townspeople—who lost their jobs when Morrison Shoes closed."

"Well…that is needed." Mayor Farley nodded to his council counterparts.

"Think about it." Stanley raised a hand and counted off fingers. "We'll need tour guides and storytellers, groundskeepers, an event coordinator, publicity, re-enactors, a cleaning staff, a historical curator. A few of the local romance authors can promote Abigail Rutledge and Thomas Baxter's love story and how she haunts the manor every night."

Adam chucked his pen onto the countertop in front

of him. "The manor is *not* haunted! How can you advertise it's haunted when it's not?"

The crowd snickered and cajoled with mutterings of ghosts circulating the room.

"You don't know that for a fact," Stanley challenged.

"And you don't know that to be true. This is crazy!" The sting of hot panic flowed through Adam's veins. "Before Phase One, this place was utopia…a safe, slow-paced village with warm people who helped one another. Life was good, and then we mucked it up with the revitalization. I don't know half the people walking the streets anymore."

"You're right," Mayor Farley said. "But that was before Morrison Shoes closed. Even though you don't like it, Phase One's tourists made it possible for some businesses to stay open. But it's not enough."

"Look…I don't want to be a downer." Adam closed his eyes to regroup, then opened them. "The revitalization is a success. Cedar Ridge looks just as quaint as Cape May. Mission accomplished." He admitted the storefront renovations, paver-stone sidewalks, and antique lampposts copied the Victorian feel of the popular south Jersey shore town.

"But, unlike Cape May, we don't have the mighty Atlantic Ocean to draw people here," Stanley said. "The manor will be *our* draw. It might be the Phase Two we've been searching for."

Adam huffed out a disbelieving breath. "You can't compare the manor with the ocean. Sand beaches, boating, swimming, fine restaurants…we have nothing like that."

"Maybe," Stanley lifted a shoulder. "We can—"

"Where's everyone gonna stay?" Adam raised his voice. "The Comfy Quilt Bed & Breakfast only has six rooms." He eyed the inn's owner sitting in the audience. "No offense, Sarah." Seeing her nod in response, he realigned his gaze on Stanley. "Next thing you're gonna say is we need a motel or hotel for everyone to stay."

Stanley eyes widened with his smile as he nodded. "That might be part of Phase Three."

"Aw...come on." Everyone favored changing the village vibe—everyone, but him. His brain understood it had to change, but his heart wanted it to slow down. He rolled back his chair, almost hitting the wall behind him, putting this craziness aside for a practical solution. "Doesn't this need to go before the planning board?"

"It will. I just wanted to let everyone know my plan. Right, Ronald?" Stanley nodded toward the Planning Board Chair who returned a nod.

"Excuse me," a woman's voice echoed from the opposite side of the room.

"Hello, Laurel," the mayor greeted.

"Hi, everyone." Standing, she scanned all the familiar faces in the meeting room.

Mayor Farley signaled for her to continue.

"The story behind Abigail and Thomas is a heart-wrenching one. Yes, we don't know for sure if the manor is haunted." A low hum of snickers rumbled throughout the room, and Laurel paused. "Just the implication of a lovesick, young lady crying at night because her true love was killed in battle brings an element of romance and drama. If you renovate the manor to its 1700s glory, it will restore the romance, not just of lost lovers, but the elegance of the estate with beautiful outdoor gardens, elegant furnishings, and opulent linens."

Concerned her enthusiasm egged on the crowd, Adam noticed how her eyes sparkled like Christmas lights when she described her vision with passion and excitement. What did she have to do with Stan's plan?

"It lends itself to china and lace tea parties, garden events, especially weddings," Laurel gushed. "The fields behind it are perfect for the re-enactments Stanley mentioned." Her gaze landed on Stan. "You're right; the manor would draw many different groups."

The hairs on the back of Adam's neck stood like porcupine quills. He didn't get it. Not the manor thing...the Laurel Eldridge thing. Ever since learning she moved back to town two years ago, whenever he ran into her, he got the sudden urge to hightail it away...far away.

He wasn't afraid of much...well, maybe bears, since he almost got mauled by one on a hike at Stephen's State Park back in the day. But that was his secret. And the biggest secret of all, the one that pressured him into panicked nightmares, was being compared to his father. Adam spent most of his life proving his honesty and trustworthiness to the world...nothing like his old man.

Tamping that fear, he glanced at Laurel again. Easy to talk to, cute in a girl-next-door way, and very driven about business. Yeah...something about her was special...but no way could he get involved with a woman who didn't fit his imaginary checklist for the perfect mate. Even though he shouldn't worry since she didn't come close to that list, he couldn't deny how his senses signaled alert.

He squirmed in his seat, distracting himself from how persuasive she sounded about Stanley's proposal. *Why is it so important?* Tourists don't buy flowers from the local florist when they come to town. *What's her angle?* "Can I ask a question?" Adam swiveled his chair so he could face the council.

"You may," Mayor Farley said.

He focused on Laurel. "I see you're on board with Stan on this one."

"Yes, I am." Her eyes shimmered under the harsh fluorescent lights. "It's the best idea presented since we started Phase One two years ago. The revitalization *you* were opposed to." Her short nod drove home her point.

She sure knows which buttons to push. Add quick on the fly to the girl-next-door cuteness. *Forget cute…she called you out!*

"I wasn't *opposed*. I wanted to make sure we did it slowly and practically." He inhaled with a rise of his chest, stiffened his neck, and exhaled a heavy breath. "People and cars are crammed in all over the place. It's great on weekdays when there isn't an event planned; it's almost like it used to be. But the weekends are crazy. The sand sculpture competition at Wilkinson's Pond in August was no beach party. The apple harvest brought in waaay too many people who drank more than apple cider."

Murmurs of agreement radiated from the audience validating his point.

"Pembrooke Farms' horse competition is this week. Don't forget the harvest festival next week. Gonna be larger than last year." Maybe he could find a way to sway their thinking. "If you're attracting people obsessed with ghosts, you're going to have strangers dressed in costumes. Think of our safety."

"Let's hope there're no clowns," one person shouted, "They give me the creeps!"

"Order, please!" The mayor pounded the gavel a few times, and laughter radiated through the meeting room.

When Adam again connected gazes with Laurel, he readied himself for whatever she'd dish out. In an odd way, her spunk was kind of a turn-on.

She sprang from her seat, her hands gripping the back of the seat in front of her. "Adam, even though you view those events as bad things, they're great for us. This town will die if we don't do something. Phase One helped, but we need more. You don't want the town to change, but it has to or it might become a ghost town."

The audience laughed again.

"Sorry for the pun." She lowered her gaze, and her shoulders rose with a heavy sigh. A few seconds later, palms up, she opened her hands toward the council. "I wish you would seriously consider this."

Adam noticed her brief glance.

Then she focused on the rest of the council members. "I'm excited about Rutledge Manor. We need it."

Adam's nerves kicked into overdrive, not at all comfortable with volleying with Laurel. No matter how many points he raised, he suffered her quick response. "Too many important things are at stake to consider before you all jump on this haunted hayride," he said. "I asked the question several times in the past, and I'm askin' it again, where the hell are they all going to park?"

"Adam, please refrain from profanity," Mayor Farley scolded, and leaning toward the village clerk, he covered the microphone with one hand. "Strike that word from the minutes."

"Crowded streets aren't such a bad thing," Laurel continued. "The slow-moving traffic gives tourists a chance to see what the stores have to offer."

"Has that helped *your* store?" Why is this nightmare such a good thing for her?

"To be honest, no." Laurel stroked the ponytail that rested on her right shoulder. "It hasn't. That's why I'm psyched about the manor. It might create a little extra business for my shop."

"How?"

"Hmmm…" She squinted and pushed a strand of wavy, brown hair from her face and squared her shoulders. "In the spring, shortly before he died, Thomas gave Abigail magnolias as a sign of his love. The morning before he died, he was going off to war, so instead of one magnolia, he gave her two…one to represent each of them. It's rumored those flowers are still in the house…that she dried and pressed them into her bible."

Adam took a second to process the connection between the history lesson and her flower shop. "So, how will that help *your* business?"

"I'll be able to sell silk magnolias as Abigail's Magnolias—provide them for the museum gift shop. Given the time period, the lady of the manor always instructed the staff to have fresh-cut flowers from the gardens decorate the inside of the house each day." Laurel faced Stanley. "I'd like to submit a bid for those flower arrangements."

"Excellent idea, Laurel!" Stanley shot his gaze to Adam. "I welcome Greene Thumb Landscape Designs to submit a bid for the initial landscaping and ongoing maintenance."

Adam hadn't thought of that. But that was beside the point. "Aren't we getting ahead of ourselves here?"

"No, not really," Stanley said. "This is what *I* propose. I'll submit everything to the planning board. Since Laurel and Adam are the most passionate about this, I'd like their help to iron out the project's pros and cons. I'd like to have it opened by Thanksgiving."

"Thanksgiving?" Adam and Laurel responded together, then looked at each other, their mouths wide open.

"Great idea!" the mayor declared. "Report your findings in two weeks. This way we'll have an unbiased report so we can make an informed decision." He banged the gavel. "Seeing no further discussion, meeting's adjourned."

Adam turned his gaze at the mayor. *What have I gotten myself into?*

****

Laurel felt her insides jump and jiggle and bounce. Finally, a light at the end of her financial tunnel.

Stanley was a genius.

The manor would benefit many Cedar Ridge businesses, and Laurel needed this…needed it bad. It had the potential to increase her business. More importantly, she could give Pop a decent paycheck for doing odds and ends around the shop and delivering flowers instead of the pittance just about covering his groceries.

Supporting Pop and the flower shop led to financial

exhaustion. "It's going to take a Christmas miracle to keep me and Pop going." She leaned closer to Jeanine. "This might be the answer we've been looking for."

"Maybe Santa can help." Jeanine snorted with a rise of her shoulders. "And while you're at it, ask Santa to help with your social life. That definitely needs help."

Laurel couldn't help rolling her eyes, then leveling her gaze on her friend. "My social life is fine."

"Two dates in two years is *not* a social life." Jeanine's laser stare accompanied her arms folded across her chest.

Laurel pushed the stray strands of flyaway hair from her face. "I don't need another lecture. This project is much more important than my social life."

"Agreed. But if you got back out there, then I wouldn't have to lecture you." Jeanine gave a sharp nod.

She loved Jeanine like a sister, but, hearing it over and over again grew old.

Ignoring the scowl on Jeanine's face, she imagined how Stanley Palmer's proposal would benefit her. Giddiness flowed through her that if approved, her flower shop, The Laurel Wreath, might bloom into the black zone instead of wilting into the red.

"This is a dream come true." Jeanine smirked. "You and the handsome Adam Carlson working together. Seems like Cupid got his months mixed up. He doesn't usually shoot his bow in October." She nudged shoulders with Laurel. "He'll have to work overtime on this one."

"Get real." Laurel tsked. "I'm not interested. He's not my type."

"Haven't you heard? Opposites attract."

Totally Venus vs Mars. "Not interested," Laurel repeated, already tired of the topic. She hadn't attended council meetings since Adam came on board. The last time she'd seen him this serious, he had opposed Phase One. Other than that, the man's smile never wavered. He always joked with people, full of fun, and not too serious. Laurel had too much on her plate to think about fun. "You date a lot." She moved back a smidge and flung her gaze toward Jeanine. "*You* date him."

"Me?" Jeanine snorted. "He's definitely not my type."

"He's *exactly* your type. He dates one person after another."

"Nope." Jeanine shook her head for several seconds. "He dates for a different reason. Rumor has it, no one measures up to his expectations. I also think he's scared."

"Scared?" Laurel gaped at her friend. "Of what? He's the most confident, self-assured person around. Won re-election by a landslide. From what I've seen, he's a flower cooler full of strength and security." *AKA control freak.* She scoffed and crossed her legs away from Jeanine. "What's he got to be afraid of?"

"Not sure. Maybe his expectations are so high because he's afraid to settle down. You know…be careful what you wish for and all that." Jeanine examined her nails and then waved a hand. "I think he wants it, but he's afraid of it."

Laurel titled her head at Jeanine and sneered. "Nice psychoanalysis coming from someone who never dates a guy longer than three dates?"

"Yes, because I *don't* want to settle down. And I

don't want kids. Nope!" Jeanine popped her lips.

Laurel studied her friend and swiveled to face her. "You always said that, but don't you want—"

"No way." Jeanine shook her head and pursed her lips. "I had my share raising kids. That's what I get for being the oldest of six. Free babysitting for Mom. Nope. I'm over it."

Laurel remembered all the times she helped Jeanine with her siblings. She loved the energy and life all those kids excited into the house. While she didn't see kids in her near future either, she wanted them—a whole houseful—especially since she grew up an only child.

But Pop and The Laurel Wreath were her priority now. And, if she were honest, diving into her business and caring for her father—even though he didn't need it—helped ease the pain of losing her mother. The tragedy she suffered at twelve-years old still burned her heart.

And her business…she worked too hard and too long to build her flower shop to its present state. That shop saved her from the grief she endured for years, bringing newfound joy into her life. The satisfaction of owning the business she loved and moving into her wonderful apartment where she "found herself" was one of the best times of her life.

But once again, fate intervened.

She had no regrets moving back home with Pop, but living with the reminders of where she had lost her mother kept the heartbreak alive.

Now fate stepped in again, although this time, presenting her with a positive option. Working with Stanley on Rutledge Manor presented a hopeful outlook that things were about to get better.

****

A few minutes later, Laurel readjusted her ponytail, smoothed the front of her jacket, and said goodbye to Jeanine. Then she marched toward Adam. Offering her hand, she presented a firm handshake, keeping it all business while resisting the warmth and comfort of his hand tantalizing her palm. "I realize the apprehension you have about the manor," she said, "I'm going to make a believer out of you."

"You are, huh?" When he arched a full, dark-brown eyebrow, a slight chuckle escaped his throat, but he didn't release her hand. "It'll take more than a sappy love story to make me believe there's a ghost flying around that old place. And even more evidence all those tourists won't change our town."

"Oh, they'll change it. They already have. But that's a good thing." A surprising, not-so-good thing was her hand still in his. She didn't hesitate to withdraw it to focus on the reason for the handshake and not the feelings it stirred.

Adam rubbed the back of his neck, and his smile waned. "A good thing for who? Have you tried to drive through Main Street on a Saturday? Or worse, grabbed a coffee at The Bean & Brew? Everyone's forced to take the back roads on Friday afternoons because traffic is snarled on Main. I can't get my truck and trailer through. It wasn't a problem before the revitalization."

"I get that. I really do—" She forced herself to keep her mind on the problem and not the darn soft tuft of hair cascading his forehead or the warmth still gracing her palm "—but for most of us, it's a huge help. If it wasn't for the new town events, I would have had to close The Laurel Wreath. Supplying the flowers for the lampposts and giant planters in the business district saved *my* business."

"Business district?" Adam moaned and pushed the hair from his eye. "Just the sound of it makes my skin crawl. We have a two-road intersection of village stores. We're not a business district, although it feels like it now." Grabbing the back of a nearby chair, he took on a sad tone. "We're ruining it all."

Gone was the happy-go-lucky guy she was used to seeing. His genuine sadness and pain at losing something precious touched her heart…the same heart that experienced the pain of loss. "I'm going to convince you we're not ruining it." An overwhelming impulse to touch him caused her to rest her hand on his arm.

When their gazes united, an odd connection lingered causing her to hold onto his arm a little longer with an unexpected awareness tingling her chest. Removing her hand, she took note of his gaze glancing at it. "We need more." Her emotions were stirred by his vulnerability, and she cleared her throat. "Much more. The ideas have to come from us so we can control how much we grow. I agree, if we grow too fast or too much, it wouldn't benefit Cedar Ridge."

****

Adam took a step back and eyed the florist. She had been a few years behind him in high school and seemed like a great person. But now, in addition to the images of a picket fence and two-to-three kids that always accompanied her, a connection spread through him like wildfire.

He shook off that reaction since she was now an

opponent—guaranteed they'd buck heads. Watching her confidence level increase, Adam suspected he'd be unable to change her mind. She was a strong, determined woman who met everything head-on, which he admired. But…

Now Stanley wanted them together to trouble shoot something Adam wanted no part of. Laurel was the real trouble in more ways than one. He didn't want to spend time with her. And he didn't want *her* to convince *him* the manor was a good idea. Things needed to go back to the way they were when he first moved to Cedar Ridge thirteen years ago when things were quiet, and safe, and secure. And that wasn't happening seeing the commitment and determination in Laurel's eyes. He suspected she'd be harder to stop than a self-propelled lawn mower.

Chapter 2

Adam yanked the gas-powered edger out of his landscape trailer, his feet pounding the pavement of the bank parking lot. It burned his butt and still haunted him that Laurel tried to steamroll him into agreeing with Stanley's project. The Greene Thumb Landscape and Design logo—artfully painted on the sides of his landscape trailer—was bright and cheerful and nothing at all like his sour mood.

"What the hell is wrong with you?" Parker Greene asked.

"That meeting kept me awake last night." Adam growled at his best friend. After tossing all over the mattress, twisting the sheets, punching his pillow, he couldn't get his mind to relax.

"Man, you gotta let it go. The revitalization is here to stay. It's best for everyone."

Adam yanked the edger's pull cord hard that the sharp tug twisted the muscle in his neck—the same muscle had knotted with the idea of the Rutledge Manor renovation changing Cedar Ridge. "Best for everyone? For who?" He thrust a hand in the air. "Is it helping Ridge Grocery? Frank Eldridge? How about Arnold the butcher?"

Parker leaned his tall frame on the handle of the zero-turn mower and stared. "Elliott's doing well at the grocery store. Frank works for Laurel at the flower shop. And Arnold's shop is okay."

"*Okay*? Okay isn't good enough." Adam dropped the edger to the ground and paced the small area, a million concerns rushing through his brain. "The monthly festivals and contests are bringing in tons of tourists. Are any of those tourists buying pork chops from Arnold? And Elliott…he always said he'd never work for his father—"

"Yeah, he did." Parker slid one hand into a pair of work gloves. "But now he likes it. Getting into managing the grocery store. Said he'd like to supply food for the manor."

Adam stopped pacing, staring at Parker. "Not him too!" He threw his hands into the air and dropped them with a slap to the sides of his thighs. "What about Frank? He's delivering flowers for his daughter. The tourists aren't helping *him*."

Laurel's sacrifice in giving up her own place to relocate back home to support her father showed her generous spirit. Working at her fledging store had to be a financial burden, but obviously, Frank meant more than her bottom line. Darn admirable and impressive in his book.

"You're right." Parker slid on the other glove. "It's gotta be tough. I'm sure she can't pay Frank much."

"Exactly." Grateful Parker understood, Adam stopped pacing. "We need this madness to end. Come up with alternative to ghosts, get our town back to normal."

"It can't. Morrison changed that. This manor thing might be the answer to help Laurel, Frank, and the rest of the town."

"Maybe, but at what cost to Cedar Ridge?" For a

long minute, silence hung between them. He cringed, waiting for Parker to recite something he didn't want to hear.

"Are you gonna re-open the shoe factory?" And there it was.

"No…Maybe…I don't know." Adam slumped his shoulders in an exhausting breath. "There's got to be another idea. And yeah…something's telling me that old factory is the answer."

"No one's got that kind of money." Parker placed a knit hat over his brown hair. "And even if they did, there's no guarantee there'd be enough jobs for everyone."

Hard to admit it, but Parker had a point. After moving from house to house, town to town, at the speed to rival an Army brat, Adam's family settled their move-weary bones into one home, in one town, for more than one year. For the past thirteen years, Cedar Ridge was home. The people became part of his extended family. Like a security blanket, they had wrapped him and his family snuggly into their fold—all warm and safe. As a child, he dreamed of a place like the idyllic village each time his parents packed them up to live in another town far from bill collectors.

"Man, you gotta let it go." Parker stepped away from the mower, facing Adam straight on. "This place is not the perfect place it is in your head. Remember when that Beek & Hoof chain opened? It almost wiped out all the eateries in town."

Adam bobbed his head with a weighty sigh. "Thank God, everyone boycotted that chicken and burger place."

"And what about that used car dealership?" Parker

pointed a finger his way. "We were lucky the Feds shut the place for embezzlement. How many of our friends got roped in by those guys, paying more money than the cars were worth?"

"See, that's what I'm afraid of." Adam retrieved the edger to get back to work; they wasted enough time on the subject. "More crazies coming in and destroying the peace."

"I know what this place means to you." Parker took Adam's lead by adjusting the lever on the mower. "You're not that seventeen-year-old with a chip on your shoulder anymore. We've got the business; so does your mom. Time to move forward."

Parker had a point. Ma fought to keep them out of poverty; didn't matter…the old man gambled away her efforts. Through it all, she shielded him and Karen from the ugliness. Once Adam found out about his father's "job," he wanted no part of him. "We *have* moved forward." He couldn't shake the open wound of his father's illegal gambling and racketeering that put their family through hell. "The best thing that ever happened was the old man spending time in state prison. At least, we got on our feet without him blowing through whatever money we saved."

Adam savored those five years when he, Ma, and Karen lived like a normal family. No stress or worry about phone calls or surprise visits from bill collectors. They chipped in, worked two jobs each to pay the debt Ned Carlson had amassed. Their rented house had been Adam's home until last year when he leased his own apartment. And Karen headed off to her dream job in Atlanta. He didn't blame her. She always wanted to see the world. Not Adam. He wanted to stay planted in one place, get married, raise a houseful of kids, and grow old right here in Cedar Ridge…the place that represented safety and security.

"You all survived okay." Parker picked up a gas can and placed the nozzle in the mower tank. "Now it's time Cedar Ridge got back on its feet with Stanley's plan."

"But—"

"Hey, man." Parker arched an eyebrow and stopped filling the mower. "Let it go. You're a respected member of the community. You need to do what's best for the town. That's why they elected you to the village council."

Right. The council. Even though he opposed the initial revitalization, he'd done his part to help those hurting. He cut a few neighbor's lawns for free and hired some to help feed their families or pay a few bills. One hundred plus people out of work in the village of 1,600 was a lot of mouths to feed. But bringing in tourists was not his idea of how to fix the problem. His decision to run for village council was the only way to help slow things to preserve the calm existence he treasured.

As far as ideas for the old shoe factory fixing the problem…he promised himself to think of something to take care of the residents.

And, unlike his father, Adam always stood by his word. But this promise seemed like the hardest to keep.

****

The next morning, Laurel channeled her good mood about Rutledge Manor into positive energy. Getting a jump on her work, she fashioned a length of kelly green-colored ribbon into a bow for a casket spray when the bells over the front door jingled.

A customer. What a great start to the day!

Sprinting from the prep-room into the front display room of The Laurel Wreath, she skidded into an abrupt stop.

Ugh! Clarice Carlson. There goes my great morning.

She forced her lips into a grin, almost certain Adam's aunt would wilt her good mood. "Clarice, nice to see you." The flower-packed display room, swirling with the heavenly aroma of flora that always soothed Laurel's soul, now became claustrophobic with Clarice's presence sucking the air from the room. "What brings you here so early?"

Posed with a tapestry-flowered handbag hooked on one bent arm, her other hand on her hip, a gleam in Clarice's eyes meant trouble.

"I need a small arrangement for my sister-in-law." She tsked and smoothed her mop of jet-black, dyed, wavy hair. "She hasn't been right lately." With an exaggerated pout, and an insincere smile, she fluttered a hand to her chest. "So, *me*, being such a wonderful supporter of all good things, I thought some flowers would cheer her up."

Supporter of good? Clarice? The woman is delusional.

Hearing Clarice raise her voice an octave and switch to her saccharine-sweet tone, Laurel cringed at the signal of more trouble.

"What a nice gesture. I didn't realize Molly wasn't feeling well." Laurel cocked her head as she recalled Adam's mother appeared to be her usual delightful, happy self last night. "She seemed fine at the meeting."

"Oh, she's a good one at hiding things, she is."

Clarice's saccharine tone dissolved.

"Certainly has *a lot* of practice keeping things under wraps," she murmured under her breath.

Molly and Clarice Carlson—married to two brothers—might share the same last name but were worlds apart. Molly was kind and generous, while Clarice was…Clarice.

"Let's see what we can do to lift her spirits." *And get you out of here ASAP.* Laurel stepped to the large, double-door cooler and pointed to one of the sliding glass doors. "How about this fall arrangement? It's cheery like Molly with autumn-colored mums in a cornflower ceramic pot."

"That's our Molly, all cheery and bright," Clarice declared again, more sarcasm dripping from her words.

Laurel cleared her throat. "Do you want to take it now, or have it delivered?"

"I'd hate to impose on delivery. It's such a shame your father—the foreman of a national company—is now forced to do such an insignificant job of delivering flowers. I don't know how a man handles something *so* demeaning."

Laurel nearly choked on her tongue. That she couldn't do more for her father was bad enough, but to imply an honest job demeaning—that went too far!

"Delivery is an important part of service *all* flower shops provide." She compressed her lips and sucked in a breath.

"All right then. Delivery it is. I'm due at the meeting of the Ladies' Auxiliary for the Knights of Cedar Ridge. I'm the president, you know." She squared her shoulders and puffed her ample bosom.

"Must be punctual!"

"No problem." Laurel retrieved the arrangement from the cooler and sprinted behind the counter. Placing the flowers on the repurposed barnwood top Pop made, she pointed to the credit card machine. "Do you want them delivered to her house or The Cookie Cottage?"

Clarice inserted her card.

"Hmmm." Clarice pointed a wrinkled finger at her chin and tapped several times. "The Cookie Cottage," she declared with a nod. "No matter how Molly's feeling, she's always at that store." Her hand swung in the air in a high, dismissive wave. "It's as if the world can't survive one day without Molly's cookies. Honestly, I don't know how she does it, especially with her no-good husband."

Most people realized things weren't right in the Ned Carlson household. But that didn't give Clarice the right to blab about it all over town. She should keep family issues private since she was talking about her brother-in-law.

Laurel bit her bottom lip to keep from telling Clarice she was nothing but a gossip and overall horrible person, so she concentrated on adding a rust-colored bow to the flower arrangement. "Molly does make the best cookies in town." Laurel shifted her gaze to Clarice for a second and shot it downward to fuss with the flowers in the arrangement. "Running her own business makes her happy. Her contribution to the community." *Unlike you, creating havoc wherever you go!*

"Sooo, anywayyy." She moved closer to the counter. "You and my nephew seemed to go at it pretty well last night."

A flush of heat warmed Laurel's face at the mention of Adam, and she pivoted, pretending to rearrange a few things on the shelf behind her, hiding her reaction at the mention of Adam from Clarice. Their ping-ponging confrontation played in her head all night, even though she tried to silence it by thinking of her proposal to Stanley.

"I'm not sure how I feel about Stanley's idea. We all know Rutledge Manor *isn't* haunted, but I do like his plan. And you're right." She tapped the top of the counter several times to command Laurel's attention, forcing Laurel to turn. "You'd be able to supply flowers, which is good since you don't have a husband. Extra money helps, what with supporting your father and all." Clarice shook her head and tsked again. "Such a shame the two of you are all alone, since your mother is gone, may she rest in peace—" she made the sign of the cross on her chest "—and you *never* married, it—"

"Oh, look at the time, Clarice!" The St. Aloysius church bells around the corner on Elm Street chimed the half hour. "Don't want to miss your meeting." Laurel rushed from behind the counter, ushering the woman toward the door. "Your members are waiting. How would it look for their president to be late? Remember, punctuality."

"Oh, yes, yes, you're right."

Laurel opened the door.

With another jingle of the bells, Clarice glanced back. "You'll take care of those flowers for Molly?"

"Of course, you be on your way now. Have a good day." Laurel released a sigh, watching the middle-aged blabbermouth parade out the door.

But then the door flew open, and in popped Clarice's head. "Don't worry, dear. About being alone, I mean. You'll find Mr. Right, eventually. People like you need to be patient. Bye-bye." With a wave and a gust of cool, fall wind, the door closed, and Clarice was gone.

If only a house would fall on her.

Waiting a few seconds to make sure Clarice didn't return—reeling in her frustration—Laurel charged into the back prep-room at the same time her father, Frank, entered the rear door from one of his *insignificant* deliveries. "That Clarice Carlson is the most mean-spirited person I've ever met!"

"Yep—" Pop agreed, his tone straightforward while he hung his quilted flannel on the hook near the door. "—that would be right. Was she here?"

"You bet she was. Rode in on her broom to remind me I'm not married, I'm supporting you, and the work we do is insignificant."

"She came to say all *that*?" Pop snickered while grabbing the morning edition of the *Cedar Ridge Sentinel* lying on his favorite chair.

"No, thank goodness." Readying herself to get back to work, she fastened a few unruly lengths of long curls into a hair clip. "She ordered flowers for Molly. It would have been worse if she hadn't bought anything."

Hearing Pop snort a burst of laughter, Laurel shot her attention in his direction. "What's so funny?"

A teasing smile spanned Pop's face, causing the crow's feet near his eyes to deepen. "Looks like there's more than one Carlson rattlin' your cage this week."

Laurel blew a stray hair from her eye, aiming a sideways glance at Pop. "What do you mean?"

"Adam," he chuckled. "You two were going at it pretty good last night. Put on a mighty entertaining show."

Darn and double darn. The flush of heat warming her face minutes ago returned, and again, she busied her hands with the ferns on the casket spray. "We weren't *that* bad." She picked at the greens, summonsing determination to replace embarrassment. "I'm a little disappointed he can't see how good it will be, but he's nothing I can't handle."

Another chuckle left Pop's throat, and he leaned against the workstation next to her. "I gotta say, it was the first time I enjoyed one of those boring town meetings. What with Stanley and the ghosts, and you and Adam…yep, pretty entertaining."

"Glad I gave you a good time." Laurel rolled her eyes and faced him, exhaling an impatient breath.

Turning serious, Pop pointed the edge of the newspaper toward her. "Adam's going to be a hard nut to crack."

"I'm not worried." She refused to let the charm he oozed distract her from her mission. "Once he sees the facts, he'll come around."

Both Pop's eyes opened wide. "I wouldn't be so sure. He's pretty dug in. I don't know why that boy's hell-bent on keeping Cedar Ridge in a time warp. He's a good guy, a little stubborn at times, but his heart's in the right place."

Laurel sent a curious glance at her father. His assessment of Adam seemed a little strange. Yes, over the years Adam proved he cared about the community, even if he wasn't a middle-aged person with a family like the other council members. He helped countless residents, including Pop several times. In fact, the two of them seemed to have a strong bond. But that didn't explain his unwillingness for the village to change.

"Don't worry about Adam." Pop patted her on the shoulder, then sat in his chair. "He'll come around."

"He doesn't scare me. When I get done with him, he'll realize Rutledge Manor is the answer to our prayers."

Frank glanced at the *Sentinel*, then turned a page. "I don't doubt it."

"Oh, I have to get in touch with Stanley to schedule a date for Adam and me to tour the manor." Laurel scooted to her makeshift desk, surrounded by boxes of ribbons and foam forms to scribble a reminder on a sticky note, adhering it to the frame of her laptop screen.

"A date, huh?" Pop peered over the newspaper, raising his gray eyebrows. "A little Freudian slip?"

Darn! "A meeting...I meant a meeting." Her face flamed hotter than a grill on the Fourth of July, and she fidgeted with the odds and ends on her desk. It wasn't a slip, but that didn't stop her reaction at the mention of his name that had her thinking all kinds of illogical things, knocking her off her game.

"If Stanley wants to meet with you and Adam, he should be the one to call." Pop rose, laid the newspaper on his chair, and placed a hand over hers to stop fidgeting. "I'll tell him to give you a call." He leaned forward and kissed her forehead, then retrieved the casket spray. "You don't have to take care of the world, you know."

"I know, but I'm excited about what the manor can do for us." With her hands twisting together, she released them in a light clap. "I can't wait to get started."

"All righty then. While you're out saving the world, I'm gonna deliver this to the funeral home."

Translation: Laurel wouldn't see Pop for at least another hour once he and Stanley started talking. "Okay, but don't take too long. I'm adding just a few more baby's breath to this arrangement, and then it's got to go to Molly at The Cookie Cottage."

"No problem. The Cookie Cottage is my favorite."

"That's because Molly always gives you free cookies." Laurel winked with a smile.

"You betcha." An impish grin stretched at his lips, and he wagged his eyebrows. "Be back in a flash."

She rushed to grab her cell phone to text Stanley and Adam. She convinced herself the giggles vibrating in her throat were about the manor…they couldn't be about seeing Adam again…could they?

****

"Now what?" Adam palmed the steering wheel, puffed his cheeks, and dragged out a long breath while his truck was deadlocked in traffic on Main Street.

If it's like this on a weekday, what the hell will it be like this weekend?

There goes a quick trip to The Cookie Cottage to grab lunch. If his mother, Molly, hadn't purposely cooked meatloaf and baked macaroni and cheese for him and Parker, then he would have gone to Lou's Luncheonette for his usual Reuben. Ah…Lou. Been going to Lou's Luncheonette ever since his first day of high school. No crowds, same customers, and Lou…a substitute father figure.

Whatever caused the traffic backup, Adam didn't

care. Mom made lunch, and he and Parker couldn't pass up a home-cooked meal made just for them, so he needed an alternative route to dodge the chaos.

With all the events, navigating his truck through Cedar Ridge's narrow streets resembled an obstacle course on a kid's game show. And Stanley wanted to bring in more tourists? Nope. Not while Adam had a say.

When an opening in the traffic surfaced, he turned onto Primrose Lane, waved at Sarah who raked leaves in front of her Comfy Quilt B & B, and sailed the back roads like an Indy driver to get to the end of town. After a line of trees, The Cookie Cottage appeared in the distance. *This traffic nonsense better stop…and soon.*

Again, he let his thoughts drift to the abandoned Morrison Shoe Factory on the edge of town holding the answer. After a few hours of brainstorming last night, he was grateful some options surfaced, and he planned to discuss them with Parker, and maybe float them passed Mom. One of the ideas had to work because if it didn't, Cedar Ridge would change forever.

****

Laurel strolled along Main Street to The Cookie Cottage with Molly's flowers in hand, walking straight into the wind announcing winter's impending arrival. She finished making the last of the Gleason wedding bows when Pop called to say standstill traffic at Main and Elm kept him from delivering Molly's flowers. If he did, he'd be late delivering at his part-time job at the food bank. Something about livestock trailers lining the entire roadway into Pembrooke Farms. She forgot arrival day for the annual horse-riding competition happened today. Since Pop sounded disappointed about not delivering to Molly—because he'd miss out on her cookies—Laurel planned to buy him a half dozen.

Passing several trailers with various equine sounds echoing from them and the distinct whiff of horses and hay, she scooted past the farm's congested entrance, continuing to the end of the block just before the Grover's Park entrance.

She spotted the old Victorian that housed The Cookie Cottage—the last building on the block before the autumn-colored trees of the park. The aroma of fresh-baked goodness wrapped her in a warm hug, reminding her of when she and Momma had baked together. The memory of ginger snaps rushed to her taste buds, forming a lump in her throat. Sixteen years since her mother's passing, and the hurt was still raw. Swallowing hard, she mounted the steps, pushing open the heavy, glass and wooden door of the bakery to enter.

"Laurel! What a pleasant surprise!" Molly lumbered her petite but plump frame from behind the glass display counter to embrace her. "It's so good to see you. What have you got there?" She nodded toward the flowers.

Each time she encountered Molly's warm welcome made her miss Momma more, and she appreciated Molly's nurturing manner.

Laurel presented the arrangement. "For you. A little pick-me-up."

Molly inspected the colorful array, then her forehead crinkled under her wispy brown bangs. "Whatever for?"

"There's a card." Laurel pointed to the small yellow square peeking out from the top.

Seeing Molly place the flowers on one of the guest tables and retrieve the card, Laurel mentally recited the inscription while Molly read aloud. *Hope today cheers you and bring you happy memories! Clarice.* Laurel stopped murmuring the words—

"Wait a minute." Molly halted. "This isn't Clarice's handwriting." She tilted her chin, turning an eye on Laurel. "You wrote the card, didn't you?"

"Guilty. It happens a lot." Laurel slanted a meek smile and lifted a shoulder. Yes, for phone or online orders, but after Laurel had rushed Clarice out of her store, she called to ask if Clarice wanted to include a card.

"Of course, I do. It's proper etiquette." Clarice's audible huff had sounded through the phone. "I'm in the middle of my meeting, write something. But make it appropriate. I've got to uphold my reputation of being considerate and proper."

Two words that didn't describe Clarice, but she was a paying customer, so Laurel included her usual short and appropriate greeting.

"Laurel, these flowers are beautiful!" Molly bent her head to sniff. "Thank you."

"You're welcome. How are you feeling today? Better than last night?"

"Last night?" Molly cocked her head and squinted her eyes. "I was fine last night. Why do you ask?"

"The flowers." Laurel aimed her chin at the arrangement. "Clarice said you were out of sorts."

"Good Lord! That woman sure loves to spread rumors. If she wasn't my sister-in-law, then I'd try to run her out of town!" She pursed her lips and tapped her forehead. "What *does* go on in her head?"

"I'm fine. In fact, I'm better than fine." She took Laurel by the hand. "I'm glad you agreed with Stanley last night. The Rutledge Manor project is just what we need."

Following Molly into the back kitchen, Laurel's stomach growled with the smell of hot sugar filling her nostrils. Warmth from the old, commercial oven helped relieve the chill from her stroll to Molly's cookie shop. "It smells wonderful in here."

"Thanks." Molly's eyes beamed. "So, last night...when you suggested ideas for the manor—especially the tea parties—my brain spun into overdrive! Sample this new cookie I just made." She handed it to Laurel. "I think it would be perfect for tea at the manor."

Accepting the cookie, Laurel widened her eyes at the heart-shaped, Linzer cookie, sprinkled with pale, pink-colored sugar and a peek of cherry preserves. Laurel took a bite and closed her eyes, tasting the soft-baked, buttery goodness melting on her tongue, followed by the slight hint of tart fruit. "Oh, wow." She kept the confection on her tongue a little longer before swallowing. "These are amazing!"

"I call them Abigail's Hearts." Molly put her hands together in a silent clap.

"Truly amazing." Laurel took another bite.

"What's amazing?"

Sputtering and choking at the sound of the man's voice, Laurel collected herself and turned. "Your mother's cookies," she mumbled with a mouthful, then swallowed. "They're perfect for the manor."

"The—whoa, let's not get carried away." Adam raised his palms, then dropped them. "Nothing's been decided." He pointed to his mother. "Don't count on gettin' rich on those cookies. This manor escapade is not going anywhere."

Molly waved a hand. "Don't pay him any mind, dear." Her hand rested on Laurel's forearm. "Adam won't be happy until all the tourists are gone." The woman spied her son over her shoulder. "That wish is *not* going to happen." Molly focused on Laurel. "We need that manor, and I'll do whatever it takes to get it going."

The warmth of Molly's touch, and her motherly ways, had Laurel longing to spend more time with her. "Thank you, Molly." She looked past the woman. "Adam, I appreciate your view on the manor, but once you see the benefit for everyone—including your mother—I'm sure we'll be able to help Stanley get things rolling."

Adam raised an eyebrow. "Do you now?"

"Yes." She nodded, confident that once he understood the facts, he'd be on board. An uncomfortable awareness wove around her as his gaze made her knees weak and her stomach flip-flop.

The stare changed when his head tilted to the side, and his eyes narrowed. "You're very sure of yourself, aren't you?"

Oh...you better believe it. "Yes." *Yes, to the manor. And yes, to controlling my sophomoric attraction.*

"And you think you can convince me this lamebrain idea is going to—" he made air quotes with his fingers "—save the village."

This time *she* eyed him, ignoring her stomach while bracing her knees tight. "Yes, it will. And it's not a lamebrain idea."

"Ghosts? Seances? TV crews? Are you kidding?"

She secured her arms across her chest, preparing for another spirited rally like the one she enjoyed last night. "There aren't any ghosts. Do you have a better idea?"

"I'm…I'm workin' on it."

Wait. Is the confident, stubborn Adam Carlson not so sure of himself right now? "Really? So, what is it?" Laurel lowered her chin to stare into his eyes. Watching him squirm was evidence he didn't have an ounce of an idea, because if he did, he would have shared it last night.

"I'm…workin' out the details." Roaming about the kitchen, he lifted a pastry crimper, examined it, put it on the counter, then gave her a sideways glance. "Gotta get all the elements straight before I present it.'

"Elements?" She raised her eyebrows. Yep…a stall tactic. "Yes, getting all the *elements* in line is important." She dropped her arms from her chest, then popped the last of the cookie in her mouth and stared with a firm chin. "How soon do you think you'll have all the *elements* figured out?"

"Soon."

"Okay, while you two joust over this *idea*." Molly moved to the wire shelf unit, "I'm going to get lunch together for you and Parker." She stretched on tiptoes for a cardboard box on the top shelf.

"Hey, Ma, let me get that." Adam sprinted to his mother's aid.

After she received the box, Molly patted his bicep.

The small gesture touched Laurel, hoping Adam appreciated his mother.

"Thank you, dear."

Molly's adoring smile caused Laurel to miss Momma even more.

"Do I smell vanilla, cinnamon sugar cookies?" An unexpected mischievous grin played wide at his lips.

"No, you don't." Molly packed a foil take-out container into the box.

Watching his eyebrows scrunch together was a treat. Laurel didn't think something as simple as sugar cookies should confuse him.

"You know those are for special occasions." Molly laid another take-out container into the box.

Adam leaned toward Laurel. "I don't get it. It sure smells like vanilla to me." Then he stepped closer. "Someone's gotta get married, die, or have a baby to get those goodies."

Okay, invading her personal space startled her a little. Not wanting to call attention to that invasion—even though her heart rate increased tenfold—Laurel just raised her eyebrows and stepped to the side a few inches. "Really?"

"Yes. Only special occasions." Molly winked at Adam.

"Why?" Laurel shuffled a step away, but not before noting the scent of cut grass surrounding him. Her controlling ex always used high-priced aftershave—said it made him feel more powerful in the board room. Never a hair out of place, and his shoes were polished to a shine.

In contrast, Adam's work boots were sprinkled with dry dirt with his uniform showing the hard-working efforts of his morning. Putting in an honest day's work proved the integrity of a person. Much more impressive than the false air of power.

"They're the best cookies in all the land!" Adam shifted from Laurel's side and placed a kiss on his mother's temple. "They have a special meaning to our family."

The exchange twisted Laurel's heart. The fun-loving charm he depended on kept her on guard, but the mother and son bond was undeniable. Adam *did* appreciate Molly, which surprised her. Laurel never expected that, but Pop—who knew him better—said Adam had a big heart, so…

"Everything okay, dear?" Molly folded a foil cover over Adam's lunch.

Maybe Laurel needed to stop misjudging Adam to see what he's all about…in an effort to convince him to agree to the manor project, of course. "Yes. Everything's fine." She refocused her attention and remembered she had work waiting. "I need to get back to the shop. Do you mind if I take half dozen cookies for Pop?"

"Of course, not." Molly came close to settle her in a hug. "You know where the bags are. Great to see you again."

"Thanks." Laurel entered the bakery storefront. Behind the glass display case, she retrieved her father's favorite shortbread cookies and slid them into one of the white paper bags stored in a slot on the back counter. She placed money in a magnetic clip on the side of the cash register.

Adam stood on the opposite side of the display case, a box loaded with two giant, foil-wrapped packages in hand. "You're not going to win this one, you know." He cast a measured gaze her way.

"Oh…I'm not?" She refused to make eye contact but lost the battle.

"Nope."

"Well, it's not *me* wining, it's Cedar Ridge." She folded the top of the cookie bag, calculating a direction to steer the conversation.

"It's important to keep things the way they used to be." He placed the box on the glass countertop.

"Change is good." While she enjoyed their bantering, she needed to gain the upper hand and get him to see her side. "You'll come around."

"Not gonna happen." He tightened his lips and swiveled his head.

Laurel strolled from behind the counter and, this time, scanned the depths of his eyes with an unwavering stare. "I've been warned you're a tough nut to crack."

And just like that, the sensation of her determination increased. "I like nuts." She pasted on a wide smile to throw him off balance before the gratification of challenging him threw her off. "They're hard on the outside, but tender on the inside. Makes me wonder what I'm going to find when I break through your shell."

Chapter 3

Game on.

The nut analogy Laurel threw down at The Cookie Cottage yesterday laid a challenge at Adam's feet—one he'd definitely win.

If Miss Laurel Eldridge intended to play that game, then he was ready, willing, and quite able to take her on. Her sweet, wholesome personality hid a calculating brain inside her cute little head, and Adam welcomed the chance to spar with someone so spirited.

He'd known strong women, but too overbearing; and also determined, driven women who lost sight of the important things life offered. But Laurel's rare, down-to-earth, self-confident combination manifested into a surprising turn-on.

Whoa!

Man, oh, man. He needed to squash that reaction. They were forced to work together to develop a report within two weeks. Okay…two weeks wasn't so bad. Probably take a few hours to show her the manor wasn't the answer. Maybe get together a day or two before the deadline, and that would be that. No sweat.

Just then, the bells from St. Aloysius Church tolled their hourly chime, cloaking Adam with a sense of security. Their trill welcomed him the first day he had arrived in Cedar Ridge, wrapping him and his family in the safe haven of the village. He'd do whatever it took to keep the traffic noise from increasing and drowning out that comforting sound.

With renewed determination, he removed Laurel, her *nut* comment, and the manor from his mind to concentrate on attaching the new belt to his zero-turn mower. He and Parker busted their butts creating the best landscaping Greene Thumb offered, proving to the owners of the medical arts building they were the right company to manicure its campus.

Struggling with wet grass made it difficult to loop the belt around the three pulleys under the blade deck. He wiped sticky grass from the back of his hands onto his pants and paused when his cell pinged. Retrieving it from his belt case, he glanced at the text.

Laurel.

—Stanley's at the manor at 5. Can you make it?—

Darn. That two-week window just got smaller.

****

Three hours later at exactly five pm, Adam drove his SUV onto the stone-and-dirt driveway of Rutledge Manor and parked next to Stanley's funeral home flower car. A split second later, Laurel's old sedan crept in from behind, blocking his vehicle while hampering a convenient quick exit. Stepping from the SUV, he ambled toward her. "A little soon to *jump* into this project, don't ya think?" He squinted at the orange glow that almost blinded him from the late fall sunset.

"No, it's not, and hello to you, too." Laurel smirked her pink lips. "The sooner we *jump*, the better."

The sparkle in her eyes reminded him of tiny lightning bug lights. Okay, scrap that. Laurel was a truckload of trouble. The kind of girl you bring home to Mom, and *his* Mom made it clear how much she loved

42

Laurel. Mom, yes; not what *he* wanted.

A rare person was needed to balance a business and keep family a priority. A little old-fashioned, yeah, but he wanted a woman like his mother. Even though she owned The Cookie Cottage, she always put him and Karen first. Ma showered them with unconditional love and lessons of determination, honesty, and loyalty. That's what he wanted. He vowed to be as devoted and to love and provide the same for his wife and kids. Total opposite of his old man who worshiped money scams over family.

He glanced at Laurel and extended an arm in a gentleman gesture toward the manor. "After you." With a polite nod, he followed on the weather-beaten, brick path leading to the manor's front porch. When a gentle breeze carried the sweet fragrance of vanilla and cinnamon, Adam peered down one side of the street, then the other.

Again?

The Cookie Cottage rested on the far side of town, and Ma insisted she hadn't made his favorite cookies. He sniffed in the subtle scent of vanilla gliding through his nostrils, questioning how the favorite, comforting smell floated all the way through the middle of the village to Hemlock Lane. As shoes crunched on crumbling brick steps, he waited with Laurel on the equally crumbling cement porch when the vanilla-cinnamon scent intensified.

Laurel took hold of the heavy, brass door knocker and grunted, pounding two strikes on the weathered oak. "Stanley better fix this thing." She shook her hand in the air, then rubbed it with the other. "Someone's going to hurt themselves."

Adam glanced at the façade of the manor. While the bricks were in meticulous shape for their age, the wooden window and door frames needed a full, paint soaking. When the door creaked opened, a whoof of musty air and old, damp wood invaded his nostrils.

"Right on time!" Stanley's smile flashed when he opened the door, his gray hair luminous from the foyer chandelier light. "Come in, come in."

As Adam followed Laurel over the threshold, he took in the massive foyer. A wide staircase stood like an old butler waiting to escort them to the second floor. Layers of chipped paint on the newel post and balusters revealed peeks of the original, stained wood resurfacing. A tired stair runner—worn at the center of each step—must have cost a pretty penny when installed to have lasted all these decades.

Parallel to the staircase, a wide hallway looked like it led to the kitchen. Adam glanced left at what he assumed a library with built-in shelves lining the walls. Light—dimmed by layers of grime—filtered through the exterior windows. "How much did you pay for this place?"

"I didn't." Stanley stepped deeper into the foyer. "Marion Rutledge left it to me. Said I'd be the last one to take care of her like my family took care of her descendants. Since she never married or had kids, she wanted me to have the house. Said no one can take better care of it than a Palmer." Stanley puffed his chest.

"Got it. Kind of like being stuck with a white elephant." Adam fingered the chestnut trim framing the library French doors.

"Not at all. I love this place. You can't get

workmanship like this anymore."

"Agreed. But…"

"Come." Stanley waved him and Laurel on, guiding them into the room on the right. "This is my temporary office."

They settled in a room with a massive claw-foot desk and two high-back chairs.

Adam didn't have a clue the period of the chairs, but the tattered, heavy-weighted upholstery gave him the impression they might be worth something if restored.

He and Laurel took the chairs while Stanley sat behind the desk. "Looks like an old parlor." Adam shifted his gaze upward to inspect the room's ornate crown molding.

"You're dead-on." Stanley's laugh echoed in the large room.

Adam and Laurel glanced at each other, then Adam shot a sideways glare at Stanley.

"Apologies for the pun." Stanley cleared his throat.

That comment reminded Adam of Stanley's original intent to relocate Palmer Funeral Home here, but the high costs had that idea dead and buried. Adam hoped the place wasn't haunted like the folklore claimed. He shivered at that possibility.

Stanley presented preliminary plans, and Laurel's enthusiasm encouraged Stanley and both gushed about potential events.

"Tea parties…tours…magnolias…Abigail and Thomas…"

The two rattled on, and Adam shifted his curiosity to the deteriorated bricks that encased the fireplace. When he left his seat for further inspection, he surmised his companions never considered the dollars and cents to restore this place, let alone support their grandiose expectations. "I hate to be the bearer of bad news"—he craned his neck to inspect the fireplace flue—"who's paying for all these renovations?" He stood; his gaze directed to Stanley. "This chimney needs to be rebuilt, or at least have a liner installed." He swept his pointer along the expanse of the room. "You've got cracked and hanging plaster, knob and tube electric. The original wide-plank floorboards are surprisingly in excellent shape around the perimeter, but the traffic areas are splintered and separated."

He plopped back in the chair next to Laurel, and a plume of dust enveloped them. He coughed, waving his hands in front of his face. "This space"—he coughed again—"might be pretty cool if renovated, but it'll cost a fortune to restore it back to life." And Stanley had no experience bringing things back to life.

"We…definitely…need estimates." Laurel also coughed. "And, yes"—she cleared her throat—"it's going to cost a lot. The estimates will let us know what we're dealing with."

"I'm working on it." Stanley tapped his pen on the desktop at rapid speed.

"The village can hold fundraisers and ask for donations." Laurel's wide-eyed expression accompanied her palms splayed upward.

The hope in her eyes held Adam's attention for a minute, but it evaporated as Stanley spouted more ideas that increased costs.

With a grumble of the events—and his unwarranted interest building toward Laurel—Adam rose from the chair, failed to swat dust from the seat of his pants, and he made his way to the triple bay windows. Blocking out the chatter of Laurel gushing about the romantic possibilities of the manor, he viewed the semi-wooded vacant lot next door.

If tourists are coming, that view isn't exactly inviting. Wait…that's Laurel's father's property.

"What do the rear grounds have to offer?" He glanced at Laurel and Stanley over his shoulder.

"What?" Stan turned his head toward Adam.

Adam pivoted and ambled to the side of the desk, his hands leaning on the inlaid leather desk top. "The outside grounds. Are they as bad as in here?"

"Adam, how about a little more positivity?" Laurel slanted a glance. "This place is grand."

"No." He stood upright, focusing on the breadth of the room instead of why it now mattered that he might have disappointed her. "It *was* grand." He made quotation marks in the air with his forefingers. "If the outside is in decent shape, you might get my vote. But the inside…" He scratched the side of his chin and groaned.

"Your vote isn't necessary." Laurel's voice grew stronger. "We need a viable plan for the planning board to approve." She waved a hand to the door. "Stan, let's tour the outside."

"You got it!" Stanley sprung from his chair, sprinted around the desk, and extended his elbow to Laurel. "May I escort you, miss?"

Laurel giggled, took hold of Stanley's arm, twisted her head, and stared at Adam. "You certainly may."

Adam watched the two co-conspirators stroll toward the vestibule, and he rolled his eyes and followed, wondering how he got roped into all this insanity.

****

Laurel's insides shimmied with each step throughout the Rutledge gardens. A giggle sputtered from her throat that with every negative comment from Adam, she countered a positive jump starting her heart.

"My vision is to have pathways in each garden," Stanley explained. "This way, we can have multiple events going on at one time."

"Gardens?" Adam's mouth opened. "What gardens?"

"Okay, Mr. Negative, you can stop now." Laurel flicked her long ponytail off her shoulder, taking a ready stance to prove him wrong. "Clearly, you can see the different garden areas."

Stepping over overgrown brush scraping against her jeans, she pointed to the west side of the back acreage. "This is a perfect spot for a garden party. Picture small, white, wrought iron tables and matching chairs. Maybe a Kentucky Derby Day with people dressed in their finest, and ladies wearing fabulous hats." *And, of course, The Laurel Wreath would supply the beautiful centerpieces and hanging baskets.* "We need wrought iron poles for hanging flower baskets. Stanley, can you put that on your list?"

"Sure." He entered her request on his tablet.

"Before you order poles and other frou-frou things, shouldn't we discuss the infrastructure?" Adam sprinted to the east side that once held a path. "There should be walkways along here, and some shrub borders dividing each of your *gardens*. At least seven rotted trees need to be removed." He pointed to the peeling bark. "You don't want a lawsuit if a tree fell and killed someone."

Stanley hesitated for a few, long seconds.

Adam groaned. "Aw, come on, are you serious?"

Laurel's stomach dropped with Stanley's delayed reaction.

"What? No. No." The older man's eyes popped wide open with a vigorous shake of his head. "Of course not. It would be even worse if someone got hurt. I couldn't live with that."

Laurel cast a second look, then refocused on the landscape. "There *is* a lot of work, but it could be beautiful." She refused to give up. This place was a huge opportunity for her and several businesses in Cedar Ridge. The manor would also draw the community together. The romantic elegance of the old house and Abigail and Thomas' love story brimmed within her heart. Oh, to have a love so strong…

Her own parents had adored each other. Their love showed every time they were together, especially when they danced. In the kitchen or living room, they laughed and joked like they were in a grand ballroom. The image of them dancing in the backyard now caused tears to form, as she remembered how Pop sang to Momma with love in her eyes.

Laurel suppressed the increased fluid burning the rims of her eyes with the memory of the last time she'd seen them dance. Momma lost her hair, was dressed in sweats that were way too big, and unable to stand on her own. Weighing little more than a child, Pop held her in his arms, placing her feet on his, and they danced. For the first time in a long time, Momma smiled.

"Belinda, you're the most beautiful woman in the world." Pop had kissed her then.

Two weeks later, Momma had died, leaving Pop devastated.

A love like theirs should have been able to flourish for decades. Laurel wanted a love like that, but fear of losing that love kept her cemented in work. Her focus forever aimed on taking care of Pop aided in shielding and protecting her heart.

"There's more than a lot of work here."

Adam's comment snapped Laurel to focus on their task. She spun around, taking a moment to clear her throat and blinked away a blur of tears when she noticed something standing near the rear of the manor. Shades of black and rust emerged into view.

Making her way closer, she realized the iron post topped with a horse head had a ring secured to its mouth. Making her way in that direction, she spotted Adam right beside her, both their hands touching the horse head at the same time.

When their eyes met, she sucked in a breath. For what seemed an eternity—but lasted a second—her world stood still. A warmth crept through her along with a sudden, unexpected attraction, throwing her off balance.

Why?

Why Adam, of all people?

Maybe the memory of romance between her parents sparked the unsettling awareness.

She heard Adam clear his throat, and then he dropped his hand from hers. As an odd urge to feel his touch again took hold of her senses, she twisted her gaze away and focused on the horse head.

"This stays," they both declared at the same time.

She bolted her gaze back to him. "Really?"

"Yes. Really." He rubbed the weather-beaten iron. "This old hitching post was original when the manor was built. You can't duplicate it."

"You mean, we actually agree on something?"

"Why do you sound surprised, princess? I'm not unreasonable. I'm cautious and practical."

One side of Adam's mouth lifted in a sexy as-all-get-out grin. Shaking herself to ignore the shape of his lips and the playfulness in his eyes, she repeated in her mind his last words.

Cautious and practical? Both necessary in business since he owned a business.

But? Princess?

That, she didn't like. Princess—as in spoiled and needs to have her own way—or princess because she's beautiful, delicate, and refined. Neither definition fit.

"This is great!" Stan announced. "We finally have agreement on something!"

Agreement in one area was not such a big deal. But in this case, Laurel guessed it made Stan happy.

Stanley entered more in his tablet. "Let's check out the front lawn!"

They waded through thick, uncut, weeds and wet grass to the front yard and gravel drive.

"The driveway needs to be paved. Drainage is needed along here." Adam pointed to the sides. "To keep it in the right time period, it should be covered in cobblestone-type pavers." He shook his head. "It'll cost a fortune."

Laurel made a mental note to research an inexpensive alternative as they discussed landscape design options within a limited budget.

"Can you give me an estimate for all the outside

work and driveway costs?" Stanley asked.

Adam whooshed a heavy sigh and scrubbed his hand around the back of his neck. "I can, Stan, but it's gonna be high. There's a lot to be done."

"Can't you and Parker work out a price on a partial project that's not too expensive up front?" Panic bolted to Laurel's stomach that Stan's budget couldn't handle the costs.

"Really?" Adam gave her a blank stare. "You mean do a half as"—he stopped—"half the job?"

The look he threw sent a you-don't-have-a-clue gaze. Well, she did have a clue, and she'd prove it. "Not half. Stages. Remove the dangerous trees and clear the brush now…we can sell them for firewood. Maybe install the driveway before it gets too cold. Then in the spring, work on the pathways, planting the shrub borders and ornamental plants."

"Ornamental plants?" Adam sputtered. "You're not even close to that stage. Look around." His arm swept the expanse of the property. "Where do you expect all your tourists and *garden party* guests to park?"

Laurel scanned the front of the property. A parking lot would detract from the beauty of the manor. Paving these front acres would ruin the peaceful gardens. Adam had a point. But defeat was *not* an option. Yes, important things like parking needed to be explored, but she refused to give up. "I know this is a lot to take on, but I've got faith we can get it done if we work together, not fight each other." She faced him square on and stared, more determined than ever.

This has to work. It has to. Or I'll lose my business.

Chapter 4

Frank snuck in the back door of The Laurel Wreath, hoping to avoid a game of twenty questions with his daughter. He had the right to see *who* he wanted *when* he wanted as long as it didn't interfere with his deliveries. Grabbing the *Cedar Ridge Sentinel*, he positioned himself in his favorite wooden chair by the prep counter appearing as casual as possible.

"Enjoy the rest of your day." Laurel's voice sounded from the display room, and within seconds, she entered the prep room with a large box and stopped short. "Whoa, when did you sneak in?"

"Who, me?" He nonchalantly folded the top of the newspaper to glance her way. "Been here a while."

"Ah, no, you haven't."

Lowering the paper to his lap, Frank eyed his daughter. He didn't mind her growing more overprotective as the years passed, but lately, when she couldn't account for every second of his day, she'd become a bit of a pain. "I've been right here. Heard you dealing with that customer." Keeping a casual tone, he smiled.

She raised one eyebrow and squinted a glare. "That *customer* was the delivery driver"—she raised the box in her hand—"the bouquet holders for the Gleason wedding." She placed the box on the counter next to him and folded her arms across her chest. "Busted!"

Yeah…he was guilty. But he needed this to end. "Okay, okay." He rose from the chair and placed the newspaper on the seat. "I appreciate you always taking care of me, worrying about me." Moving closer, he set a hand on her shoulder. "I'm okay. I've moved on."

"I know, but Momma—"

"Momma is in here." He pointed a finger to his heart. "She always will be. I'm a *big* boy. I don't need you to mother me. Your mother *never* mothered me." Seeing the far-off stare in his daughter's eyes proved him right that her paranoia of losing him kept her cemented in the past. "Sweetie, it's okay. Living in the past isn't healthy. You aren't my keeper; you're my daughter who selflessly came back home and keeps me going with odd jobs. But you need to get out and have fun."

"I have fun." She grimaced and then her face brightened. "Just the other night, Jeanine and I went shopping."

"That's not fun. You hate shopping!"

"We—"

"How about going on a date?"

Her lips pursed in a frown. "I have." Picking up a length of ribbon that she ran through her fingers, with her chin down, she peeked from a sideways glance.

"Two dates in two years?" His hand rose to hold up two fingers.

"You sound like Jeanine."

"For good reason. I know you had a rough time with Richard, and I'm proud you sent him packing. Although, something tells me he didn't get the message."

"Thanks." She lifted a shoulder. "Didn't do

anything special. I was tired of him telling me how to dress, what to eat, and what to like."

"Yeah, showering you with high-priced material stuff you didn't want. He tried to turn you into someone you weren't." He saw a defensive expression shift on Laurel's lips. His little girl had a good head on her shoulders. She didn't need to defend the egotistical jerk. "That guy wasn't worth your time," he persisted before she answered. "There's someone out there for you…one who's worthy of you."

She let loose a humorless chuckle. "Pop, no one is worthy in your eyes."

"That's not true. Someone like Adam is worthy. Or even Parker or Todd."

Laurel dropped the ribbon onto the counter, lowered her chin, and aimed her gaze into his eyes. "Parker has a girlfriend, and Todd is still grieving the loss of his wife. I wouldn't make a good substitute mother for his two kids."

"You'd be a great mother. You mother me all the time."

Laurel puffed out a heavy breath. "Mothering, dating, and me as a stepmom is avoiding the subject." She wagged a finger in his face. "You're hiding something. Where were you for two hours?"

Frank released a long sigh. "There was a lot of traffic, then I stopped by the Muffins 'n More to get those muffins you like. I met some people, got to talking, and I'm back. No harm done." He patted his arms, thighs, and head. "See, I'm fine. Nothing happened." Seeing the return of her arched eyebrow meant she was cooking up a question he didn't want to answer.

"Where are the muffins?" She narrowed her eyes.

Darn. "The muffins?"

"Yeah." She crossed her arms over her chest again. "The ones you got for me?"

"Ah…" He glanced the prep room. "I must have forgotten them. You know how it is once I get talking." He raised his right shoulder and leveled his right palm toward the ceiling. "It slipped my mind."

Okay, okay. He'd have to come clean, but he wasn't sure his strong-willed, independent daughter's vulnerable side would be opened to the truth. He wondered if she ever would. She needed to leave the past behind and live in the present. But right now, he needed to curb her curiosity.

A delivery truck horn sounded outside the shop's back door.

Just in time to save the day. "I'll get that." He rushed to the door. "And speaking of talking"—he yelled over his shoulder—"when I come in, I want to hear how your meeting went with Stan and Adam."

Laurel mumbled something incoherent.

But he didn't stick around to decipher it, so he headed through the back door in a flash, away from her questions.

****

As Laurel watched Pop escape through the flower shop back door, everything tilted off kilter. Again, he acted weird with his whereabouts, and Adam acted even weirder by agreeing that the hitching post stays.

What is going on?

Stanley's hardcopy preliminary proposal stared up from the top of her desk. Rutledge Manor had the positive potential to change Cedar Ridge and everyone who lived there—including Adam Carlson. But Mr. Stubborn denied it. No matter how upbeat her enthusiasm, she couldn't convince the young councilman to be logical.

"What are you saying?" Pop carried in a case labeled *precut wood* for her keepsake boxes.

She lifted her attention from the prelim. "What?"

"You're grumbling."

Laurel leaned forward and rattled her head. "Things don't add up. One minute, Adam is saying 'no, no, no' to everything at the manor. Then—out of nowhere—he agrees the hitching post needs to stay." She threw her hands in the air. "Who does that?"

"Times like this confuse me. I'll never understand this younger generation, especially you." He shook his head and placed the box on the work bench. "Maybe Adam needs time to see the manor will work. Or maybe not. If he agrees about the hitching post, doesn't that show he's open-minded?"

"Open-minded?" *Pop is losing it.* Dropping her pen on the desk, she slumped in her chair. "He's not open-minded at all!"

"Sure, he is. That boy's been through a lot. Had to grow up fast." Pop whooshed a loud breath. "He used to tell me stories about how they moved every time Ned put the family in financial trouble. Give him time."

"He's *not* a boy." *Definitely a man. No boy causes a rippling heated reaction through me like he does.*

"You know what I mean." Pop opened the case of wood with a box cutter. "Has Adam said why he's against the project and the village revitalization?"

Laurel waved a hand in the air, more to ward off the reaction Adam caused than to dismiss Pop's

57

question. "Something about not wanting the village to change."

"Nah...it's got to be more than that." Pop examined the wood slats he withdrew from the box. "I'm willing to bet when you find out why he's hell-bent on not wanting things to change, you'll understand him better."

She weeded fingers through the hair at her temples. "I don't need to understand him better. I need him to agree the manor is what we need. He's so stubborn."

Pop sputtered a chuckle. "Now who's being stubborn?"

She'd show Pop...and everyone else...that Adam truly was stubborn, unreasonable, and not dedicated to saving Cedar Ridge.

****

Adam sat in his truck at the job site and snorted, remembering the delight on Laurel's face while she had ticked off the landscape stages she claimed would work for the manor.

When he had cited the long list to Parker, he heard his business partner scoff. "No problem. And I got a bridge to sell you."

After a few laughs, he and Parker gave serious consideration how to accomplish the tasks; but not in the stages Laurel imagined. Maybe over time, they could transform a reasonable amount of the grounds back to life in four stages, which sounded odd for a proposed funeral home site. But the cost...well, he needed to discuss that with Laurel and Stanley in hopes they'd be open to lowering their expectations.

The two-week deadline weighed on Adam's shoulders, and as much as he didn't want to rush into this crazy project, he semi-conceded to Parker's belief that this was a great opportunity for Cedar Ridge.

Time to text Laurel.

—Got prices for manor grounds. Tonight, 7:00 at diner?—

A few minutes later, a return text pinged his phone…

—Sorry. Can't. Have a date.—

Date. He nodded.

Wait…a date?

****

Two days later, when the mayor had called requesting Laurel and Adam meet with two councilmen who served on the Village Improvement District Committee, Laurel jumped at the chance. The brainstorming meeting to raise money for the village's share of the manor project should address Adam's financial concerns.

So much depended on tonight's outcome—her pulse increased that things were progressing. She entered the Acropolis Diner, shaking off a shiver, appreciative of the restaurant's warmth cloaking her on the cold October night. "Hi, Phyllis." Laurel greeted the server and glanced right toward the counter area and left to the dining room.

"Hey, Laurel. They're in the back. Follow me." Phyllis led Laurel through the busy diner. "Ernie reserved the table so you wouldn't be interrupted."

Ernie from Donaldson's Hardware and Harold from Jenkinson's Corner Store were a perfect combination. Both men owned businesses for a long time. If the four of them managed to get this portion of the village revitalization to work, then the project stood to be a success, which promised to provide The Laurel Wreath with much-needed income. Putting her brick-and-mortar business back in the black would be a godsend without relying on her online keepsake box sales to keep her afloat.

Laurel followed the middle-aged woman—who'd been working at the diner for a few decades—and tried to temper her rippling anticipation.

"There you go." Phyllis pointed to the table. "They're all seated."

"Thanks." Laurel's stomach did a surprise flip-flop at the sight of the back of Adam's head of thick, black hair. The sudden pounding of her heart drowned out the sounds of the diner. *No way.* She refused to let that bothersome reaction sidetrack her mission, so she squared her shoulders and headed straight for the table.

"Laurel!" Ernie stood with an outstretched arm. "We were just saying we need your good sense to break a stalemate."

Adam stood to face her.

His fixed attention produced the same tantalizing reaction settling in the pit of her stomach that hit her at the manor's hitching post. She forced her gaze away and fussed with her jacket zipper to ignore feelings she had no business feeling. "Am I late?" She focused on Ernie and noticed he was a little grayer than the last time she saw him.

"No. Not at all." Harold Jenkinson stood in the old-fashioned tradition of greeting a lady. "We're excited to get things moving. I mentioned a few ideas to see if anything sticks."

Adam held and offered an empty chair opposite him.

Surprised by his manners, Laurel placed her jacket on the back of the chair, sat, and tried not to appear flustered. "Thank you."

"What can I get you, Laurel?" Phyllis placed a menu in front of Laurel and pulled an order pad and pen from her apron pocket.

With a quick glance at the table to see everyone's order, Laurel stifled a quiet giggle. "I'll have a large hot cocoa, please."

"Whipped cream?"

The warmth of a smile inched across her lips. "Yes, please."

Phyllis winked, and the crinkle of her smile replaced the tiredness in her eyes. "You want colored sprinkles to top it off?"

"That would be perfect!" Laurel giggled out loud this time when a wave of giddiness overcame her.

"Are we five years old again?" A glint of humor glistened in Adam's nutmeg-colored eyes when he pointed his beer bottle.

"No, *we're* not." She turned her gaze to the others. "I rarely go out to eat. This is a treat." Pointing a finger toward Adam's drink, Laurel focused on the brown bottle. "Is that your usual?"

"You betcha. Only thing I drink."

The familiar brand with the blue ribbon was her father's favorite, too. Her ex, Richard, detested beer. When he wasn't impressing his co-workers with a bottle of high-priced scotch, he lowered his standards and referred to craft beer as *slumming it*, degrading working-class beers.

Somehow, she didn't see Adam needing to impress anyone, always confident, never exhibiting any pretense. Richard and honesty didn't go hand in hand. He fit into her idea that a non-committed relationship kept her heart safe...the only positive in dating him. In her heart, honesty set foundations of relationships with everyone...friends, co-workers, family, and a lifetime partner.

Uh...lifetime partner? Stay focused!

Glad the men couldn't hear the thoughts in her head, she darted her gaze to see if anyone noticed an unwelcome blush warming her cheeks. Zeroing in on the older men helped to jump her back to reality.

"I remember those days when I could drink anything"—a wide smile crinkled the crow's feet at the sides of Harold's eyes—"but with this cold weather, I need something warm." He pointed to his cup. "It's decaf so I can sleep."

"You got that right." Ernie raised his coffee mug in a salute.

"Luckily, I'm not at that point, yet." Adam motioned his chin toward Ernie's cup. "I drink a few cups of high-test every morning to get going. After work, a nice cold one hits the spot."

"Okay, okay. Enough small talk. We have a job to do." Harold faced Laurel. "I've got some ideas to raise money for the manor"—he flipped a thumb toward Adam—"although, your boyfriend doesn't like them."

Pow! She bugged her eyes out and felt a repeated surge of heat shade everything from her neck up to a bright-red. "He's not my boyfriend!"

"Harold, uh..." Adam's hand grasped his neck and rubbed. "I, uh, I'm flattered you'd think that Laurel and I..."

Lowering her head, she darted her gaze to her

knotted hands resting in her lap while her stomach rolled with nerves.

Laurel and I, what?

A long, troubling few seconds clicked by.

What made Harold say that?

While it was considerate of Adam to use the word *flattered*, his comment did little to alleviate the awkwardness.

That he said he was flattered made her feel better, but…

"No. Nope. We're *not* together." His chin lowered, and he rotated his beer bottle between both hands.

Ouch. Laurel shot her gaze up and tightened one hand over the other. A little too blunt for her bruised ego.

So much for considerate.

"Oh…" Harold's gaze roved between them. "The way you two were going at it the other night at the meeting, I thought…" He scrunched his lips to one side. "You held her chair when she got here. Guys your age don't do that."

"Well…they do if they're gentlemen." Adam raised his head to view her. "Especially when the lady is as…nice as Laurel."

Nice?

That's it? Nice?

Grandmothers are nice.

Church ladies are nice. Well…except for Clarice.

Thank goodness, she avoided the dating pool. More important things needed to be dealt with instead of this type of humiliation.

Why did she allow her ego to be hurt by Adam's unintentional rejection?

What these two, kind gentlemen assumed didn't matter. She protected her heart by concentrating on her business and Pop. And Adam…well, she wasn't aware he dated in a while, but he had in the past—not the commitment type.

Not *her* type.

Her mind had wandered away from the reason for this meeting, so she set her brain back on funding and not why it mattered that people believed she and Adam were a thing.

****

Keep it real. Adam took a swig of beer and let it slide down his throat, hoping the delay would help dodge more comments of him and Laurel as a couple.

Dating—not his thing these days. His last girlfriend, Sophie, didn't work out—just like the rest. Confused by the odd chemistry between him and Laurel, he recognized chemistry didn't equal the long-lasting, marriage-leading relationship he wanted.

Besides, Laurel didn't fit his checklist.

Although, every time he found himself with her, he couldn't stop images of picket fences, swing sets, a houseful of kids, and even a dog from popping into his mind. She seemed like the dinner-at-home-type, snuggling-together-on-the-sofa-kind of woman who represented all kinds of homey stuff—stuff he inwardly wanted.

But the same needling dilemma resurrected questions that always followed him.

Was he enough for someone like her?

Was he the kind of man she deserved?

Was his DNA predetermined to take after his old man, even though he fought it every day of his life?

All that didn't matter. She seemed consumed by her business. While he respected Ernie and Harold, they didn't know squat for thinking he and Laurel were together.

The overwhelming smell of vanilla sugar cookies again yanked him back to his surroundings. He sniffed and took in the vanilla scent that revived comforting, childhood memories.

Ahh...now it made sense.

Laurel.

He offered a chair, and his favorite smell drifted over him. Probably perfume or the gunk women put in their hair. He took care not to glance Laurel's way. No need giving the old guys unwarranted ammunition.

"So, here's where we could begin." Harold steered them back on track. "The Harvest Festival this month can be our kickoff. Then—"

"The Harvest Festival?" Adam and Laurel simultaneously uttered, turning their gazes to one another.

He withdrew, but not before he noticed the flush of pink forming on her creamy, white skin. The tiny freckles just under her eyes seemed to brighten. He never noticed them before. They were cute.

"Yes, the Harvest Festival," Harold continued. "The pumpkin regatta, the pumpkin-chunking contest, the pie baking contest, and the Great Pumpkin Contest raised a lot of money last year. We can use some of that revenue for the manor expenses."

Sliding his attention from Laurel, Adam held up a staying hand. "Hold on there, Charlie Brown." Not wanting to be disrespectful, Adam hesitated before shooting Harold down. "Sounds like a good idea, but that money is appropriated for the senior citizen's group." He studied Laurel then. "Right?"

"Right." She nodded without glancing his way, and she withdrew her tablet from her bag and typed.

Organized...pretty impressive.

"Good idea. We need to keep track of everything." Ernie nodded toward Laurel. "Adam's right. We need something separate from the events we already have. Something *big* to fund the expenses."

Adam breathed out a swoosh of air. Finally, someone agreed.

"How about a Christmas parade as the kickoff?" Ernie paused while Phyllis placed the hot cocoa in front of Laurel. "That'll give us a month and a half to plan."

Adam's short-lived relief escaped in a quick breath. *Jeez, these people don't get it.* Cautioning himself to a tactful answer, he watched Laurel lick whipped cream from her spoon that caused him to lick his own lips. Drawing his gaze away, he tried to concentrate on Ernie's words but missed them due to the distraction.

Parade, whipped cream, parade in six weeks. Oh, yeah.

Blocking out the image of Laurel's mouth, he stared at Ernie's aging face. "Another good idea that should also be done *next* year. A big parade will need at least year to plan."

"I agree." Laurel sipped her cocoa and placed the cup on the table to enter more in her tablet.

Adam hoped it was to scrap the parade until next year. "Good. That's the second thing we agree on." He remembered the warmth of her hand when they both touched the hitching post.

Man…you gotta stop. Where is this interest coming from?

"Next year?" Harold raised a bushy, white eyebrow wrinkling his forehead. "We don't have that kind of time. A few of us will be lucky if we're able to cover our mortgages for six months, let alone a whole year."

"I know, Harold." A sympathetic stab for the struggling businesses sliced through Adam's gut. "Unfortunately, *you* don't have enough time to get a Christmas parade off the ground. There's too much to consider. Financing, marketing, logistics—"

"We'll just have to forego those small details and run with it," Ernie interrupted.

What?

How had Donaldson's Hardware survived three decades with that kind of business sense?

Adam traveled his gaze to Laurel whose green eyes flashed wide.

She hitched one shoulder.

A tiny smear of whipped cream at the corner of her mouth teased him—begged him to remove it with his fingertip. Instead, he grabbed hold of his beer bottle and drew a long swig.

"Gentlemen, I think we need to approach this a little differently." Laurel wiped her mouth with a napkin.

"How?" the three men chorused.

Okay, he was grateful she drew his attention away from her mouth, but what was she up to? Pulling his focus from her lips, he zeroed in on her eyes, but that might have been worse with their determined gleam showing she had the answer. Damn, she was compelling.

"A compromise." Laurel tipped her chin in a short nod.

Man, oh, man, oh, man. *Here it comes*. On more than one occasion, he witnessed Ernie's and Harold's inflexibility regarding village council decisions. Eyeing the two men, he noticed how one squirmed and the other tapped his spoon on the table. "A compromise—okay." Adam figured he'd take Laurel's side to see where it landed. "I'm in. What'd ya have in mind?"

"To keep costs down, the parade should be all local units—the high school band, police, scouts, clubs, especially the fire department because everyone loves fire trucks. But we *have* to have Santa…maybe he can ride on the last fire truck." With a brief pause, the brightness in her eyes dulled, and her shoulders sagged. "Problem is, they won't attract outside visitors. We need someone with a huge regional draw. The parade needs to do double duty—bring people to town."

"You're right," Ernie pipped in. "We also need someone or something to get people interested in visiting the manor."

Adam rolled his eyes, sat back in his chair, and drummed his fingertips on the tabletop, trying to minimize the sarcasm in his voice. "Why don't you get Trevor Lawrence for next year's parade? He should draw in a lot of people."

"Excellent idea!" Lightness returned to Laurel's expression.

"Scott Lawrence's son?" Harold asked. "Wasn't he in that TV talent competition?"

"Yes! *Homegrown Superstar*," Laurel responded, all happiness and joy. "He came in fourth, but he's got a huge fan base."

"Great thinking, Adam." Harold raised his coffee mug. "Where do you think the parade will march from, Main to Hemlock?"

Adam slumped in his chair. Resting both elbows on the table, and aiming his gaze at a chip in the laminate tabletop, he struggled to consider ways to slow things. "Yeahhhh…that makes sense."

"What if we have the parade watchers follow the parade to the manor?" Ernie added. "We can end with a Christmas tree lighting outside the manor."

"Tree lighting?" Adam scoffed and raised his gaze to focus on the two men. "Every town has a tree lighting. Ya need something to *wow* the people."

"You're right!" Harold agreed. "You really know how to plan a parade."

"Ah…no. I don't." The fear of getting dragged into this lunacy prickled Adam's nerves. The thought of finance popped into his mind, and he sat up. "You need different units to attract people. The village alone can't fund everything."

"You're right, we can't." Laurel entered more into her list. "Even with local units, making it a success is going to cost money." She lifted her attention from her tablet and stared across the room. "Doesn't Brett Meyers work for L&L Lars?"

Adam squinted. "The candy company?" Lowering his chin, he leaned back in his chair and tilted his head. "Where you headed with this?"

"Maybe he can get the company to sponsor the parade?"

Adam raised his eyebrows and nodded. "It's a long shot, but it might work. Would be a big help."

"Got it." Laurel noted it.

He liked how they complemented each other on ideas, even though they didn't see eye to eye. He still wanted to put everything off for a year, hoping all the hype would die down to allow more time for people to reject the idea.

When Laurel's green eyes connected with his, he couldn't deny how relief inched through him. The reality that he liked working with her blocked the conversation from his ears.

"We need subcommittees to plan the different events like you have in the Village Improvement District Committee." Laurel directed the idea to Ernie and Harold. "We can start with the holiday kick-off parade the first week in December, but we'd have to begin plans for it ASAP."

He never got this close to notice how graceful her lips formed her words. He sagged his shoulders, and his breath deflated that her attention was on the other men—another feeling he didn't understand. With Laurel, everything seemed magnified—dizzying confusion, surprising disappointment, intense anticipation.

Pull it together, Carlson. This is Laurel. Practical, dependable Laurel Eldridge.

The fearless conqueror who charged ahead after what she wanted with an undeniable charm. A double whammy that he needed to stay away from, but her scent of vanilla enticed him to take notice of the warm, cinnamon-colored strands of her hair flowing around her shoulders. Delicate freckles running in flowing swirls over her cheeks and nose.

The longer the conversation about the premature Christmas kick-off parade continued, the more Adam grappled with his puzzling reaction. His thoughts jumbled, and right now, those thoughts overshadowed the urgency to slow the parade.

"Okay, are we in agreement?" Laurel asked.

Ernie and Harold chorused a resounding, "Yes!"

"Adam?"

"Sure. Sounds good to me." He didn't have a clue. Laurel's enthusiasm lured him deep into her little world.

"Meeting's adjourned." Ernie slapped his hands together in one loud clap. The two men and Laurel rose from their chairs.

Adam stood along with them, coming out of his Laurel-induced haze, and wondering what he had just agreed to.

****

Why is he staring?

Laurel lowered her head, pretended to straighten her jacket, and waited for her three companions to leave their table. The intensity of Adam's gaze, and the good fortune he no longer blocked the start of their plan, had her heart fluttering again. Moving forward with the Christmas parade *this* year gave Laurel's heart double reason to flutter.

Ernie extended his hand, signaling Laurel to lead.

Easing passed him, she fixed her gaze on the floor with the elation of the parade swirling through her thoughts. Just moments ago, Adam agreed to hold the parade now. But she viewed different emotions that had drifted across his face. One minute, his eyes were mellow and complacent, then they appeared confused, like reality kicked in as if he wasn't sure he liked the plan. Seconds later, they had shifted to mellow again.

What's going on with him?

"So, Laurel..."

Harold's voice diverted her attention.

"Is Frank planning to enter the bowling fundraiser for the church?"

She did a double take and glanced at Harold. "Oh...ah...he isn't sure. He twisted his ankle a few days ago. Doesn't know if it will be healed by then."

"How swollen is his ankle?" Adam stepped closer.

She inhaled the pleasant, woodsy fragrance of his masculine aftershave. Not the obnoxious, overpowering aftershave her ex, Richard, used. "The size of a grapefruit." She positioned her hands to form a circle. "He's wearing a hiking boot on one foot and a slipper on the other. You should stop by the store to see him tomorrow."

"I think I will." Adam removed his jacket from the back of his chair.

"He'd enjoy that." Having Adam stop by to see Pop caused a rise of butterflies dancing in her stomach. Years had passed since that reaction pulsated through her. Adam visiting her father on her own turf, without discussion of the manor, might give them the opportunity to get along better...for the project's sake.

"It won't be until early afternoon." Adam put on his jacket. "Parker and I are taking care of the grounds over at Morrison Shoes. I can stop by during lunch."

"Perfect!" And right now, viewing his huge smile, it seemed Adam liked the idea, too. His eyes twinkled like fireworks, and then, opened wide. Without warning, he rushed toward her, then passed, brushing her arm.

Laurel's breath hitched, and she sank her

shoulders, realizing she was so wrong about Adam's reaction. Her foolish hope that he shared the same feelings had her face flaring once again in red heat. All those dancing butterflies in her stomach died in an instant, crashing thud.

Adam stood—a mere four feet away—hugging a redheaded woman.

Chapter 5

Laurel's body tossed; her limbs flailed. In between consciousness and sleep, she slowly drifted back, back to the same spot her mind refused to release...seated at Momma's bedside. "I love you, Momma." She held tight, not wanting to let go. She cringed at the brittleness of bones and veins in Momma's hands.

"I love you, too," Momma whispered, her voice weak and tired...so, so tired. "Now, go to bed." Momma coughed a choking sound, almost unable to breathe. "You've got a big day tomorrow."

Laurel stood, leaned on tiptoes over the hospital bed Pop had placed in the living room, reaching to kiss Momma's forehead. She stepped away, stretching her lips into the biggest smile, even though her heart was sad. "I'll see you in the morning before I go to school."

Momma nodded and whispered again, "Good luck at the science fair."

"Will you kiss me for luck before I leave?"

A faint smile stretched Momma's lips. "I always do."

But the next morning, Momma was still sleeping, and Laurel watched Momma's chest barely rise and fall.

Pop gave her that good luck kiss, promising to see her at the science fair.

But Pop never came—Aunt Louise did.

And when Laurel arrived home, the corner of the living room where Momma's hospital bed rested was empty. It was gone.

And so was Momma.

****

"It happened again, didn't it?" Pop walked into their kitchen, and his gaze landed on the perfectly set breakfast table.

"No, it didn't." Popping two slices of rye bread into the toaster, Laurel hesitated to make eye contact.

"Yes, it did. You always hover over me when you have one of those dreams."

The warmth of his hand covered her shoulder.

"Sweetie, you've got to let it go. It's been sixteen years. We never have to worry about Mom suffering anymore."

"I know. I'm fine." She stepped away and clasped her hands, her gaze bouncing around their small, cozy kitchen.

"Mom will always be with us. It's okay, we're okay." He snatched the toast before she did, sending a smirk her way. "Mom would want us to live, not just exist."

"I'm *not* existing…" She took a seat on the opposite side of the table.

Even though Pop said he'd been cheated that Momma had been taken too soon, he also said how grateful he'd been for their time together.

But she had been cheated, too. She was kept from saying goodbye to Momma. And, instead of doing what other girls did at twelve, thirteen, and fourteen, she had arrived home from school each day to take care of the house. Did her best so Pop didn't have to worry. He'd had enough to deal with.

"You rarely go out and have fun." He pointed his butter knife in the air.

"I have fun." Convincing herself of the veiled fib, she poured milk into her bowl, flattening the cereal with the back of her spoon. "I've got the shop and my friends." She peeked sideways at the rough way he spread butter over his toast.

"The shop and your friends are good. But you need to open your heart and find someone special. Your friends all have someone in their lives. You need that, too. But not someone like the last guy."

"Don't worry about that. Control freaks are off limits." *Won't make that mistake again. Another reason I need to ignore these crazy feelings for Adam. That, and the fact that he hugged that redhead last night.*

"Good to hear." Pop took a bite of rye toast. "Keep looking." And then, he licked his lips, and a wide grin turned into a full-blown smile. "The right guy is probably right in front of you. Keep your eyes open the next time you see him."

She hated disappointing Pop and had done so when she had dated Richard. Even though they had little in common, Richard wasn't the man she'd spend her life with so he was safe to date. Pop had good instincts about people. She should have listened after the first time he met the *city slicker* as he called him. Pop and Jeanine appeared to band together to gang up on her about her dating life.

Ah....Jeanine!

She slanted a cat-like smirk her father's way. "Jeanine doesn't have anyone special." She slurped a spoonful of cereal. *There...that will end the discussion.*

"Jeanine?" Pop hooted. "I don't think there's a guy out there who can keep up with that girl." Pointing his toast, he lowered his chin. "Mark my words—when the right guy sets his sights on her, she won't know what hit her."

Laurel chuckled at that one. Deep down, Jeanine wanted someone to share her crazy life. Maybe Pop was right. But losing someone Laurel loved had been too painful to live through at twelve. Of course, she was no longer that little girl, but she couldn't risk feeling that kind of pain again. Dealing with the anxiety of losing Pop, or even Jeanine, or if she gave her heart to a man, consumed her with worry. To fall in love and have a family would fill her life with so much joy, but could she bear the pain of another loss?

****

Adam woke and stared upward at the light from the sunrise that peeked through the blinds to paint shadow lines on the ceiling. Even that distraction didn't stop an unsettling gut reaction in the pit of his stomach. His sister, Karen—home for the weekend—surprised everyone. Ma gushed that her successful little girl—who made it big in Atlanta—took time for a visit. And Adam held that same pride for his sister's success that she worked for the number one beverage company in the world.

But the excitement of seeing Karen last night also supplied two surprises. One, she'd become a redhead. Two, she'd shown up with his buddy, Parker, causing the uncomfortable twist forming in Adam's gut.

Parker had been in on Karen's arrival. Probably an innocent conspiracy, but Adam was well aware of the decades-old crush Karen had going on for his best friend. He hoped more to this pairing didn't exist than just a *friend* helping another *friend*. Knowing Parker dating Heather, he didn't want his little sister getting hurt, even though he trusted Parker would never set out to hurt Karen.

Pushing that worry from his mind, he lifted his body from bed and started his morning routine. Yanking clean clothes from his dresser, he stretched a navy, long-sleeve, logo-printed shirt over his head, then plodded to the closet for matching navy uniform pants. Sliding one leg in, then the other, he remembered last night when Laurel suggested he visit her father. Yeah…that'd be a good distraction from the Karen and Parker situation he hoped wasn't a *real* situation. And Laurel would be there. Perfect.

Wait.

Perfect? Why?

Perfect opportunity to sway her thinking about the manor…or perfect to explore why she piqued his interest at last night's meeting at the diner?

The manor had to be the reason. Impressed with how they agreed on a few things and her efficiency organizing their plans, he figured his interest had nothing to do with how her straightforward honesty drew him in or how her wholesome looks were a refreshing change from women who primped and troweled on tons of makeup.

Nope…none of that should distract him from his goal…to persuade her the village project is a mistake. Not sure how receptive she'd be, he'd guarantee no shortage of her giving it to him straight.

He headed to the first job of the morning at the old Morrison Shoe factory out on Rt. 94. When lunchtime rolled around, he planned to skip his usual habit of grabbing a Reuben at Lou's Luncheonette and head to The Laurel Wreath to see Frank. Maybe even talk to Laurel…about the project, of course.

****

Adam parked at The Bean & Brew where Evan always had his coffee order ready—one for him, one for Parker. Then to Jenkinson's Corner Store where Harold had his lottery tickets waiting. More reasons why he didn't want Cedar Ridge to change.

When he stepped out of his SUV, he enjoyed a good-day feeling spread over him, but he stopped when he approached the coffee shop. His good feeling crashed at the sight of Russell Chapman standing inside the glass door of The Bean & Brew.

The man pointed two fingers on one hand at his own beady eyes, then leveled those same fingers at Adam in the silent gesture…*I'm watching you.*

Adam grabbed the door handle, entered, and walked passed the portly aging man toward the counter.

"Up to no good as usual, Carlson?"

"Russell." Adam dipped his chin in a single nod, kept his gaze straight ahead and refused to further engage with the former councilman.

"Keeping an eye on you. Making sure you don't walk away with the village's money."

"The village money is safe, Russell. No need to worry."

"Not the case." Chapman narrowed his eyes and sneered. "With your family history, everyone knows you can't be trusted. Noticed you're expanding your business."

Adam's peripheral vision caught Chapman

79

directing his lecture to the customers.

"We residents need to watch that our youngest elected official isn't using village funds for his own use. Especially since he ran an illegal campaign."

Chapman's regurgitated claim was getting old. Adam never had a traffic ticket, much less the appearance of impropriety with his campaign. Purging his father's sordid legacy from following him seemed impossible. Not just the election, but Adam lived his entire life above board and honestly. "I don't want trouble, Russell. Just want to get my coffee and go to work."

"Oh, you're already in trouble. Just a matter of time till we get proof." Chapman raised his voice. "But don't worry, folks. I'm on it."

Adam ignored the former politician but sensed Chapman was staring. He rubbed the back of his head to make sure Chapman's laser stare hadn't bored a hole.

Evan rushed his slight frame from behind the counter to escort Russell out of the store like a bar bouncer.

Adam heaved a shuddering breath, not sure how much longer he could put up with Chapman's threats. "What a pain in the—"

"You okay, buddy?" Evan asked when he returned.

"Yeah, I'm fine. Election was eleven months ago, and he still can't accept that I won."

"Can't believe he thought his son could beat you."

Adam retrieved his coffee order from the counter. "Guess when Chapman stepped down, he assumed his son would replace him."

"He's supposed to have heart problems." Evan took his place behind the counter. "Looked okay to me."

"No worries." Adam pivoted toward the door, coffees in hand. "Hopefully, he'll get over it," he announced over his shoulder. "Eventually."

****

Two days flew by in a whir of machinery and muscle. Leaves were well under way with their kaleidoscope of colors. In a few short days, that glorious foliage would turn brown, fall from their trees, and the Greene Thumb Landscaping task turned into winter storm mode. This time of year added an increased workload, but the good fortune of securing the Morrison property maintenance prevented Adam from seeing Frank the other day as planned. The biting autumn air cleared Adam's brain, but it didn't stop Chapman's threat from a few days ago to still taunt him. The threat wasn't the first…wouldn't be the last. The man never accepted that his son lost the election.

Okay…no reason to dwell on it. Time to make good on a promise. Parking in front of The Laurel Wreath, Adam came upon Frank Eldridge sweeping leaves from the sidewalk, limping with short strides. "Hey, Frank!" Adam closed his pickup truck door and met Frank on the sidewalk.

"Adam!" A welcoming smile broadening Frank's face. "It's been a long time."

Adam extended a firm hand, grateful to see the man moving around. "How's the ankle?"

"Not bad. Laurel mentioned you'd be stopping by." Frank rested a solid hand on Adam's shoulder. "Glad you did."

Damn. Days had passed since Adam promised to visit Frank, but the owner of Morrison Shoes had him and Parker working overtime. With the property now listed on the market, the owner's request for extra work helped Greene Thumb's cash flow, but it messed with their route schedule. Time flew by, and Adam hoped he hadn't disappointed Frank by not coming until now.

He dipped a hand into his shirt pocket. "Here…I got these for you."

"Well…I'll be." Frank examined the small, beige and black tickets. "You got my lottery tickets!"

"I asked Harold if you'd been in to get them, but with your ankle and all—"

"Yeah. The healings longer than I thought. Gets stiff as a board in the morning. Takes a good hour to get it going."

Ahh…the reason Adam hadn't seen him at Jenkinson's each morning. "I figured you'd want them. Harold printed them." Another reason to keep Cedar Ridge the same.

Frank studied the tickets. "Yep. These are my numbers. What's the jackpot?"

"Two hundred forty-seven million."

Frank put his hand on Adam's shoulder again. "Son…if I win, I'm sharin' it with you."

An unfamiliar quiver vibrated through Adam. He never had a close relationship with his own father, so Frank's generosity embraced him like a warm, yet uncomfortable, hug. "Nah, Frank. Those are *your* numbers. I've got my own. Maybe we'll both win."

"The least I can do is pay you for them." Frank leaned the broom handle against the clapboard facade of the building. "Come on in. I'm sure Laurel'll be glad to see you." Frank limped into the flower shop.

Adam followed taking note of the empty store.

Made him feel bad to take Frank's money. Had to be hard on the guy after all he'd been through. Although, he seemed to be making the best of it with flower deliveries for The Laurel Wreath and also delivering for the food pantry. Through it all, the man appeared happy.

"Laurel!" Frank's voice echoed through the empty store. "We got company!"

Adam snorted, examining a funky arrangement of greens with spiky orange flowers. He envisioned Laurel's negative reaction to Frank calling him *company*.

Laurel stepped into the storefront from the prep room door and glanced at her father. "We have company?" She scanned the storefront.

"We do!" Frank waved two hands in Adam's direction.

He snickered at Frank's action that reminded Adam of a game show hostess. *I wish my old man was like Frank.*

"Oh, hello, Mr. Carlson." She pivoted and fussed with a bucket of carnations. "What brings you here?"

"You did." He noted her cheeks flared hot red. *Hmm…that's interesting.* "Came to see how Frank's ankle is doing."

Laurel raised a hand to her mouth. "Oh, right." She spun away and rearranged a few displayed fall arrangements. "It must be great to have Karen back." She rotated a potted mum still not looking. "Although, I almost didn't recognize her with the new hair color."

"Yeah, she's been changing it up lately." He lifted one shoulder with a head tilt. "Last time, it was whitish blonde."

"Will she be home long?" Frank asked.

Adam glanced at Frank, his mixed emotions about Karen and Parker crawled along his spine. "Just a week. She wanted to surprise us with news of a big ad campaign she's spearheading."

"That's nice." Laurel plucked a few carnations from the bucket and nearly brushed his arm as she scampered to a prep table.

What's with the cold shoulder?

"Well, then, that's good news."

Frank's upbeat tone sounded as if Adam's sister had just won the lottery.

"I'll make sure to congratulate her when I see her." Hooking his arm on Adam's shoulder, Frank leaned in close and motioned his chin toward his daughter. "Don't mind Laurel. She's been a little cranky...business hasn't been good."

Adam recognized the fact with a nod, soaking in the bonding he never had with his father, Ned. He concentrated on Frank's assessment of his daughter. Laurel wasn't her usual cheerful self. The dark circles under her eyes, and the overall slump to her shoulders, spoke volumes that things weren't going well.

"Pop, give it a rest." Laurel bounced her gaze between Frank and Adam. "I'm a little busy; if you don't mind, I'll leave this male bonding."

"You're not *that* busy." With a brief glance at Laurel, Frank directed his comment to Adam. "Gleason wedding from last weekend—drove her crazy with bridezilla's last-minute changes. The prep room looks like a hurricane blew through. Ribbons, flowers and wire all over the place."

Frank dropped his arm from Adam's shoulder and

faced him, his hands splayed at the ready. "Can you imagine releasing ten doves at the church? Laurel designed a flower-covered cage for them." Even though it sounded like a wild idea, Frank's eyes gleamed, and he snorted.

"I heard about it." Adam suspected Laurel wouldn't consider something like that when she got married. He relaxed and leaned against the counter. "Where'd ya get the doves?"

"Not me." Laurel lifted her hand to her chest and tottered her head. "The bride's mother found them online. I was just responsible for the cage. Which brings me to my point...I need to clean. Sorry." She pivoted toward the prep room doorway.

"All she does is work." Frank waved a dismissive hand. "That girl doesn't know how to have fun."

"Oh, I wouldn't say that." Adam shot a glare at Laurel's back. "She did have a *date* two nights ago." Saying that word made Adam's neck and shoulders tighten as he wondered about the guy. He noticed Laurel's shoulders hitch with her abrupt stop before she got to the doorway.

"Date?" The end of the Frank's word rose. "Two nights ago?"

"Yeah." Adam was surprised that even though they lived together Frank didn't know.

Laurel spun around, the glare in *her* green eyes shot angry beams across the room.

"Going to the movies with *me* isn't a date." Frank scoffed and directed his gaze to his daughter.

"With you?" Adam released his jealousy in a rush, and he sputtered a laugh.

She lied! Laurel Eldridge, the poster child for

85

honesty, had actually lied! Adam intended to bust her on this one. *Oh, this is gonna be good.*

"Yep. She's been my movie partner ever since Belinda passed."

That pride in Frank's voice played with Adam's emotions. He would have given anything to have Ned show him that kind of pride. But parental pride accompanied love...an emotion his old man lacked. He watched the transformation of Laurel's face reddened again. Her lips puckered, and her eyes narrowed.

She shot a laser-stare at her father. "We planned the *date* a few weeks ago, right, Pop?" She then turned a glare on Adam, her voice tight and deliberate. "It wouldn't be right to cancel at the last minute."

Adam breathed a snort through his nose. "Hey"— he stepped toward her—"I think it's great you have that kind of relationship. Sharing stuff with your father is something I've—"

Don't go there.

"It's not like he doesn't have anyone else." Laurel wove her arms together over her chest. "I've been telling him to ask Joan to end the monotony of being stuck with his daughter. But he won't."

"Joan's got better things to do." Frank looked away at the mention of the woman who worked at Muffin's 'n More. "Besides, who else would I see a movie with?"

Adam envied Frank's love for his daughter. But she had a point. And from Frank's deflection, the man clearly had an interest in Joan. "You know, Frank." Adam stepped closer and, this time, hooked his arm on Frank's shoulder. "You could do better than Laurel." He snickered, attempting to ease Frank's embarrassment while staring into the simmering heat in Laurel's eyes. "She's a little cranky, if you get my drift. Joan would make a more enjoyable movie partner." Adam dropped his arm, tilted his head, and grinned at Laurel while placing the opposite hand on his heart. "In my humble opinion."

Frank let out a hearty belly laugh. "Now you're gettin' the hang of it!" He leaned closer to Adam again. "Laurel's a little set in her ways, but she's a good girl. Always does the right thing."

Adam agreed. That's why he needed to sort through the baffling jealousy at the mention of Laurel dating.

Over the past few weeks, unexplained thoughts of Laurel interrupted his life at the oddest times. Even though he hadn't seen her for a few days, he remembered their two-week deadline approached— probably the reason she disrupted his thoughts. And those cute freckles floating on her cheeks called out to say, *Hey, stupid! I'm the one you're looking for. It's been me all along!*

Adam shot his face toward the door. Time to get out of there when freckles started talking. "Well…ah…I've taken up enough of your time." He extended his hand to Frank. "Glad to see you're on the mend. I'll catch you at Jenkinson's once you're up to it. Take care of that ankle, Frank."

"Will do. Don't be a stranger. Stop by anytime." Then Frank popped his blue eyes wide open. "Why don't you stop by the house on Sunday for some football? The game promises to be a good one."

"I'd like that, Frank." Thrilled at the invitation, Adam glanced at Laurel and hoped she would, too. "I'd like that a lot."

"Good. Maybe Laurel will whip up some appetizers." Frank pitched a thumb at his daughter.

"Sorry, caveman." Laurel approached the prep room door and responded over her shoulder. "I've got plans on Sunday."

"Another date?" *Another fake date?*

She turned with her chin down and flashed a slit-eye glare. "No…Jeanine's birthday. A bunch of us are taking her out."

Not a real date…great! "Girls' night out?"

"Yes."

"Good." He cupped his hand over his mouth after the word slipped out, then slid his hand to his neck. "Uh, good. Good that we guys can hang out…ya know, watch the game."

"Then it's a date," Frank proclaimed. "Game starts at four." He extended another firm handshake and patted Adam's opposite shoulder.

"I'll be there." Glancing toward Frank's daughter, he nodded a goodbye. "Laurel."

"Wait!" she called in a hurry. "The Christmas kick-off parade."

"What about it?" Adam's heart did a happy, little jump that she'd given him reason to stay a few minutes longer.

"We need to plan a meeting."

"Okay." Adam gave a half shrug. "That's *your* thing. Whatever plans you make are fine."

"Not mine." Her mouth molded in a grimace. "Yours."

"Me?" *What was she talking about?* "Why me?"

"Because you're the parade chair."

Adam dropped his jaw like it hit the ground. "I'm what?"

Chapter 6

Laurel stared wide-eyed at the door Adam had walked through. "Do you believe that?"

"What?" Pop focused on the leaves floating in on the shop floor from the wind when the door opened.

"He didn't know he's the parade chair." Hands clutching the sides of her head, she fought the urge to yank her ponytail. "Who functions like that?"

Pop took hold of the broom and swept. "Pretty well, I suspect. He's a good businessman."

She slid her hands along the sides of her neck and massaged the tension stiffening her muscles. "He might know business, but his people skills—"

"Are just fine." Pop stopped sweeping and raised his eyebrows. "Lighten up. You're too serious. The boy's got a lot on his mind."

"Seriously?" She dropped her hands to her hips. "Did you hear how many times he said the word *date*? He's more worried about who *his* next date is." Angling her head, she shot a glance from the corner of her eye. Yes, she sounded petty, but Adam didn't get it.

"Ha!" Pop leaned against the counter to rest his ankle. "Sounds like that little, green-eyed monster is getting the best of you."

"Are you kidding?" Realizing her tone rushed a little too defensive, she inhaled to regroup. "Adam is way off the mark for me... an aardvark would be a better pick."

Pop laughed.

That same belly laugh he let loose when Adam made that snide comment a few minutes ago about her being crankier than Joan.

My own father turned on me. Really?

Dealing with Adam was difficult enough, she didn't need Pop adding to the frustration. "This isn't funny."

"And neither is your vow to swear off men." Pop's laughter faded. "You need to get out there. If your head keeps telling you all guys are bad, you'll never find love."

Her *mind* had played tricks, convincing her Adam's good traits outweighed the bad while her attraction guided the way. "I can't deal with another controlling guy. Adam is irresponsible and controlling." She shook her head to hammer the point while a ribbon of panic and waning resolve wove through her. "No way…been there, done that."

"I agree, but that jerk you dated is making you think Adam is controlling. He's not. He's confident. There's a difference."

"It's—"

He held up a hand. "Admit it. You're crazy about the guy."

"What?" A swoosh of defeat wilted her willpower, and she struggled to hide it. Taking a deep breath to gain strength and set Pop straight, she opened her mouth—

"Don't deny it." He rested both hands on the tip of the broom handle. "You've been carrying a torch for him forever. Your mother and I used to joke about it."

"What?" She buttoned her lips shut and stiffened both arms to her sides like a child who'd been accused of something she didn't do. The urge to stamp her foot for good measure boiled inside. But she wasn't eight years old, and those old tension releases were futile in the big-girl world.

A crush on Adam? Why did Pop and Momma think that?

Sure, at twelve years old, when she recognized boys were no longer gross, she remembered thinking how cute Adam had been with his dark eyes and gorgeous black hair. Then her world upended, replacing boys with more important, grown-up responsibilities.

Raising her chin again, she leveled her gaze on Pop. "Adam is irresponsible. Everyone's survival depends on the manor and this parade, and he doesn't care. Doesn't care if we all have to close our doors for good." *There. That ought to steer the conversation away from my supposed torch.*

Pop arched a salt-and-pepper-colored eyebrow. "A little melodramatic, don't you think?"

"No." She picked off a few dead petals from a nearby cooler bucket of mums to slow her frustration. "He fought us with the Phase One Revitalization. Now he's doing it again with the manor and parade."

"The way I hear it, he's just cautious. Seems to me he's looking out for everyone. Doesn't want the village in so deep they can't get out."

"Where'd you hear that?"

He eyed her and offered the trash bin.

"Right." She nodded, cupping the wilted petals in her hand. "Hanging with the guys at Jenkinson's."

"Give him a chance. He's a great guy with a good

head on his shoulders."

"I try, but then he does something like this." Dropping the petals into the bin, she rubbed her palms together. "Doesn't he know he's supposed to get the ball rolling?"

Pop replaced the trash bin in its spot. "Everyone is not as OCD as you. Give him a break. He'll do it in his own time."

She stretched her eyes double their size and stepped back, tripping over a Halloween display. "I don't have obsessive compulsive disorder." She secured her balance and composed herself. "I don't procrastinate. I just like to get things done."

Both Pop's eyebrows lifted. "Really? I hadn't noticed." He took hold of one of her hands. "Look…You care *too* much for the town…and him. Admit it, you both have a lot in common."

"We don't—"

"Don't waste your time." He waved the other hand. "I know that look."

"What look?" *Darn…I hate that my expressions are so transparent.*

"The look on your face when Adam's around. That's the same gaze your mother used to shine on me whenever I came near her." Pop leaned forward and kissed her forehead. "Hold onto that feeling, sweetie. It doesn't come but once in a lifetime. Savor it. You'll be glad you did."

Laurel let his statement germinate a minute. In the past few weeks, she found herself thrown together with Adam. Even though they both owned businesses involving foliage, and both loved Cedar Ridge, they never seemed to be on the same page.

Maybe drive and determination to get things done could also be the flip side of stubborn. He and Parker had built a thriving business. Maybe his practical business side would see the benefit of the two projects.

Would Adam do right by the parade?

"Sophie…" She stepped out of her father's hold, convinced Adam's head wasn't in the game. The other night at the diner, Laurel had mistaken Adam's sister, Karen, for Sophie. When she saw Karen was who had kissed Adam on the cheek, jealousy that had replaced her standard rational thoughts bothered her even more.

"Sophie?" Pop asked.

"His last girlfriend." With her tone flat, she picked up a watering can and made her way to the sink.

"How long ago was that?" Pop returned the broom and dustpan to the closet. "From what I've heard, he's not dating anyone now. What's the problem?"

Until he finds another woman to fill the void. "He jumps from girl to girl." Laurel filled the can under the faucet and accidently sprayed herself with water. She wiped her face with her shirt sleeve. "How can he focus on what needs to be done with the parade when he's always dating?"

"I guess he's searching for the right girl." Pop walked past her and settled himself on the stool, propping his bad ankle on the lower shelf below the counter. "The way I figure it—sooner than later—he'll get his head straight and settle down. Just in time to realize you belong together."

Settle down. Just like Jeanine mentioned.

Both Jeanine and Pop made giving Adam a chance sound so simple—so natural. But two birds were needed for the nest to be strong, and she wondered if

Adam had it in him to be committed to one person. She also didn't want to be one of those he'd left in his wake when he flew away.

****

Another meeting at Rutledge Manor and Adam wanted answers. He bolted through the library doors. "Can someone tell me how I became the Christmas parade chair?"

Stanley and Mayor Farley—seated on an old, love seat sofa—removed their attention from a pile of papers to the intrusion.

Laurel, seated across from the men, snapped her head to look his way. "You volunteered when we all met at the Acropolis, don't you remember? You said it was a good idea."

I did? Oh, man.

At the end of that meeting, he experienced twisted thoughts with a sudden interest in Laurel that he hadn't paid attention to the discussion. He vaguely remembered saying, *yes, good idea*, to something, but of course, the preoccupation of his brain created a distraction. With her sugar cookie fragrance now seeping through his nose, he slid a few steps away from the distraction. *Better pay attention.*

"It's a good idea with your experience guiding people, you know, your employees." Winston Farley returned his attention to whatever papers he and Stan had been studying.

"Employees?" Yeah, he did have a few seasonal guys who helped with spring and fall cleanup. Snow plowing, too. But that wasn't enough experience to enable him to run a Christmas parade the entire village counted on within an *unreasonably* short timeline. With the commotion of a circus sounding from the foyer, Adam craned his head to see the three octogenarians everyone in the village depended on. Wherever they went, the air was always sprinkled with a little chaos.

"The guys are here!" Stanley jumped from his seat to sprint through the open, French doors into the foyer.

"The cavalry has arrived!" George Statler bellowed, waving his cane in the air, his voice echoing into the library.

"You weren't in the cavalry, George," his buddy Howard Waldorf corrected. "You were in WW2."

"Darn right, I was. Saved that famous general's butt back then, and I'm going to save Stanley's right now."

"Only a miracle will save Stanley right now," Adam mumbled.

Laurel elbowed his side as she stood beside him.

"What?" He glanced her way. "It's the truth."

"Don't be so negative," she murmured. "We're here to help."

As they walked together across the creaky, wood floor into the foyer, the weight of the parade responsibility freaked him out.

"We'll be working a few hours," Howard Waldorf announced, his tuft of shocking white hair bright under the foyer light. "Then we're headed over to The Bean & Brew."

Every day for the past year since Evan's father, Tom, had died, Howard, George Statler, and Walter Buchanan helped Evan and his mother, Arlene, run the coffee shop.

When Evan's wife had run off on him and his daughter, he struggled to move back to Cedar Ridge.

Evan had been to hell and back, and Adam celebrated having Evan home where everyone supported him—where he belonged.

"Stan, we're going to whip this place into shape," Walter Buchannan, the former police detective said in his soft, gentle way. "What do you want us to do?"

Adam respected these three men who had helped more people than anyone he knew. Even with their advanced ages, they were part of the Greatest Generation, and Adam appreciated they'd get things done.

"The wallpaper in the front parlor has to be torn down," Stanley instructed. "Start there, but only go as high as you can reach. No ladders, okay?"

"Ready, willing, and able." George stood at attention and saluted.

"You haven't been able in years," Howard commented.

"I'm retired. I'm not dead. I still know my way around electric." He pointed to his head. "All my years at the electric company is still in here."

George's years at New Jersey's biggest electric company benefitted everyone in the village. Each one of the men had a level of expertise.

"Let's get this job going without any fanfare." Howard patted Stanley's shoulder. "What about the wallpaper in here and on the staircase?"

"Don't worry about that." Stan swiped a hand in the air. "I've got a crew coming in tomorrow to deal with the removal for all the high spots. They've got the proper ladders."

"What's *that* going to cost?" Adam spied the large amount of square footage covered by wallpaper.

"I'm w-working on it." Stan diverted his gaze from Adam. "But…right now, you, Laurel, and Winston have to iron out the Christmas parade."

Adam watched Howard grab Stan by the shoulder and guide him to the side of the foyer.

"You havin' financial problems with the renovation, Stan?"

Howard had spent years in the finance department at the brewery in Newark. Everyone enjoyed when he used to supply a few cases of beer when they all got together to work on a village project.

"Ah…" Stanley scratched his temple. "The entire project is going to cost a little more than I thought. The manor's on the national register. Gotta stay within the state historic preservation guidelines. That adds to the cost."

Howard nodded and angled a glance at the ceiling.

Adam figured a plan might be cooking in Howard's mind to bail Stanley out since Howard was known to be the village money guru and had a way with investments.

"Adam!" Winston waved him into the library. "We need your input on the parade theme."

Adam entered the room, seeing Laurel already seated next to Winston on the love seat she referred to as the settee.

She raised her gaze from papers spread atop an old, period-style table.

With Stan on Adam's heels, the men sat on two, high-back chairs opposite her.

"What are the theme choices?" Winston directed the question to Adam.

"Theme?" He just found out about being parade

chair, now Winston wanted a theme? *Don't people just show up and march down Main Street?*

"Yes, a theme." Winston drew his eyebrows together. "What are you planning?"

Okay, this just got *real* uncomfortable. Adam *never* did anything without being prepared. With the way he grew up, he learned to always prepare for the worst; this way, when the worst didn't happen, he hit the jackpot. But this…planning a parade…developing a theme…he squirmed in his chair, hating the feeling of inadequacy.

"I know!" Stanley's posture straightened. "How about The Three Ghosts of Christmas?"

Adam shot a glance. "You mean the story of Scrooge?"

"Well, yes and no." Stan toggled his head from side to side. "Since it's rumored to be haunted—and keeping with the haunted theme—why not incorporate it into the parade!"

"This place is *not* haunted!" Adam slapped his hand to his thigh. The more people talked about ghosts, the harder it would be to dispel the rumor. He was about to continue—

"Stan, you've been to the third floor." Laurel plopped her palms down in her lap and shook her head while briefly closing her eyes. "There's nothing or no one up there. From everything I've read, Abigail was a lovely person with a kind heart. She's not haunting this place."

"Exactly!" He felt a rush of gratitude, glad Laurel put this ghost craziness to rest. He understood the everyday occurrence of Stanley dealing with death, but he was taking this way over the top. "Parade goers are among the living." He eyed Stanley. "Something a little more upbeat seems the way to go. How about we go with, I don't know"—Adam scratched the back of his head—"maybe something like Christmas, Santa, candy canes, presents…"

"Present, that's it!" Laurel nearly jumped off the loveseat.

"Presents?" Adam squirmed again, a little surprised about Laurel's excitement of something materialistic. "You want the parade to be about gifts?"

"No. No." The luster in her eyes aided her freckles to appear to dance on her cheeks. "The word present. Christmas Past, Present, and Future."

Relief washed over him that she wasn't one of those women who believed receiving was better than giving. "Yeah, I'm liking that! Not as creepy as the ghost theme." He shot his gaze at Stan for a second. Then he refocused on Laurel. "We can highlight things the village offered in the past and how things are now."

"Yes." Laurel bobbed her head several times. "Colonial Christmas of the past, like when Abigail lived here. Christmas of today for the present, and then the future when the village grows and changes."

Changes? Um…not too enthusiastic about that, but Adam had to admit the theme was a winner. He sprang her a thumbs up. "Yep, I think we have a theme!"

"Excellent," Winston bellowed. "You make a great team."

Adam glanced at Laurel whose eyes beamed like Christmas lights. "Yeah, Winston, you're right. We do make a great team." He noticed Laurel's cheeks brightening.

"Now, you two sit and devise a plan of attack."

The mayor puffed his chest. "I've got to leave…have a meeting with the Board of Ed. I trust you'll keep me abreast of your plans."

Adam hid a chuckle with a sharp nod. "Abreast." He suppressed a laugh at the mayor's attempt at sounding official, and also, that Winston acted like he created the idea himself. "Yes. Definitely." He heard a soft snicker escape Laurel's throat. He liked how she got his sense of humor. More and more, he found himself enjoying their time together and liked how he could be himself in her presence.

They talked over a few immediate parade items, and Adam overheard Stanley talking with Howard Waldorf again in the archway between the foyer and parlor. When the chaotic sounds of George Statler and Walter Buchanan removing wallpaper made it difficult to hear, Adam excused himself from Laurel to join the men deep in conversation.

"Tell me what you need, and it's yours," Howard said to Stan. "But there's a catch."

Stan laughed. "There always is."

"I'll loan you the money, provided you take good care of me on my way to the Pearly Gates." Howard laser-pointed a serious stare at the funeral director.

"Don't worry, Howard," Stan softened his voice. "I always take good care of our dearly departed. Especially those who are friends." He patted Howard on his shoulder. "You'll be in good hands."

"You better," Howard warned. "Or I'll come back and haunt you for real."

Adam worried that even with Howard spotting Stanley's expenses, it wouldn't be enough for this fiasco…and then what would they all do?

****

Deadline day and Adam felt his comfort level drop lower than the leaves swirling outside. Even though the cold weather settled in, his internal temperature rose high enough to roast a Thanksgiving turkey. The awkward silence of the municipal meeting room added to his building tension, and he clamped a hand on his leg to stop the shaking. The manor's high repair estimates and unreasonable timeline seemed impossible to achieve, and he didn't know how to stop the expectations from the village residents, especially the business owners.

Laurel flew in from the restroom like a butterfly set free and perched herself in the next seat. "Don't worry." She nudged her shoulder to his. "I'll help."

Her broad smile shimmered like Christmas tinsel cheering up the large, lackluster room. He posed a worried eye and nodded, hoping not to squash her enthusiasm. "Thanks."

Winston Farley's voice emanated from the lobby.

Adam jumped in his seat. *Okay, chill.* He hadn't been this nervous since the first day of senior year. Not knowing anyone in the regional high school had freaked him out with hundreds of unfamiliar faces. Now, he didn't want to disappoint everyone, especially Laurel. That old familiar feeling came back to plague him. He thought he had outgrown that trait, but *this* nervousness had to do with crushing Laurel's hopes and the practicality of the project. And what would be the change in the village if the project was approved.

Behind Mayor Winston Farley—following like a good minion—Planning Board Chair, Ronald Whitmore, scurried to his seat on the dais followed by the rest of the planning board. The mayor conferred with the board for a few minutes, and with boisterous bragging, he laughed at his own jokes and then took his seat in the audience.

With a bang of the gavel, Chair Whitmore opened the meeting, stated all paperwork was in order, and addressed Adam and Laurel. "So, what have you to report?"

Adam shifted his concern to the effect on the village. The short, two-week deadline the village council imposed didn't give much time to get more information. He and Laurel compiled the mountain of necessary paperwork, but the unsettled feeling that the numbers didn't add up still gnawed at him. He hated being unprepared, especially since he and Laurel had rushed through their individual figures a few minutes ago in the lobby. He couldn't program his business mind to a comfortable level that their combined findings weren't positive.

But that didn't stop Laurel's optimism when they had spoken. She viewed the entire project through rose-colored glasses.

He didn't want to burst her happiness bubble, but the reality was *not* rosy. While she considered his view pessimistic, he called it realistic. Landscape costs were too high, even after he and Parker crunched the numbers for the four stages they envisioned.

The reno for the manor busted Stanley's budget. If the funds were available, the timeline might enable them to get most of the work done. But no way Stan could produce half the money necessary for all the *extras* Stan and Laurel dreamed about even with Howard Waldorf kicking in a large chunk.

"Ahh…it doesn't look good." Adam stood with papers in one hand, massaging his neck with the other hand. The prospect of the project seemed bleaker when he presented the figures to the planning board. Even though he didn't think the project stood a chance at completion, he hated to be the one to crash it to a screeching halt. But someone had to be the grown-up in this fantasy with a reality check—even if it hurt. "The parade will generate interest, but I'm not sure it will generate money." He hated knowing his assessment disappointed Laurel. "And then there's parking." Shaking his head, these facts had to be crushing Laurel's hopes. "I don't know…where are we gonna park everyone who comes to town?" A calm washed over him when he finished, even though he squashed Laurel's dream. "I'm sorry," he whispered.

Acting like he hadn't said a word, Laurel leapt from her seat and recited all the ideas and costs they had submitted in the presentation packet. She had taken Stanley's preliminary proposal and gone through each item in detail for the board.

Adam had to hand it to her, she was efficient. As the momentum of Laurel's speech kept ever positive, recent comments from everyone in Adam's life streamed through his mind.

Mom had scolded him. *Everyone in the village needs this project! You can't stop progress!*

Evan was all in. *I need a boost in sales. My father's dream to keep The Bean & Brew going will die without the manor.*

Even Parker sided with Laurel. *It's gonna help a lot of our friends. Time to let the village grow, buddy.*

But what hit him hardest were Lou's words. *It's*

not worth it for me to keep the luncheonette open. Business is down. I might as well retire.

Lou gone? He'd hate for Lou to be forced into early retirement. In a matter of minutes, everything had changed. But at the same time, for things to stay the same, for things that *really* mattered, this crazy project of Stanley's might provide some relief to those hurting. And maybe—just maybe, it wasn't crazy after all.

"So, it's my belief," Laurel concluded, "this project will draw more people and result in more revenue for the existing businesses."

She sat beside him, her eyes sparkling like they had when she first floated into the meeting room. This project meant the world to her. Every word she uttered, every action she took proved her dedication. She genuinely believed the manor would save her business and everyone else's, too. Somehow, wanting to give her what she wanted mattered.

A surge overcame him to do everything in his power to rescue Laurel and the village. Against his better judgment, he rose from his seat. "Even though it's going to be almost impossible to accomplish with the lack of funds and short timeline," he addressed the planning board again. "We might as well give it a try. It's gonna take a miracle for this to work. But Christmas is a time for miracles. I'm"—he cast his gaze at the hope in Laurel's eyes—"*we're* up for the challenge."

With Laurel now watching with trust and gratitude like he just saved the world, he'd make sure he'd stand by his word and keep his promise to the village and to Laurel.

But how in the world could he make that happen?

Chapter 7

The weeks flew by in a blur. Veteran's Day arrived with orders for honorarium wreaths to be displayed in front of the two veteran halls and the memorial section in Wilkensen's Pond. Thankfully, a florist in the next town ran short and asked Laurel to send six wreaths. She worked overtime to bail out a fellow business owner with a generous payout for the last-minute workload. Every little bit bolstered her income since new business rarely entered her shop.

Laurel scanned The Laurel Wreath display room taking note of the modest fall arrangements stocked with hues of oranges, browns, rusts and yellows. Unfortunately, those creations would provide minimal sales. Leftovers after Thanksgiving were given to dinner guests as a thank-you for joining her and Pop for the holiday that they celebrated on Thanksgiving Sunday.

An exasperated sigh filled her chest at the reality of being behind in the holidays. Days before Halloween, TV ads kicked off their Christmas blitz. Cedar Ridge showed signs of the season when The Book Nook's window showcased all the new Christmas releases. Arnold's Pork Store draped a large, holly-decorated banner across his window for holiday orders.

The few Christmas items she displayed were mistletoe and angels with a few sprigs, and several cherubs hung in various spots around the store. Sitting at the counter, she polished the maple exterior of a keepsake box and realized she should have followed the early lead of promoting Christmas. But to her and Pop, Thanksgiving—the forgotten holiday—gave them the opportunity to give thanks to the people in their lives. But she needed to bite the bullet to order poinsettias and create a few Christmas pieces of dried and silk flowers to place in her window to entice more customers. Maybe have Pop retrieve the Christmas Ferris wheel from the basement to put in the front window.

The bell secured to the front door jangled from its perch.

Before Laurel raised her gaze, she sensed her visitor.

For a moment, he didn't say a word—just stood opposite the counter, the scent of fall leaves and his personal musk floated into the air.

"Hello." She looked up to be captivated by the gold flecks twinkling in his brown eyes, and she expelled a silent gasp. "How's it going?"

"Busy." He didn't break the connection of their gazes. "That thunderstorm two days ago stripped every tree. The leaves are piling up fast."

"Fall clean up?" She made sure to keep it casual while tingles of awareness dotted her insides.

"Yeah, but that storm was bad, not typical for this time of year." He withdrew his gaze and redirected it to the counter. "It's a lot for Parker and me." Leaning a hip against the counter, he pushed up his sweatshirt sleeves and surveyed the shop. "Parker wants to hire the snowplow crew to help clear everything, but I've got a feeling this winter's gonna be a doozy, so I'm holding off."

"Hard to hold onto those pennies when you know you're going to need them."

Without a word, he seemed to consider her statement, then nodded. "Point taken." He leaned his head forward, a fraction above hers. "What are you doing?"

A strange shimmer of heat coursed through her, causing her heart to flutter, and she lowered her head to focus on the wooden box in her hands. She tempered her tingled reaction by buffing the corners of the box. Fighting the urge and losing, she drifted her gaze toward Adam's eyes that reminded her of gold-drizzled, chocolate truffles. *I love chocolate truffles.* Laurel swallowed hard as he stared expectantly, and she wondered how to control these inconvenient thoughts.

"What are you doing?" he asked again, his head lifting away when he straightened.

With the vision of chocolate melting away, she needed to say something, but—"What?"—simply left her lips since this growing, impractical attraction stopped her from hearing his question. Maybe Momma and Pop had been right. Maybe she did have a deep-seated crush on Adam from long ago without realizing it.

"What are you working on?" His finger circled the keepsake box resting between her hands. "Did you put those small flowers into that little box?"

"Oh, um…" *Stop daydreaming.* "Yes. It's an online order." She shifted her gaze from the box to his strong hand. The retracted sweatshirt sleeve revealed a blue vein snaking his arm like an impressive river surrounded by mountains of muscles. Laurel cleared her throat. "I, uh, sell keepsake boxes from my website."

"You make them?"

She nodded, surprised at his interest in her work. Richard never cared about her business. "Pop makes the wooden boxes, according to the order request. I insert the dried flowers under glass and line the inside with satin."

"It's nice that you and your father work on those together." He arched a dark eyebrow. "How's it going?"

"It helps pay the bills." The awkward discussion about her bottom line reminded her of when people talked about their salaries. She'd spoken about it several times with Pop and Jeanine, but they were family. They understood all the work of running her business. Yet, she found talking with Adam easy. He was a business owner, too, so they shared similar issues. Although, his business did well, while hers...

Wow...stop! Adam is taking an interest. No negative thoughts allowed.

She always held hope that someday soon the old Morrison Shoe building would sell to another large company returning prosperity to the village. But hope didn't pay the bills. Like Pop preached over and over again, she needed to stop living in the past. Time to think positive.

The manor should increase her cash flow. And while she enjoyed talking with Adam, she remembered his stubbornness about the project and how he now flipped in favor. They were making progress; another positive. And, Adam proved his flexibility by agreeing to run the parade, even though he wasn't at all comfortable.

"I'm impressed." Tiny lines bracketed his eyes, and his lips curved into a smile. "You've got a creative eye. Thanks for helping me with the parade. In case you didn't notice, I'm in over my head."

Laurel let loose a chuckle, glad his honesty carried her back to reality. "Yes, I noticed. I'll help as much as I can. With Thanksgiving two weeks away, I'm hoping to be busy since the Harvest Festival is this weekend." She held up two crossed fingers. "I'm hoping I'll be swamped."

"Well, that's good, isn't it?"

"Definitely! Mid-November through Valentine's Day is my profitable time. It's the only way I'm able to hold my head above water."

"Okay, here's something that might make you happy." He leaned against the counter again, inching closer and graced her with a quick smile warming her to her toes. "The village council wants the manor opened by December first. And—they suggested Stan hire you to provide all the decorations."

She jumped from her stool and sprinted from behind the counter to stand before him. "Are you serious? This is great!" She spread her arms and hugged him, questioning if the heated shimmer she had a few minutes ago caused the impulse. But he hugged back!

She pulled away, peeked up, and saw his huge smile. Whether for her decorating the manor, or that she hugged him, his smile conveyed support and comfort and oh, boy…

"There's more." He placed his hands on her shoulders, positive encouragement deep within his eyes. "Stan wants you to decorate each room with a different Christmas theme, ya know, to go along with our

Christmas Past, Present, and Future theme."

She blinked several times. "Wait. What do you mean?"

"I don't know." He removed his hands from her shoulders and sliced his hand upward with a shrug. "It's that time period stuff I'm not good with."

Laurel's insides jumped and hopped and skipped a happy dance. She liked it better with Adam's hands on her shoulders, but this news took away the disappointment of no longer feeling the warmth of his touch.

"Do they want one room in colonial times, another in Victorian, another in the 1920s?" A hand at her temple, she envisioned the possibilities. "I can't imagine they'd want a futuristic Christmas with a silver tree and modern decorations in a room for the future theme."

"I know nothin' about decorating. I'm the outdoor guy."

He placed his hands on her shoulders again.

She almost swooned.

"I have full confidence you'll pull this off." Sliding his hands down her arms, he squeezed both her hands. "If anyone can, it's you."

"Thanks." She squeezed his hands, too, not wanting this moment to end. "No one's ever supported me like that. Well, Pop and Jeanine, but they don't count. They have to support me."

"Guess you're not hangin' with the right people." He released her hands and took a step back, sending her a sideways glance. "Did I hear you were dating a corporate type?"

The joy that permeated her seconds ago

disappeared in a snap. She lowered her head and pretended to fix a nearby arrangement. "Um…I did. Been over a while." She gazed and attempted a casual conversation, but her insides tensed in defense at the disapproval in his voice.

"Richard, right?" Adam arched both eyebrows with a questioning curve to his eyes. "How did Frank feel about that?"

Not wanting to reveal Pop's opinion, she needed a distraction with a change of topic. Lifting a Thanksgiving arrangement, she bypassed him to place the flowers in the window display. "Did your parents like Sophie?" Oooh, when the words left her lips, she whizzed her head to see his reaction.

Adam snickered before he answered and shoved his hands into his sweatshirt's front pockets. "Wow…good memory." After a few seconds—"Sophie was a long time ago. Mom tends to ignore the women I date. She says I've got my head up my…butt…when it comes to women."

Laurel chuckled at the image of Molly standing with her hands on her hips, lecturing Adam about his choice in women. "What about your dad?" Now it looked like Adam's turn to wander the store.

His chin lowered, and a frown accompanied a harsh snort. "The old man doesn't care." His voice was laced in pain, and he yanked his right hand from his pocket and scrubbed it along the back of his neck. "Ned's a non-issue." He then rested his gaze on her. "What about you?"

"Me?" She opened her eyes wide and quickly lowered her eyebrows when she realized they were raised at the question.

"I betcha Frank wasn't too keen on you dating that guy. And, worse, I bet Jeanine felt the same, too."

How did he know? Had they told him?

Laurel slowly inched her way from one arrangement to another, shuffled them closer for no reason other than to make sure her defenses weren't exposed. And then Pop's words poured into her ears. *You need to date a guy worthy of you. A guy like Adam.*

She hoped Pop didn't discuss her dating situation with Adam, especially with the idea she was crushing on him, which until a few minutes ago seemed ridiculous. She wasn't looking for a guy right now...too many other things were a priority. It did bother her that Pop kept telling her to get on with her life. But that came with risks. Risks her heart was unwilling to take.

****

Okay. Time to back off.

Adam shifted his gaze to inspect the rack holding floral inscription cards, not focusing on them, but giving Laurel a few seconds to regroup.

They both plunged into defense mode discussing their dating lives. From Laurel's reaction, her and her ex weren't as serious as Adam had heard, and he had no intention of talking about his former girlfriends or his old man.

When she had jumped to her feet and hugged him minutes ago, fitting neatly into his arms, he pictured her in a cozy, little house running into his arms. He felt unnerved because his brain had him right there next to her in that cozy, little house hugging her back. "So, back to the manor." He removed his gaze from the cards and tried to extinguish those homey images. "My council counterparts suggested you handle the

Christmases inside. They want me to provide all the natural Christmas trees for each room. I'm not sure that's a good idea."

He watched Laurel's tightened lips relax, and she angled her gaze. Good. Awkward dating conversation successfully sidestepped.

She narrowed the rims of her eyes. "Will you have a hard time getting them?"

"Nope"—he shook his head—"not at all. Usually get them from a farm on 94."

"For your jobs or for home?"

"Three, for home." He usually didn't explain, but of course, he anticipated Laurel's next question when she opened her mouth. "One for my apartment, one for the Cookie Cottage, and one for Ma's house."

"Oh. Wait—the one at the Cookie Cottage last year was huge." Her eyes grew wide, and her mouth fell open again. "Why so big?"

"Um…" He tipped his head back and tightened his lips. "One year we didn't have a tree. The next year, Ma got a two-foot plastic one at the thrift store. No lights, a few ornaments we made from things around the apartment. It was fun making those ornaments together." He cleared his throat…the bittersweet memory always choked him. "Anyway…I still have that plastic tree. It's on my TV stand every year as a reminder of where we came from. But now, I get the biggest trees I can find."

"From what I saw, yes, you do. I'm sorry you had to go through that." She tilted her head and scrunched her lips. "I'm not sure we can convince Stanley to forego trees. They've been an American holiday symbol since the 1800s along with mistletoe." She rocked her head from side to side several times. "You can't decorate without either of them." She plucked a sprig of mistletoe from the bunches hanging from a circular display on a corner oak table.

"I agree about the tree." He pointed a finger to the sprig. "Mistletoe, not so much."

Laurel slanted her eyes half open and pointed the mistletoe toward him. "Mistletoe is *extremely* important."

Adam sent his gaze to follow her hands sweeping the width of the store.

"There are all kinds of myths." She rocked the mistletoe in her hand. "The one I believe to be true is kissing under it is a prediction of happiness and a long life."

"Really?" He folded his arms across his chest. Yeah, he didn't buy it. "What about the myth if you kiss under one, it's a promise or something about marriage?" Right before his eyes, a timid version of Laurel replaced the confident one he'd come to know. As she stroked the ends of her ponytail, she lowered her eyelids, like she believed in *that* myth more than the others, but wouldn't admit it. "Well?" He lowered his head and hooked two fingers to his chin waiting for an answer.

"There's that, too. But a long life is more important"—she bowed her head and fingered the sprig—"especially to the ones you love."

Her comment hit him like a fifty-pound bag of fertilizer.

What a dope.

That she'd focus on the long-life version instead of the marriage myth made perfect sense. He couldn't imagine what twelve-year old Laurel must have gone through when her mother died. That situation seemed to make her stronger, but now she exposed her vulnerable side.

They both had been hurt as kids; and even though their experiences were different, emotional scars were hard to lose.

Adam had a feeling Laurel's broken heart prevented her scars from healing. He wanted to wrap her in his arms to ease her pain, but they were working partners—protecting her in a comforting hug was off limits.

"See." She pointed to the mistletoe placed in the doorways and throughout the store.

He hadn't noticed the one suspended just shy of where he stood until he looked up. He slowly slid his feet a few inches away from the one dangling above with its bright-red bow and white berries staring down. "A little overkill, don't you think? It's not even Thanksgiving yet."

"You can never have enough mistletoe. How about those trees?"

Trees, right.

"I'm concerned about a fire hazard."

Out of the corner of his eye, he took note that not only were a lot of mistletoe hanging, little angels also rested in every nook and corner. Probably a reason for that, too, but he needed to concentrate on the tree issue. "If we get those real-looking, artificial trees, we don't have to worry about them going up in flames."

"Oh, I hadn't thought of that." Laurel settled herself back on the stool behind the counter. Resting her elbows on the wood, she outstretched her arms and folded her hands. "But artificial trees cost a fortune."

"Yeah, that's what the council said." He joined her at the opposite side of the counter, hoping together they'd find a solution. "The mayor asked if I could get real trees donated from one of my suppliers."

"Is that possible?"

He glanced at her hands folded across the counter…wanted to touch them, but he slid his attention to the wooden keepsake box. "Yeah, it's possible and practical on a cost level; but again, I'm concerned about the safety." He lifted his eyes and met her gaze while fighting the urge to touch her. "Can you decorate them without lights?"

"I can, but it won't be the same." Angling her head, she bit her bottom lip. "LED lights don't heat up. They might work."

"Right. But then someone's gotta make sure to water those trees every day, twice a day in the beginning." He pondered that fact for a moment. A few seconds and… "I'd be willing to alternate days with someone, maybe…a cute, head strong florist who loves mistletoe." Like magic, Laurel's eyes shown like the night stars. He'd come to appreciate how expressive they were.

"Cute?" She sat straighter, and her eyebrows went upward. "No one's ever called me cute."

"Again, you're hanging out with the *wrong* people." He tweaked the tip of her nose. She deserved someone who appreciated her. "What do you say?" He went with the urge to wrap his hands around hers. Right now, he'd do whatever he needed to keep a smile on her face, and it scared him. His feelings were growing by the minute, and even though he wanted to stop them, his brain just continued to ride along. "If you're willing to share the responsibility, then I'm with you."

"Really?"

Adam breathed out a laugh. Watching pure joy radiating from her face, he found himself traveling on her happy train. "Yeah. It'll be fun. If you need someone to hang any high decorations, let me know. The ceilings on the first floor are super tall, especially in the parlor and library."

She withdrew her hands from his grasp, and her lips drooped into a pout. "I'm not so short that I can't climb a ladder." She sat straighter again, planting both hands on her hips, and she cocked her head to the right and squinted.

He enjoyed her tough girl attempt. "No, you're not too short. You're just the right height." He sent a reassuring grin until her expression softened. "I bet there isn't anything you can't do. Ya know, going at it alone isn't as practical as letting people lend a hand."

"I know, but I don't want to impose." She settled her hands in her lap. "You're busy with all those leaves. I can always ask Pop."

"Ah, no, you can't." He pointed his finger toward the floor. "Remember his ankle."

Her brows knit while her lips pursed. "Oh, right, the ankle." And then her lips relaxed, and she smoothed her hands over the countertop a few times. "Okay, thanks. I appreciate it."

"Really?" Adam stepped back and placed a hand to his chest. "You're going to accept my help?"

"Why not? I'm asking a few of the ladies to help fix the draperies. I'd be a fool not to have a big, strong, handsome guy do the heavy work."

Adam approached the counter to lean his elbows on its top, taking hold of her hand that now fiddled with a pen. "Handsome, huh?"

From the top of her turtleneck to her forehead, her skin glowed a deep shade of red. "Did I say handsome?" Her eyes grew large like sunflowers.

"Yeah, ya did." He stayed right there, right in her space, soaking in the longing between them. She probably didn't want him to know she considered him handsome, but he liked that it slipped.

"Oh, I meant…strong." With a not-so-confident nod, she yanked her hand from his. "*We* need a *strong* man for the heavy work." Sliding off the stool, Laurel shifted to the far end of the display room.

"Yeah, you said strong." Busted—like a kid with her hand caught in the candy jar. He let a loud laugh erupt from deep within his throat. "I guess I *thought* I heard handsome. Must be mistaken. I'd be happy to help you—I mean *all* the ladies."

Since he caught her expressing her true feelings, he figured he'd change the subject so she wouldn't be so defensive. "You know, it's been a while since I got excited about the holidays. Usually it's just Mom, me, and Karen—when she's able to come home. Mom makes it special, but it's not like all those commercials with big families and a giant turkey on the table."

"What about your father?"

Damn—his good feeling just withered. "Let's just say, the spread the casinos lay out blow Mom's meals out of the water."

"Oh, I'm sorry." Her hand rose to cover her mouth.

"Nah…it's okay. More enjoyable without him. It's something to be thankful for." That familiar resentment tightened in his chest. The old man was the last person he wanted in his life, especially during the holidays. "Mom makes our favorites. Always fusses to make it special for me and Karen."

"We all fuss for Thanksgiving." She approached him in a few strides.

"Pumpkin pie?" he asked.

"No, actually, Dolores spoils us with her homemade, sweet potato pie."

"Hmmm…sounds delish. Mashed potatoes?"

She nodded and giggled. "With gravy."

"Yum…"

"Good enough to join us? I'll add whipped cream for the pie." She winked.

Whipped cream? Memories of her whipped cream silken lips at the diner blindsided him. *Whoa…stay focused!* "There you go again, taking care of everyone."

"I love doing it. Fills my heart. Makes it feel more like a holiday."

Adam took in her words while gratitude overwhelmed him. "Thanks for getting me involved in this project. It *does* feel like the holiday."

"I'm happy to give you the holiday spirit." She withdrew a few long-stemmed mums from one of the cooler buckets. "I'm serious. You and your family should join us. We celebrate on the Sunday after because I'm busy with deliveries until dinner on the holiday."

A cradle of appreciation swept in to fill his soul that she wanted to include him, but… "Thanks for the invitation, but Thanksgiving is about family."

Placing the mums on the counter, she looked him straight in the eye. "*Family* is being surrounded by people you care about." She picked up her clippers, nipped, and shortened the stems. "Pop and I had Evan, Arlene, and Julie over last Thanksgiving. It was their first holiday without Tom. I didn't want them to be alone." She motioned her chin for him to hand her a few mums.

Adam retrieved the flowers from the cooler bucket. "Evan mentioning it. That was really nice of you."

"It's what anyone would do. I like having a houseful. The first holiday without my mom was painful. I pestered Pop to invite anyone who was alone. The next year, Walter and Dolores Buchanan, George Statler, and Howard Waldorf came with their wives. After Kristie passed, your buddy, Todd, and his kids joined us. Every year, the guest list grows. We're grateful to share the holiday with our friends."

Even though she purposely put a large distance between them, he intentionally headed next to her, shoulder to shoulder, handing her mums. "Your mission to take care of people is a big responsibility. Doesn't it get to you?" He gathered the stem pieces and dropped them into a nearby trash bin.

She glanced his way.

His stomach flip-flopped at the glimmer in her eyes. He wanted to take her in his arms to tell her why she was so special. He stared at her for a moment, and the warmth of being with her released a comfort that sent a panicked vein to his nerves.

She stared back, and then broke the stare. "Giving is much better than receiving."

Falling behind in collecting the stems, he needed to focus on the conversation and not how she made him feel. "You don't really believe that, do you?"

"Oh, yes, I do. You just helped me with these stems. And I'll bet you love volunteering at the rec center."

He studied her, thinking about her ability to take everyone under her wing, accepting them. "I like doing stuff with you. The rec…gives me a chance to give back to kids who grow up in bad family situations like—" He stopped. "You've made your point."

"Good. So, think about Thanksgiving Sunday. I'd…*we'd* love to have you. Let me know. I'll talk to Molly about what to bring."

Noticing the additional slip, he just nodded as a satisfying vibe whirled through him. Laurel and Mom planning a holiday meal for the ultimate *family* holiday. Mom *loved* Laurel. He could picture them laughing and having a good old time like family. Exactly what he always wanted.

Laurel.

Home, hearth, and family.

A partner who would fit right in, making his world whole.

And those images scared the hell out of him.

Chapter 8

Boy...were her insides happy...and her outsides almost giddy!

Laurel bounced in her work station chair, no longer bothered that her Internet search came up with a big, fat zero. Glancing at the neat organization of her flower shop prep room, unfortunately, proved that her lack of business kept it orderly. But right now, that didn't matter.

First, Adam's agreement to the manor project thrilled her beyond belief. And asking her to help with the parade proved his commitment. With those hurdles accomplished, hope added excitement to those tasks.

Second, she realized how in sync she and Adam were yesterday when he jumped right in cleaning mum stems beside her like they'd been working together forever.

But now, with the end of her workday nearing, Laurel's search for a manufacturer of *affordable* 18th-Century-type paving blocks for the manor driveway had left her discouraged. Add to that, an email that her cellophane rolls were on back order until after Thanksgiving, and frustration had her looking forward to closing for the day.

So, for the third time in as many days, surprise hit her with an unexpected dinner invitation from Adam when he called a few minutes ago. His compassion-laced voice soothed her when she briefly explained her exhausting day. She had no intention of complaining; it just blurted out in a rush. And then...

Since you've had a hard day, why don't you come over? I'll make you dinner.

Dinner?

She hardly took Adam as the cooking type, but she wouldn't pass up the invitation. A meal she didn't have to make was a luxury. But before she got her hopes up, she did a reality check. Was Adam's definition of *making dinner* ordering takeout? It didn't matter. She'd appreciate whatever he served.

After closing her shop, Laurel climbed the outside steps to the old Craftsman-style house where Adam rented an apartment. Taking in the welcome of the front porch, a pair of white, wooden rocking chairs sat beside colorful mums she remembered Adam's landlord had purchased at The Laurel Wreath. Colorful, fall-patterned pillows sat on each chair along with a stuffed goose dressed like a pilgrim. She pressed the antique doorbell button under the second-floor sign beside the glass-pane door original to the 1930s house.

Thundering footsteps sounded from inside, and then the door flung open. "Hey! You're here!" Adam welcomed her with a surging smile and outstretched arm.

"Wow, something smells good." Laurel followed him up the narrow staircase to the apartment. "Did you actually cook?"

He stopped mid-flight, turned, and looked down at her. His hand flew to his chest, and his lip dipped into a pout. "I'm crushed you'd think I'd invite you to dinner and serve takeout." His brown eyes sparkled like chocolate diamonds, and his pout morphed into a playful smile.

"I didn't mean to—I don't know how you had time to cook after working all day."

Pivoting, he climbed the stairs. "I went along with Parker's idea to have one of our snowplow guys come in today to help with the cleanups. We finished early so it was a good night for us to meet."

Ah...Pop was right. Adam is flexible. Laurel arrived at the top landing and entered a small, square hall leading to his second-floor apartment. "Actually, it's a good night. Not having to cook is like a vacation. This is the best!"

Seeing his extended hand, she slid her arms from her jacket handing it off.

He draped it next to his jacket on one of the hooks on the wall.

She liked how the two garments hung side by side. And standing this close in the small space sent butterflies fluttering her insides. She'd stay this close, right here, in this spot, for the entire night inhaling his just-showered scent. That, and his warmhearted welcome had all the frustration of her *exhausting* day fading away. "Thanks for inviting me." Did that sultry voice come from her? While she wanted to savor the generosity he showed, she didn't need to make a fool of herself by gushing.

"No problem." He swept his arm for her to enter the apartment. "I like to cook. Don't always have time, but I do okay."

She inhaled, recognizing the spicy aroma. "Something smells great."

"Chili, salad, and burn 'n serves."

She chuckled. "What are burn 'n serves?"

"Refrigerator rolls. Mom made them with special dinners. They were always light and fluffy."

"Oh, I haven't had them in forever. Now I'm even hungrier." *But, wait.* "Why burn?"

This time, he chuckled. "When I first got this place, I had Mom and Karen over. To make it special, I made the rolls. Didn't realize Mom's trick was to use parchment paper. Mine burned on the bottom. So, I dubbed them burn 'n serves."

Laurel quirked her lips to one side. "They're special, and we're having them tonight?"

"Yep."

"With or without the burn?"

He laughed. "Without, *definitely* without."

"Good. I'm trying to stay away from charcoal these days."

Walking into the small but neatly arranged living room, she felt a lump form in her throat when she noticed the small, plastic Christmas tree sitting on the TV stand. She fingered a small branch and admired the few homemade ornaments that looked like they were made by a child. She expected a large-screen TV since he loved football, but a modest-sized screen sat next to the tree on a rough-hewed, wooden stand. She stepped closer. "This is an interesting piece."

"Thanks. I made it."

"Really?" Running a hand along the textured wood, she admired the work of crafting the piece.

"A few years ago, Parker and I made wooden window boxes for one of our customers. Was the first time I did something like that."

The heartwarming tone of his voice mirrored the

pride in his eyes.

"It's good, ya know, to make something tangible that someone appreciates. Like your keepsake boxes."

She spread her fingers across her chest. "I'm surprised you remember those."

"Of course, I do." He slid his hands in his jean pockets and rocked on his heels. "I remember everything about you."

Laurel lowered her hand and found it difficult not tear up. Richard barely remembered things concerning her, which, in hindsight, was her fault for dating him for the wrong reason. Not fair to Richard, and not fair to herself. Thankfully, Adam and Richard were nothing alike. She blinked a few times to clear her vision. "Um…" She purposely surveyed the room to clear her head. "What other pieces have you made?"

He showed her the bookcase stuffed with landscape design manuals and horticulture reference books. He lifted his fist to his mouth and cleared his throat. "There are a few pieces in the other room"—he pointed a thumb in that direction—"but I can show them to you another time."

The other room…his bedroom. Laurel liked how he respected her enough not to put her in an uncomfortable position.

Guiding her to the small kitchen, he showed her the message center affixed to the wall. Every piece he made was attractive and practical. He proved to be practical in his business decisions, the village revitalization projects, and equally practical in his home.

Home… Memories of the apartment she left rushed to her mind. Her sanctuary from the world. The yard sale specials bought on a shoestring budget had given her such pride. Now they all sat in the back of Pop's garage.

"Here, sit." He offered a chair at the oval table set for two.

Laurel noted the mismatched bowls and utensils provided a charm to the place settings. She never had a man other than Pop cook for her. And he held a chair just like he did when they met Ernie and Harold at the diner meeting. In all her time with Richard, he never held her chair. Even at the fanciest restaurants, he always seated himself in the perfect spot to see who was present for *networking*.

Laurel slid a spoonful of chili into her mouth and closed her eyes. "Mmm...this is soooo good," she said with a mouthful, forgoing her manners.

"Glad you like it. It's the one thing I've mastered." He passed the burn 'n serve plate.

"You can make it for me any—" She held her tongue and took a biscuit. "I, uh, I rarely eat a meal I haven't made myself. This is a treat."

"You sounded pretty stressed when I called...I had to do something to help."

"I *really* appreciate it." Especially since he took the time to show he cared.

"Doesn't Frank cook for you?" Adam separated a dinner roll and began to smear it with butter.

"He's always there to help, but I usually come home from work and throw together something quick. He's offered, but I've been doing it ever since Momma died...just part of my day." She inclined her head sideways and shrugged her right shoulder.

"Does he know how to cook?"

Laurel huffed a laugh in between another spoonful.

"I'm not sure. Even when I had my own apartment, I cooked enough every night to give him leftovers for the next day. He just had to nuke it."

"You spoiled him." He popped a bit of roll into his mouth.

"I guess." She held her spoon in her right hand that rested on the table edge and leveled her gaze across the room, thinking of all Pop had been through. "Pop's great. He deserves to be spoiled."

"And we're back to you always doing for others." Adam reached across the table and rubbed a fingertip over the back of her hand. "You need someone to help you break that habit."

The gesture touched her while it also created a little rush of excitement. "I don't need a shoulder to cry on, if that's what you mean."

"I think I've got pretty big shoulders."

Laurel pulled in her lips and bowed her head, afraid to make eye contact. She'd love to rely on someone's shoulders—not to take care of her—but to share her dreams and even her troubles. Pop and Jeanine were great, but having a close relationship seemed more of what she wanted, even if she insisted she didn't have the time. She yearned for someone to listen with an understanding ear and be honest when she needed a dose of reality.

Peeking up at the sincerity in Adam's eyes, Laurel suspected he might be that someone, which caused fear to settle in the pit of her stomach. She cleared her throat and took another spoon of chili.

With dinner over, they cleared the table together, and their bantering made her relax in a way she hadn't in a long, long time. She enjoyed their easy conversation, his company, and the comfort of his home. He provided a safe environment, where removing the walls she'd built to protect herself weren't so daunting. She'd become a bundle of stress and worry supporting those walls sturdy and strong for the past sixteen years. The security and caring Adam provided was something she needed to explore, especially since the tension she always carried seemed to melt away.

With the dishes loaded in the dishwasher, they sat again at the table to get to work.

"We need a Grand Marshal." Laurel checked the list on her tablet, not sure of the best choice. "The mayor?"

And then they both shook their heads at the same time. "No," they uttered.

"I'm thinking it should be someone with a larger fan base." Adam tapped a pen on the tabletop. "Don't get me wrong, Winston's a great guy. I just don't think he can draw anyone from out of town."

"I agree." She nodded and gazed across the room. "We need someone…"

A few seconds of silence passed, and they yelled in unison, "Trevor Lawrence!"

He high-fived her. "Yep, we're a great team."

Seeing his fixated stare, she liked how they were in sync, remembering their discussion about the *Homegrown Superstar* contestant during the meeting with Ernie and Harold. Her optimism about Adam's dedication to this parade increased with every agreement.

She twisted the end of her hair as his stare sent tingles sprinkling within her like magical fairy dust. "Okay, I'll contact him to see if he's available." She focused on more notes entered into her tablet to gain control of the tingles. "Now for the most important parade guest, one everyone will be looking for."

"And who's that?" Adam leaned forward, his attention solidly on her.

"Santa Claus!"

"Oh, right, I forgot about him. He *is* most important." He hooked his right hand under his chin. "Who do you have in mind?"

"We've got Ernie, Harold—" Laurel ticked off a list of candidates. "—and the guys...Howard, George, Walter—"

"No." Adam shook his head, and with an elbow on the table, pointed his pen to the ceiling. "What do you think if the three guys ride in a special car after the grand marshal with signs on the doors that say *Greatest Generation?*"

"Oh, Adam...I love it! A tribute to their sacrifice to our country and honoring them for all they do for Cedar Ridge. Perfect!" Her tablet got a workout today with her fingers punching in the idea with her concentration on the parade details and not on giving in to the connection they shared. "So that leaves Ernie and—"

"I'm not feeling either of those two." Adam plopped his pen onto the table. "Don't get me wrong, they're great guys, but Santa needs to be jolly, someone kids can relate to."

"We can't rent a professional." Worrying about their budget, Laurel felt her excitement deflate. "We don't have the money."

A twinkle appeared in Adam's eyes, and they widened. "What do you think if we ask Lou to be Santa?"

"Lou…of course!" The owner of Lou's Luncheonette would be perfect. "You know, for a guy who claims he doesn't know how to run a parade, you've got great solutions."

"Thanks. I guess I had to get into it to realize the planning wasn't as bad as I thought. You make it easy. I'm enjoying it."

"Glad to hear it. You being all-in makes my job of assisting a lot easier." She enjoyed it, too…she never thought she'd want to spend more time with Adam Carlson. But now, she couldn't imagine not working with him or seeing him as often. Now she wasn't looking forward to both projects ending.

An awkward silence followed. Almost as if one of them should say something about the direction of their working relationship.

Friendship?

No, not really. More was brewing…something stronger, but Laurel refused to acknowledge it. After all, as much as she wanted one, she didn't have time for a relationship. She cleared her throat and glanced at the checklist, thankful that more needed to be discussed to break the silence. "Let's offer horse-drawn carriage rides."

"Portable toilets," Adam added. "We're gonna need *a lot* of them."

"Carolers at the manor."

"Police directing traffic."

"Roasted chestnuts and hot cocoa vendors." She kept pace, adding items on her tablet.

"Road barricades." He wrote on his notepad. "I'll need to contact Pete at the Department of Public Works."

"A goal thermometer…" Laurel lifted her attention from her tablet to focus on the questioning frown on Adam's lips. "So, everyone can see the funds raised."

"Okay…good idea." He looked up at the ceiling and squinted his eyes. "A staging area. We need to figure out where to start the parade."

"A beautiful Christmas banner across Main Street to welcome everyone."

"Yeah. All those people." He huffed a heavy breath. "Again…where's everyone gonna park?"

"Umm…I'm seeing a pattern here, Mr. Scrooge." She abandoned her tablet to stare him down across the table.

He tilted his head and pursed his lips. "You mean where you're thinking of all the frou-frou things again?"

"And you're being a downer with all the logistical, practical stuff." She arched an eyebrow and quirked her lips.

He leaned back and snorted. "Someone's gotta keep you in check."

She liked how their different approaches meshed, and she pointed a finger. "And someone has to let you expand your mind and have fun."

"Hey." He raised both hands in the air. "I'm the king of fun. Clogging the streets with tourists isn't my idea of fun."

"I see we're still on opposite sides when it comes to the revitalization."

"Opposites." He stroked his chin. "Hmm…you know what they say…"

Yes, opposites attract. And right now, she focused on her list to hide the flush heating her face.

Opposites, yes, but she and Adam complemented each other, both with the ability to lead, but sometimes—though she'd never admit it—leading grew tiresome. Huge responsibilities weighed at times that weren't welcomed. When Adam took the lead, he merely led, not as the control freak she had envisioned.

Um...get back to the real reason for this dinner and not how much you admire him. "What about a tree lighting?"

"Nope. It's been way overdone. Too ordinary."

She positioned her elbow on the table and rested her chin in her right hand. "What are you thinking?"

He left his chair, stood in the center of the kitchen while his playful smirk, and joy-filled eyes framed his face.

Goose bumps formed on her arms, as she awaited the answer.

"Picture the manor in total darkness."

"Dark?"

"Okay, maybe one light on the porch."

"Not very festive." She stretched her lips to grimace. "Creepy, like a haunted house."

"I'm not done." His hands rose to hold off. "The carolers are waiting for the parade to land at the manor. Everything is dark. People gather, wondering what's going on. The carolers start singing something like *that song about joy coming to the world,* and instantly, the manor lights up, the entire building is decorated in an awesome light show and then...ready?" He moved closer. "Wait for it…"

"What? What?" Her insides sizzled.

"Fireworks!" Adam's hands splayed in the air, imitating an aerial display. "Shot off from the back gardens, exploding over the manor."

For a moment, she couldn't speak. His planning proved he wanted the project to succeed. Slowly, tears escaped from her eyes.

"What…what's wrong?" He turned, grasped her hands, and tenderly rubbed them with his thumbs.

"W-where are you getting fireworks this time of year?" She struggled to gain control of her gratitude for his serious commitment.

With a tilt of his head, he lifted one shoulder and winked. "Easy. I got a guy."

"A guy?"

He nodded and wagged his eyebrows. "Don't worry. It's all legit."

Laurel released a laugh and continued to laugh which was better than tears streaming her cheeks.

He dropped her hands. "Okay, what's the joke? You hate it?"

"No!" She smiled, calming her laughter. "I *love* it!"

"Funny way of showing it. Tears and laughter?"

"I do. I do. I do!" She sprang from her chair.

He stumbled back.

She hugged him.

Just like he did in her shop, he hugged her back.

The action seemed natural, like something she'd always done. Safety, security, and a thrill surrounded her within his arms. But…*Oh, my God, what have I done?*

She withdrew an inch, and when their eyes met, the urge to stay put strengthened and overtook her logical side. Finally, her brain kicked in.

You can't do this!

Everything in her world flipped upside down.

Adam made her happy and made her feel alive. And that was the problem. *You lose people you love.*

Adam was everything her heart wanted, but her brain screamed, *NO!*

Chapter 9

The next morning, Laurel needed a distraction from the embrace of Adam's arms last night. Oh, how she wanted to kiss him, but that reaction had to be off-limits for now until she figured out her feelings. Were those feelings gratitude for his efforts to save Cedar Ridge, or a true, deep-down emotion that he might be the one?

She entered The Bean & Brew at ten a.m. and was greeted by the guys—George, Howard, and Walter—sitting in their usual seats against the inside, brick wall of the coffee shop. And just like her shop, the coffee shop was empty.

Every small store in the village suffered. And while Adam agreed with the project, he now understood the urgency that tourists flooding the streets would help, not hurt the village. And he should. Evan Cavanaugh was one of Adam's best friends. A person would have to be dense not to realize Evan and The Bean & Brew were hurting.

Evan's mother, Arlene, serviced the counter, exactly who Laurel needed to see.

"Good morning!" Arlene greeted, dressed in a pink-and-baby-blue plaid flannel shirt, jeans, and a Bean & Brew bib apron tied at her waist. "Feels like snow out there. You want your usual to warm you?"

"Sure. But I need a favor. Help with the manor

project." Laurel hoped Arlene's involvement would occupy the shop owner's mind on something besides the store's wilting bottom line and first anniversary of her husband's death. Laurel's heart experienced Arlene's pain in both concerns.

"I'm not good with a hammer." Arlene deftly assembled Laurel's tea.

"Don't worry, Arlene!" George yelled from across the store, pointing a finger straight into the air. "We're handling the renovations."

Walter and Howard nodded like a pair of bobble heads.

"Thank goodness, George." The middle-aged woman chuckled. "Last time I used a hammer was to hang a curtain rod."

"Great!" Laurel faced Arlene. "That's exactly why I'm here. Some of the draperies in the manor need mending and cleaning. Would you be willing to help with fixing them?"

"Absolutely." Arlene nodded several times and smiled. "I'd love that." She rested her hands on the counter and gushed, "There's a lot of buzz about the manor." She leaned in close to Laurel and lowered her voice. "I'm so excited. Maybe The Bean & Brew could supply the manor with teas and coffee for their events? I don't want to step on anyone's toes, but it would *really* help the store."

"Excellent idea!" Laurel glanced at the ceiling as an idea percolated, then set her gaze on Arlene. "That would work perfectly because Molly is experimenting with new cookies for tea parties. Maybe you could combine forces with cookie and tea pairings."

"That would be wonderful!" Arlene clapped her

hands with a new sense of glee layered in her voice. She slid Laurel's *Flowers make me smile!* mug of tea across the counter.

Laurel liked that everyone stored their own mugs in the shop, making The Bean & Brew feel like a second home.

"We can have holiday favorites," Arlene cooed. "Hot chocolate, mulled tea, peppermint coffee! Perfect to go with Molly's candy cane cookies!"

Satisfaction that Laurel provided purpose and happiness to the widow wove a delighted ribbon around her heart. It also afforded her with some much-needed female-bonding time. Teaming with the ladies to fix the draperies would give Arlene something to look forward to, and joining forces with Molly to pair desserts would provide revenue for The Bean & Brew and The Cookie Cottage. Laurel loved the win-win for both women.

"Okay." Laurel grabbed her mug. "I'm off to Muffins 'n More to see if Joan can help us, too."

"Good idea. Many hands make light work!"

"Exactly," Laurel said over her shoulder as she strode toward the door. "I'll call you to set up a time. Thanks, Arlene!" She turned her attention to the guys. "You boys save your energy. Stanley's got a few more jobs at the manor."

"We've got plenty of energy. This kind of work keeps us in shape." Howard glanced right and left at his friends. "We've got our tool belts ready. Right, boys?"

"You betcha!" George saluted. "And as long as I have my trusty cane, I'm good to go."

Walter's eyes radiated pride as he looked Laurel's way. "My sweet Dolores packs us lunch every day when we're on the job."

"Gotta keep those muscles strong." Laurel raised a hand in a thumbs-up at the *boys'* whose combined ages totaled at least 240 years. But in their minds, they each were no older than thirty. "See you at the manor!" Laurel trekked the length of Elm Street with the cold wind pushing against her as she made her way to the corner of Main and Hemlock—her destination, Muffins 'n More. So far, the bake shop seemed the only place in town that turned a decent profit because of their scrumptious muffins, doughnuts, and pies. This time of year, everyone from surrounding towns visited the village for apple cider doughnuts brimming with cinnamon-apple filling oozing out in one bite. Laurel had no willpower for the glazed blueberry, though, and didn't care that whenever she ate one her tongue and lips blazed a wild shade of blue.

She stood on line behind three people. Oh, how she wished for a line of three at her flower shop. She'd be lucky if she had two customers at the same time. All online deals that the large flower chains offered made competing hard. And those tele-floral contracts were way above her financial threshold.

Joan greeted her with a broad smile bracketing her lips when it was Laurel's turn. "Laurel, did you enjoy those blueberry doughnuts I sent you?"

"Doughnuts?" Laurel cocked her head. "When?"

"This morning." Joan grabbed a rag and wiped crumbs from the counter into her hand. "Frank came especially for them."

Ah, no. He came to see you; although, he'd never admit it.

Pop's lecture about letting go of the past played in her mind. Had he moved on? Maybe because *she* hadn't, he worried about her reaction to his interest in Joan. "I haven't been back to the shop, but I'm sure they're there." She folded her hands to rest on the counter.

"Enjoy them." Joan patted her hand. "So, sweetheart, what can I do for you?"

Such a lovely woman. She felt wrapped in a warm embrace each time Joan called her sweetheart. If Pop liked another woman, Laurel wouldn't mind if it was Joan. While no one could replace Momma, Joan was truly a good person. Their pairing would be interesting to see if anything developed. The two would be cute together. Joan's tall height matched Pops, and with her blonde hair and willowy frame, she and Pop resembled a middle-aged version of that famous fashion doll couple. But her reason for the visit wasn't to play matchmaker. "Joan, I was wondering if you'd like to help Arlene and me with the manor project."

"I'd love to work with you!"

"Thank you, and I'd love to work with you, too!" And she meant it. She imagined working with Arlene and Joan might be what it would have been like if Momma had survived. Surrounded by the older women enveloped her like a comforting hug from heaven. And right now, a hug from heaven was just what she needed because her growing feelings for Adam had her world in flux…and she didn't have a clue how to stop it.

****

Upon entering the crowded Cedar Ridge Recreation Center in the evening, Adam spotted Laurel. "It would have been great if Mayor Farley told us about this lights' donation ahead of time." The sarcasm in his voice slipped out. "We *are* the ones organizing this parade, right?"

Laurel nodded and stood near the double-door entrance with her tablet in hand. "I guess Winston thought it would help because of the short timeline."

"The timeline *he* gave us." Adam scanned the dated, dark paneled multi-purpose room. "But I gotta admit, it's a great idea to donate Christmas lights."

"We need white lights, but they're bringing other colors, too." Laurel checked her tablet spreadsheet. "I like the idea of outlining the fire trucks in white lights. What do you want to do with the rest?"

"The scouts and the veterans are making floats." Adam pointed to a few scouts in uniforms standing near the front double doors. "Maybe they can use them on the floats." And then he caught her staring.

She lowered her chin and gave him a subtle smile. "Thank you."

"For what?" He guided her through the crowd and shot his gaze her way.

She hugged her tablet to her chest. "For taking this parade seriously."

Adam stopped and pinched his brows together. "Why wouldn't I?"

"Well..." She stopped, too, and pulled in her bottom lip. "You weren't too excited about it in the beginning."

"I'm excited about it now." He leaned in close. "Fireworks...boom!" he whispered for her ears only. He liked that they had a secret no one in the village shared. Sure, he'd have to tell Stanley who he suspected would be equally excited, but he'd make sure to tell him not to mention it to Clarice. If she found out, all of Sussex County would know within an hour. Right now, it was a special secret between him and Laurel.

"Oh, there's Arlene and Joan." Laurel motioned with her chin. "I need to talk to them. Be right back."

A crowd of residents—armed with hundreds of holiday light sets—crammed themselves into the drab, outdated meeting hall. Strings of white, red, green, and blue lights, in all shapes and sizes, tangled and twisted atop folding tables haphazardly positioned throughout the room in complete disorganization.

Adam realized the mayor sent out a call for lights without an idea of how to handle it. No plan, no guidance…just chaos. Proof that rushing into this whole fiasco was disastrous without a proper plan, especially since Mayor Farley persuaded Stanley to have the manor grand opening the first of December. That left twenty-two days churning Adam's gut about the lack of time to complete everything.

People milled about—talking, laughing, spreading happiness and good cheer. For a moment, Adam soaked it all in. He'd known most of these people for over a decade and treasured being part of such a close-knit, welcoming community—one of the major reasons he didn't want Cedar Ridge to change.

But right now, this donation social gathering wasn't working. The logical voices in his ears shouted that someone needed to take charge. He should probably be the one, but most of the residents didn't understand his hesitation with both projects. Even though he'd helped with the manor—and was now the parade chair—Adam could tell people didn't trust he was on their side. He didn't blame them. Laurel had convinced him both projects were necessary, so he wanted this lights donation to work. Obviously,

Winston Farley wasn't taking charge. He spied the mayor across the hall still in campaign mode, even though he easily won reelection four days ago.

The person to handle this mess must be a resident. Someone who loved Cedar Ridge.

Someone like Laurel.

Her infectious excitement about the project convinced many to contribute. After all, it was hard saying, "No," to the friendliest, kindest, most-caring person in the village.

Adam scanned the crowd. With nearly every resident packed in tight like a new roll of sod, finding her seemed impossible. Maneuvering through the mass of bodies, he roamed his gaze through the packed hall, hoping for a glimpse of the top of her wavy brown hair.

Nope. Not happening. Not when many of his friends tried to engage him in conversation. Nodding to each when he passed, he might have spotted her, then suddenly—

His stomach dropped when a surge of caution wove through his blood.

Russell Chapmen stepped in front of him. "This mess is all *you*. That's what the town gets when they elect someone with no experience," the former councilman spewed. "You've got no business running this parade and less credibility to advise the manor project."

Adam massaged the side of his neck. These confrontations with Chapman were getting old. "This is Winston's gig. You know there's no stopping him when he's on a roll."

"Someone better stop *you* before you ruin this town." He moved closer.

Adam inched back nearly choking as Chapman's hot breath projected a putrid smell of cigars. First instinct was to shove the guy out of his way to finally put an end to his threats. But he was better than that, and he spied the older man. "Don't you have a heart condition? Shouldn't you be home resting?"

"My personal life is none of your business."

Aware of the rapid beating of his own heart, Adam chomped hard and clenched his jaw. "Get off my back," he ground out. "I'm on the council now. Your son lost; get over it."

He sidestepped the guy, wondering if Russell planned to stop him. Then he spotted Parker and Tom waving him on near the kitchen entrance. Bumping and twisting through the crowd, he reached his friends and inhaled a deep, clean breath to rid the smell of Chapman's nasty habit.

After trading handshakes and playful shoulder punches with his friends, Adam semi-relaxed, even though his heart rate hadn't slowed. Taking control of his composure, he surveyed the crowd to resume his search for Laurel.

"Hey, what's up?"

A touch of concern deepened Parker's voice.

"You look like you saw a ghost!"

Tom slapped Adam on the shoulder. "You haven't been hanging out on the third floor of Rutledge Manor, have you?"

Adam focused on Tom. "W-what?"

"Ghosts…" Tom circled his finger at Adam. "The manor?"

Ugh…the heavy groan rumbling from his throat had both his friends sending him suspicious glances.

"How many times do I have to say it? The manor isn't haunted!"

Tom snickered and rested an arm on Adam's shoulder. "I know *that*, but you're as white as a g— sheep. What gives?"

White face, quick heartbeat. Guess Chapman got to him. "Chapman's at it again."

"More threats?" Parker asked.

"I can call my contacts at the county…see if they can put an end to this."

Being the newspaper editor, Tom's connections to everything in the county and state gave him access to a lot of prominent people. "No!" Adam didn't mean to snap, but he didn't want to tick off the guy even more. Besides, this was a local matter; no reason to involve the county. He pictured Tom's headline for the next edition of the *Cedar Ridge Sentinel—Former Councilman Harasses Replacement*. "No," he softened his tone. "Nothin' I can't handle. I appreciate the offer."

"Whenever you need it, let me know." Tom elbowed him. "It's the least I can do for all the times you helped me."

"Yeah, especially in high school," Parker broke in. "He saved your butt plenty of times."

"Hey! It wasn't my fault the football team always picked on me!" Tom pushed his glasses higher on his nose.

Parker sounded a hearty belly laugh. "And the wrestling team, basketball, soccer—"

"They didn't know what they were doing!" Tom faced Parker and stood tall, as if to make his slight frame taller.

Parker moved closer and looked down at Tom.

"You videotaped their games and matches and told them what they were doing wrong. I would have picked on you, too!"

"Guys, guys!" Adam held up a hand between each of them. "Let's not rehash what went down back in the day. We're all okay now, and that's important." He studied his two friends as he laid a hand on each of their shoulders. He was one lucky guy to have them—Parker and Tom, and Evan, and Todd, too. They had accepted him his first day at Ridge High. The five would do anything for each other. They were a brotherhood because none of them had a brother.

"Hey, did I mention I sent a story about Rutledge Manor to *NJLocal*?" Tom asked. "They like the attention Stan is getting from the *Historic Network*. They're printing it."

"The reno isn't finished." Adam wasn't sure if he was grateful or upset with Tom. "Donations are slow, and the parade…it won't stream in enough money." He tried to find a way to slow things, but everyone jumped the gun. "I don't know, Tom. I guess thanks are in order, but are you sure bringing the media in is a good idea?" He cringed when the image appeared in his mind. "More people will want to come here."

"Exactly! More people, more money they spend." Tom studied Adam. "I guess you're still not okay with this?"

Laurel and the entire village counted on the project's success. He sighed at the idea he was an army of one—a losing army. Time to concede that rushing Rutledge Manor's opening answered everyone's prayers. "Tom…I'm okay with it. I love this place. I just don't want it ruined."

"Uh…I guess you're not going to like this, then." Tom cringed. "I contacted *The Star Journal*, too."

Adam hung his head, exhaled a strangled breath, and looked at Parker, and then at Tom. "I guess the manor's been giving you a lot to write about in the *Sentinel*?"

Tom nodded several times, his glasses bobbing with each nod. "Advertising is up twenty percent. Especially when I hinted it might be haunted."

"You did *what?*" Adam's head hurt like he'd been hit with a shovel.

"I mean, it's not. I didn't outright say it was. Since Abigail died there in the 1700s, and it's been abandoned for years, many *suspect* it's haunted."

Adam scrubbed a hand along his jaw and around the front of his throat, winding it to massage the back of his neck. Yeah, newspapers needed an angle, and Tom desperately needed more paper sales, especially since everyone got their news online. If that one *hint* increased sales for one edition, hopefully, crazy ghost chasers wouldn't get wind of it. After all, it's just a local paper.

Adam released a surrendering breath and placed a reassuring hand on Tom's shoulder. "Twenty percent is good news. I'm happy for you." And he meant it. Tom had put in long hours, carrying on his father's legacy with the *Cedar Ridge Sentinel*.

Both Tom and their friend, Evan, had a sense of pride and obligation to fulfill their fathers' dreams as they took the reins of their family businesses. Adam wanted nothing to do with his father, let alone the old man's art of scams and illegal gambling.

"There you are." Laurel stepped alongside Adam

and said "hello" to Parker and Tom.

"This place is a mess," Adam addressed why he'd been looking for her. "Someone needs to take charge. No one knows how to relate to all these people better than you."

"I agree," Parker said.

"You're the only one to handle this chaos." With her organizational skills, she'd be the perfect choice. She'd also be the perfect person to come home to every day.

Wait…What?

Adam's brain slowed like one of his lawn edgers running low on gas. He shook his head in hopes of knocking some sense into it. Since their dinner together, Laurel consumed his thoughts and left him restless with no direction on how to handle his ever-growing feelings. He glanced at Parker, then at Tom, neither aware of the turmoil going on in his brain. Luckily, they had switched the conversation to Rutledge Manor.

Ah…now it made sense.

The manor.

He'd been so concerned lately with the change in their peaceful village that craziness took over. The only person to share the same concern to slow things had been Laurel. They were the voices of reason over Stanley and the village council. Two responsible, logical business owners who understood how to run things.

"Any progress in finding Abigail's diary in the manor?" Tom asked Laurel.

Adam barely paid attention to their conversation and chuckled over how she'd been enamored with the whole Abigail and Thomas romance.

Listening as she talked with Tom, Adam glanced at the freckles running across her small, upturned nose. They gave her a sweet, girl-next-door look. Although, her timid appearance didn't match her strong personality…now *that* attracted him. Nothing was more appealing than a woman who was comfortable in her own skin.

Who was he kidding? Laurel consuming his thoughts had nothing to do with the manor. He glanced and spotted the playfulness in her green eyes. They sparkled like glistening snow that filled him with an unexplained warmth while she explained her search for Abigail's diary.

And then it hit him…his gut twisted again along with his chest tightening. An unexpected surge of something much deeper, more emotional than attraction hit him like a sledgehammer.

And he couldn't stop it.

Chapter 10

"Look." Adam led Laurel to one of the tables laden with piles of lights at the rec center.

The warmth of his hand on her arm distracted her from the tight-knit sweater stretching over his chest.

"There's no organization." He swept a finger along the expanse of the tables. "People are asking what to do, but no one's guiding them."

Boy...he looks good tonight. Ooo...better pay attention.

"Did Winston explain what he wants to do with everything?" She stared at the lights, instead of Adam, but his presence captivated her attention again, so she focused on his eyes. The concern on his face troubled *her,* because she'd never seen him like this.

"No. Not a word." Adam directed his chin toward the area where the mayor stood. "He's too busy campaigning."

"Still?" His closeness caused her internal heat to rise. When his hand slid down her arm and encased her hand, awareness tantalized her insides.

Okay, enough.

Sure, they worked well together. And the night he cooked dinner for her had her thinking she'd like to share more of those moments...*a lot* more. But she needed to help correct this problem. "If Winston isn't taking charge, this isn't going to work." She spied the mayor talking to a cluster of people. "We need a plan."

"I was kind of hoping you'd take charge on this one," he said.

"Me?" Her free hand sprang to her chest. "You're the chair."

"Yeah, but everyone likes *you*." He gestured a finger toward her. "A few of them aren't too happy with me right now."

"They're fine." She flung her free hand. "Even the mayor likes you taking charge." And she did, too. He proved to be a take-charge problem solver, not a control freak.

"More like dragged into it," he murmured. "Look, if we put our heads together, I'm sure we'll think of something."

"Well…" Laurel looked around the crowded room and thought a minute. "We need more than you and me to pull off this parade."

"Definitely." Adam nodded, his gaze steady.

Nothing came to mind…and then— "Subcommittees!" She remembered how they had discussed it earlier.

"Right, the subcommittees," he confirmed. "Come on, let's go find Winston." Adam took her by the arm again, guiding her through the crowd toward the mayor.

"Excuse me, Winston," Laurel interrupted, ignoring the caress of Adam's hand on her arm. "Can we talk to you?"

"Laurel, Adam!" The mayor glanced at Adam's hand where he grasped her arm. "I'm surprised to see you *together* tonight."

She gently pulled away…no need to encourage any false rumors.

"Ah…we're…not together." Stepping away, Adam's eyes instantly widened, rushing his gaze from Laurel to Winston.

Oh, why didn't she have the ability to disappear? Strike Number Three—Adam's reaction to Winston's comment hit her like a water-filled bucket of flowers. Ouch and double ouch. Just another example of the irrationality of her newfound attraction.

"Oh, sorry about that," the mayor said. "I just thought…because you were holding her arm…that you were a couple."

They snapped their heads toward one another.

How people assumed they were together mystified her. She noticed Adam searching her face as if for a response, but she didn't have one. She twisted her ponytail end and smiled weakly, even though her ego wilted.

Adam broke the connection and addressed the mayor. "Since we work well together"—he glanced back for a second, as if that fact had given validity to Winston's comment—"to tackle this lights project, we'd like to form a parade subcommittee with a chairperson for different sections?"

"With Adam as the overall parade chair," Laurel joined in, "the subcommittees can take care of things like coordinating units, distributing the lights to the fire trucks—"

"And the floats—don't forget the floats."

"Yes, the floats." Hearing no nervousness in Adam's eager reply, she found herself drawn into his enthusiasm. "And the assembly and mapping out the parade route."

"I've done it already." Adam bounced his

eyebrows and stretched his lips into a wide grin. "Logistics are kind of my thing."

"You did?" She almost screeched with the proof that he was totally in.

"I like it!" Winston Farley raised his chin in a nod and patted Adam's shoulder. "Don't forget to come to the council for approval of any ideas."

"We will." Relaxing a little, Laurel bobbed her head. "We'd like Ernie Donaldson and Harold Jenkinson to serve on the committee since they were in on the parade idea from the start."

"Excellent idea. I'll go talk to them right now." He lumbered away in the direction of the men.

"Great." Adam cradled his right arm across Laurel's shoulders.

Prickles of goose bumps peaked over her skin. The sandalwood smell of his aftershave drew her face to turn toward him. Strange. She'd never experienced that reaction from the few times Richard put his arm around her. Her entire body melted this time in the protection of Adam's arm.

"We're a great team," he whispered as he leaned in close.

That action left her in a swirl of confusion, and she refused to acknowledge that she now craved his attention. Like a cowboy on a white horse, he rode into her life, forcing her to open her heart to save her from herself. But…would she let him?

****

The next day, Laurel and Jeanine sat side by side on the dais of the municipal building meeting room as auditions droned on. One by one, individuals and groups stepped forward to show off their singing talents for the manor opening.

Jeanine threw her pen down. "What do we do with him?" She aimed her chin to old Mr. Benjamin, who not only sang monotone, but was surely tone-deaf.

Laurel tapped her fingertips to her forehead, studying the list of auditioners. "When the Ugly Sweater Singers sing the drummer boy song, he can sing the *bum, bum-bum, bum* through the song. Like the little drummer drumming the beat for the singers."

"That…would…work! You're a genius!" Jeanine high-fived her. "But what about the rest of the songs?"

"I dunno," Laurel shook her head and perused the list. "One problem at a time. What do we do with Clarice Carlson? There aren't any screeching cats in carols."

Laurel glanced at the people facing them, all enthusiastic and openly nervous about singing for the opening. Then she motioned her head to where Clarice posed. "Look at her sitting there all smug and confident, expecting to have a staring solo. This is a group effort to create the atmosphere of a traditional, old-fashioned Christmas celebration. The only stars allowed are the ones hanging on the Christmas trees."

"Mix her in with the First Holy Church Choir," Jeanine said flatly. "Maybe they'll drown her out."

"Nope…" Laurel shook her head. "I'm pretty sure there was some bad blood between them."

Jeanine threw a sarcastic glare at Laurel. "Name one person Clarice doesn't share bad blood with."

"Right." Laurel pointed her pen toward Jeanine. "But the church choir is wearing vintage costumes that the county historical society is loaning them. Can you imagine the kind of chaos Clarice would cause if her costume didn't outshine everyone else?"

Jeanine put her head in her hands. "Why is that woman such a pain in the—"

"Don't go there." Both Laurel's wrists rested at the edge of the counter, fingers splayed upward. "This is the fun part, where everyone comes together to participate." She released a restrained breath and stood.

"Okay!" She raised her voice to address the crowd. "Can we have the eighth-grade middle school come forward to show us what you've got?" She sat and checked her list.

Just then, Adam sprinted into the meeting room from the side door and plopped in a chair alongside Jeanine. "Made it…perfect timing. I love when the kids sing!"

"Did you hear that?" Jeanine bumped her elbow against Laurel's. "He loves kids."

Laurel ignored her BFF and didn't look at Adam, even though her heartbeat surged knowing he was only three feet away. She swallowed hard and focused on the music teacher. "What are the kids going to sing today?"

"The song about sleigh rides," the teacher gushed with pride.

"That's my favorite!"

Laurel watched Adam bounce in his seat like he just won the lottery. He definitely liked kids which made sense since he volunteered at the rec center, and he was great with Todd's kids. But right now his anticipation surprised her.

The kids jumped into their performance.

Relief washed over her that, at least, the kids, the church choir, and the Ugly Sweater Singers were more than sufficient for their needs.

Adam leaned in front of Jeanine and directed his comments to Laurel. "This is great! More of that holiday spirit. Thanks!" he whispered while keeping his gaze on the kids as they sang the *calling yoo-hoo* part.

Is he rocking in his seat to the tune?

When they finished, Adam cheered and clapped wildly. "What do you think?" he asked when he finished his applause. "We gotta showcase these kids."

Laurel studied the list, figuring out the placement of the three groups.

"How about if the church choir and the sweater singers stroll Main Street to draw interest in the stores," Adam suggested. "Then they stroll down Hemlock to the manor so people will follow them to the opening."

"So, what do you want to do with the kids?" Jeanine's head pivoted back and forth between Laurel and Adam.

Laurel scribbled a quick idea on the paper in front of her. "Got it! We don't want the kids walking at night for safety reasons. We'll position them at the manor where their songs can welcome people as they gather for the opening."

"Are people going to stand around and yell 'Merry Christmas,' " Jeanine asked, "or are you doing a tree lighting or something?"

Adam shook his head. "Nope. I've got a guy hooking me up with something spectacular."

A niggle of worry had Laurel biting her bottom lip. She loved Adam's plan for the Christmas fireworks, but would it actually happen?

"A guy?" Jeanine asked with a snicker on her lips. "A guy who does what?"

"Something spectacular." He fanned his hand in

the air. "Don't worry about it."

A huge grin turned up Jeanine's lips, and she nudged Laurel's arm. "Don't worry. He's got a guy. It will be *spectacular*."

While Laurel had hopeful anticipation, she held her brain cautiously at bay in case Adam's plan didn't pan out. She rolled her eyes at Jeanine's admiration for Adam and constant insistence Laurel date him.

She thanked the music teacher and told her she'd be in touch about the schedule.

The kids filed out of the meeting room amongst cheers and laughter. Oh, to be that age again. But then Laurel had been their age once, then she lost Momma, and fun had been stripped from her life. Those heart-wrenching memories were interrupted with a chime of her phone.

"Is that *him*?" Jeanine questioned.

Laurel nodded without looking up and frowned at the text message.

"Him?" Adam asked. "As in the infamous, *Richard*, him?"

"Yeah," Jeanine said. "It's been two years. The guy can't take a hint. Don't get me started."

Laurel ignored their comments and read the text.

—Wondering how you've been. Maybe we can get together. Bet you miss me.—

Miss me…is he serious? Her insides boiled at his arrogance, but she refused to show it so she wouldn't get the third degree from Jeanine. "It's nothing."

"Date text?" Adam asked.

"Where are you meeting him this time? Oh, wait, let me guess. Giorgio's." Jeanine directed her comment to Adam. "That's where they always go. Dick's favorite place."

"Dick?" Adam's eyes bulged with his brows stretched upward.

"Jea…nine!" Laurel cringed at Jeanine's nickname for Richard, although, right now, the name fit.

She glared at Laurel. "Sorry. *Richard.*" Jeanine looked at Adam again and nodded. "I think Dick fits him better."

An annoying burst of laughter erupted from Adam. "Nice, Jeanine." And with that, he rose from the chair. "Ladies, if you'll excuse me. I've got a *date* with Mom. She needs a few light bulbs changed at The Cookie Cottage, and she's a little too *short* to reach. I'll see you 'round."

Laurel took note of the *date* remark and *short* comment.

After he left, Jeanine glared. "What's *wrong* with you? He loves kids. He's good to his mother. Why aren't you going after him?"

Why does Jeanine keep harping about this? "You know why. End of discussion." Yes, Adam oozed good qualities, not to mention he got along really well with Pop. She refused to burden her heart with the stress of worrying and wondering if a loved one would be taken away. Every time Pop caught a cold or complained of an ache or pain, she insisted he run to the doctor. Eventually, she'd have the family she always wanted with the man of her dreams, but not now.

"You're the only one who can't see Adam is a good man," Jeanine lectured again. "Look at what he's doing with the parade and the manor. Considering his disapproval from the beginning, he's diving in headfirst."

Laurel hesitated, then continued keying her handwritten notes into her tablet. "I see everything he's doing." She didn't want to admit it out loud. Besides, she needed to concentrate on the vocal auditions. "Adam's extremely loyal to Cedar Ridge. He's been great, and I'm grateful everything is running smoothly with the short deadline. Whether he's a good man or not doesn't matter. He's good for the town."

"And he's good for *you* and good *to* you. You need to give him a chance. He's totally into you."

"What?" Laurel stopped typing and whipped her gaze toward Jeanine.

"You heard me. The man is moving heaven and earth for you."

Now Jeanine was wrong. She and Adam grew closer, but him being *into her* had to be in Jeanine's mind, even though with each day, Laurel grew more and more into him. Still…the *idea* that Adam might be interested was just nonsense. "He's doing it for the town." She waved a dismissive hand and focused on her tablet.

"Wake up. He's doing it for the town, but he's also doing it for *you* because he knows how important it is to you. The rest of us are benefitting from his love for you."

Love?

Love?

She leaned away from her friend and squinted her eyes. "That's impossible." Adam constantly dated different women. No love existed in that. "I admit…he's a nice guy, but there is no way he's in love with me. We don't even know each other that well."

"The way he looks at you, if he's not in love yet,

he will be soon."

A thread of panic caused her thoughts to cloud. Caring about Adam was difficult to admit, but to have others see that Adam cared truly scared her. Taking a chance on getting hurt—no way. "I want a family someday. But I want someone who'd be a good father...like Pop."

"You just saw how excited he was when the kids sang. He volunteers at the rec center and is a terrific godfather to Evan's daughter, Julie." She popped a palm to her forehead. "What more proof do you want?"

Laurel tried to push away the panic and took Jeanine's words to heart. "I have noticed how he is with Todd's kids, especially since Kristie died. He's really good with them."

"Ah...I see that faraway look you've got going on. You're feeling something for him."

"I don't know." Laurel waved both hands in front of her face, then clutched her cheeks. "Maybe he's good with other people's kids. But father material?"

"Get out of your own head." Jeanine huffed. "You *need* Adam."

She dropped her hands into her lap. First Pop sang Adam's praises. Now Jeanine. Everyone seemed to believe they would be good together. Adam, himself, had said they made a great team. But a team and a couple were too different things. From what she'd heard, he never stayed in a relationship long. Maybe because he had been with the wrong women.

What made everyone think she'd be the right woman? She certainly didn't.

And...was he the right man?

****

Two weeks had passed, and Adam hadn't given Russell Chapman a thought...until Chapman stood behind him in line at The Bean & Brew, his cigar breath on the back of Adam's neck.

He'd be forever thankful to Howard Waldorf and Walter Buchanan who left their seats unnoticed and approached Chapman with a question on how the village planned to install more handicapped crosswalks on Main and Elm Streets. The two octogenarians didn't know the former councilman had nothing to do with crosswalks, but Adam appreciated the distraction.

"Don't worry, Adam." George Statler limped toward Adam, his cane clicking with each step on the tile floor. "We've got your back."

His counterparts steered Chapman aside, enabling Adam to skirt to the counter, grab the coffees Evan had waiting, and exit the coffee shop. He jumped in his 1970s muscle car, thinking about the irony of the three senior citizens protecting him from a middle-aged man. Walter, Howard, and George were three of many men he admired in Cedar Ridge.

Laurel had already arrived at Rutledge Manor when he parked behind her car. She stood at the fence lining the property, and that sledgehammer reaction hit him again. Seeing her face him, he quickened his pace.

"Don't you have an SUV?" She squinted in the fading sunset.

"I do." Her hair was tied in the messy ponytail she always wore, but a few strands snuck out of a scrunchy thing secured at the top of her head. He resisted the urge to move the hairs from her face. "I have this, the SUV, and my pickup."

"Three vehicles?" She then stroked the hair away.

"You can't drive all three at once."

"True. The pickup is for work, the SUV is for off-roading or scooting around town cuz it's easy to park, and *this*"—he pointed toward the dark, green body with the black vinyl roof—"is my pride and joy."

"That's not the kind of car I'd picture you in, but it looks fun to drive."

"It is. Especially on nice days like this." The November temperature had risen to a balmy fifty-three degrees, which for Sussex County, New Jersey, was like a spring day. "Although, it's not great in the snow."

"Aren't three cars a bit much?"

Adam wasn't sure he wanted to relive those old memories. Never revealed his reason to anyone but family. Yeah, three cars were overkill, but he bet instead of judging him, Laurel would understand. He leaned his forearms on top of the split rail fence bordering the Rutledge property and studied the wooded lot next door. "When I was a kid, I used to walk everywhere."

"I did, too." Laurel copied his stance on the fence, as she overlooked her father's property. "Everyone in Cedar Ridge did."

"Yeah, but your family had a car. Mine didn't." He waited a moment for it to sink in.

Turning her head, she sent a questioning glance his way. "No car?"

"Nope." Staring at his work boots now, he shook his head. "We had one once, but it was repossessed." He looked at her then and sucked his lips inward, then let them out with a pop. "Mom didn't have money to get one so we walked everywhere."

"Even to school?"

"No, we were bussed like you were here. Going to church, shopping, everywhere else, we hoofed it." The old resentment resurfaced, tightening his chest. From town to town didn't matter where they moved, the memory of kids laughing at him, Karen, and Mom for walking everywhere still echoed in his brain.

"That must have been hard on your mother. Hard on you and your sister."

"Yeah, it was." Forever be imbedded in him would be that transportation equaled independence.

"So, that's why you have three vehicles, so you never have to walk again."

Grateful that she understood, he released a relieved sigh. They connected on so many levels—one of the reasons he'd been finding her more and more attractive. "You get it, don't ya?"

"Hmm, hmm." She nodded and swiveled her chin to his car. "So why this car?"

"When I was sixteen, before we moved here, we lived in PA." He stood then, facing her, wanting to share his story. "Driving age is sixteen. All the kids got cars. All but me." He shook his head several times and looked out into the distance. Pushing the hurt aside, he focused his gaze her way. "I worked my butt off mowing lawns and shoveling snow for anyone who'd hire me. I vowed, someday, I'd have a new car like those kids received for their sixteenth birthdays. But, of course, that didn't happen." He hesitated with a flood of emotions rising in his chest. "Um…" He cleared his throat. "When…when I had the opportunity to buy this little beauty, I couldn't pass it up."

"It's in excellent condition. How did you afford it?"

A chuckle from deep in his throat released the lump that had formed. "The car wasn't always like this. The restoration took a full year to get it running." And then he felt a surge of pride replace the pain, and he stood tall with his hands on the top rail of the wooden fence. "A few years to get the body work done. Another year to save for the paint job. The work was a labor of love."

"A childhood memory. That's sweet."

"I wouldn't call it sweet, more like necessity." He rested his arms on the fence again, the hurt still raw. "My friends busted me about driving an old car, but it makes me happy."

"That's important." Her lips relaxed into a smile, and she laid a hand on his arm for a second. "Just seeing the pride on your face and hearing it in your voice says the car means a lot to you."

"Yeah, it does." Yep. He was right. She got it. She *really* got it. Unlike a lot of the women he dated. Being with Laurel now became just as important as spending time with Mom and Karen. She made sure everyone she cared about was happy and had everything they needed. She treated everyone like family. Something Adam had been searching for in the uncountable number of women he dated.

"So, what are you doing out here?" He stood and pointed to the overgrown acreage, forcing himself to focus on the land to keep his thoughts from hoovering over how her kind, gentle, spirit grew from the self-assuredness of knowing herself. She didn't try to be someone she wasn't. Nothing phony about her.

"My father's property." She stood, too, pushing her hair from her face again when a light gust of wind blew.

"It's way overgrown."

He motioned his chin at the property. "What's the plan for the land?"

"My parents had so many hopes for it. Pop was going to build Momma a ranch-style house, you know, one floor." She stretched her arms wide toward the empty lot while a joyful smile shone on her face. "Momma wanted a large front porch running the length with rocking chairs to watch people and cars go by and porch sit with friends."

"That sounds nice. Like a great retirement dream."

"That was the plan." She dropped her arms, and her smile faded. "Momma wanted a vegetable garden right over there." She pointed to the far side of the property. "She wanted Pop to remove a few of those trees near the fence for the sun to shine on her flowers. Pop wanted a shed out back for his tools and," she deepened her voice, "other manly things." And then she giggled.

Adam understood the love she had for her parents, envisioning the dream house, the garden, and the shed. That the property laid dormant for more than a decade was a shame. He wished he could take away Laurel's sadness that accompanied her memories.

When a stronger gust of wind surprised them, rocking Laurel to keep her balance, Adam steadied her, enjoying her softness in his arms. Seeing the shocked expression in her eyes, he withdrew and cleared his throat, hoping to save the awkward moment. "Um…does Frank still plan to build?"

With a pause, Laurel scanned the land. "Can't afford it. He has a small pension from Morrison and just Social Security. All the money he saved for the property paid Momma's medical bills."

Adam nodded. "Keeps paying the taxes and insurance on it?"

"Yes. Guess he's forced to decide sooner than later. Those expenses aren't worth hanging onto the property."

When the wind blew again, this time Adam swiped a length of her wavy hair from her eyes and held his thumb on her cheek for a moment. He locked his gaze onto her eyes that overflowed with a longing that touched him in ways he couldn't explain.

Laurel broke the connection, looking past his shoulder toward the manor. "We're *not* here to discuss Pop's troubles. Stanley's inside waiting."

Adam angled his head and shoulders toward the manor, studying the small, crowded driveway. "And a few others, too, from the looks of those cars." He motioned a hand for Laurel to lead the way.

When they entered the manor, he saw all the wallpaper had been removed from the foyer, and a fresh coat of paint in colonial blue covered the walls. Newly stained, decorative trim surrounded the archways, windows, and staircase. His friends, Todd and Parker, were on opposite ladders, securing a chandelier. "Wow, that puppy must have cost a fortune." Adam examined the beauty of the light fixture.

"Nope." Sarah Hoffman walked into the foyer, carrying a small box of candle-shaped light bulbs. "That's the same one that was here. I cleaned it with white vinegar, and then wiped it with brass polish. Looks good as new."

"I'll say." Adam gazed upward. "How'd you get so good at that?"

"A lot of practice renovating her house," Laurel

167

stated, "turning it into The Cozy Quilt Inn."

Right. Sarah had worked at Morrison, too. Her husband wasn't the most ambitious guy, and Sarah did what she needed to keep food on the table. Just like Mom had. "Didn't Todd do a lot of work for you?" he asked Sarah.

"I did." Todd groaned from atop the ladder and struggled with the heavy fixture. "She's a pretty good apprentice."

Sarah chuckled. "Yep, I know my way around *You Do It* TV. You can learn to do just about anything on those videos."

"Is that Joan's car out front?" Laurel asked. "I need you both to give some pointers on how to fix moth holes in the draperies in the bedroom upstairs."

Sarah nodded and posed a slanted glance Laurel's way. "Which one?"

"The one with the pink, fabric-covered cornices."

"Okie, dokie." Sarah placed the light bulb box in the safety of the foyer corner and joined Laurel climbing the stairs.

Adam didn't know what a cornice was, and as long as Sarah did, he'd concentrate on the renovation portion. Watching Laurel climb the stairs and then fall out of sight left him wanting to follow, but that was way over the top. Pivoting on his heels, he entered the parlor where he saw Stanley staring at his laptop. "Stan, this room looks great." He stood across the funeral director's desk.

"Hmm, hmm," Stan mumbled, void of his upbeat tone with his focus fixed on the laptop. "The guys did a good job in here."

Adam glanced around the room. "The guys, as in

George, Howard, and Walter?"

Stanley shot a quick glimpse at Adam over his screen. "Yeah, just because they're older doesn't mean they still can't get stuff done."

"I didn't mean that." Adam stepped closer to the fireplace. "It's just that these ceilings are high."

"The tapers took care of the high spots," Stanley mumbled again. "The guys did the rest."

"That's impressive." Adam ran a hand over the wall, amazed how it now looked new. "George uses a cane, Howard is hard of hearing, and Walter is so laid-back, you'd never know he was a detective back in the day."

"Don't judge a book by its cover," Stan barked, his eyebrows knit together with his eyes concentrating on the laptop.

"Hey…" Adam took a seat across from Stan's desk. "You havin' problems?"

Stan scratched the top of his salt-and-pepper-colored hair with one hand, then did it with both. "I'm over budget." He finally pulled his gaze from the laptop and looked at Adam. "A lot over budget."

Adam leaned forward. "For what?"

"The heat died." Stanley dropped his hands onto the desk with a thud. "That wasn't in the budget."

"Fix or replace?"

"Fix." Stan puffed out a heavy sigh from his bottom lip. "There's no way to replace it. The cost is at least twenty-five grand. Way over the budget Howard gave me and the donations we collected."

They hadn't worked this hard and come this close to the finish line to be sidelined. Seeing the despair on Stanley's face said it all. Adam searched his brain.

"What about the *Historic Network*? Aren't they paying you?"

Stan shook his head. "Not for the first visit. It's a short segment to determine how much interest it gets streaming and on their social media platforms. If it goes into a reality series, then they'll pay."

Adam rubbed a hand across the back of his neck and sighed. "So, it's not a done deal?"

"No." Stan closed his eyes and shook his head again.

That meant the revenue from all those history buffs coming into town wouldn't start until after the manor opening. Same with the tea parties, author signings, and other events Laurel dreamed up. "Okay, Stan. Don't sweat it." Adam stood and leaned his fingertips on the edge of the desk. "We'll come up with something. You concentrate on everything else. I'll figure this one out."

Stan left his seat and grabbed Adam's right hand. "Thanks, Adam. You don't know how much it means. I know you were against this whole project in the beginning."

"It's not the project, Stan; it's the crowds. Look, if it's gonna help the village and good people like you, I'm in. Don't worry, I've got this." Adam left Stan and braved the cold outside to clear the overgrown brush on the side of the manor. The few cars parked from the volunteer work crew butted up against one another, making his job difficult. Without enough room for these few cars, where would they park those for the events?

But tourists wouldn't come if he didn't figure out a solution for Stan's heating problems. Once he finished with the brush, he'd find Parker to garner some good advice and helpful suggestions. If they put their heads together, they'd find a logical solution. The manor project needed to be a success. Adam wanted to fix this, not just for Stanley and Cedar Ridge, but for Laurel. Her giving heart—without pretense—accepted him, flaws and all. She didn't fit his checklist, but now he realized she was exactly what he needed.

****

Laurel and Sarah found Joan ironing the draperies in the beige bedroom on the second floor. She banked on the time away from Adam to clear her head. Her body had gone into all-systems-go when his fingers grazed her cheek a few minutes ago. Her reaction didn't surprise her, but Adam's did. This time, she was sure he had the same feelings.

"Those draperies will be amazing when they're all pressed."

Sarah's words gave Laurel something to concentrate on other than the pleasure of Adam's touch.

"They sure are. Great decision reusing these, Laurel." Joan pressed the iron to the drapes with steam rising to her face. "I used the hand-wash cycle, and they came out looking like new."

A heavy sigh rose from Laurel's chest, released with a prayer of relief for both the draperies and the distraction. She glanced at the ceiling to give thanks that the older woman knew exactly what to do to restore the drapes. "They're beautiful. Wasn't sure about their condition with all the dust covering them. I thought they'd be headed for the garbage."

"Not a chance. You can't get this kind of quality anymore," Joan said.

Sarah motioned her head of chestnut-colored hair toward the older woman. "That's one of the things I love about Cedar Ridge—people aren't afraid to dig in and work hard for something. Look what we've achieved."

"I'm grateful everyone volunteered." Laurel considered herself lucky to live in such a giving community. "Thank you both."

"It was *my* pleasure." Joan's beaming smile showed she meant it. "We all thrive on hard work."

"Or some of us hardly work," Sarah murmured in a flat tone.

From the looks of it, the sight of the draperies seemed to please Sarah, but now a frown downturned her lips. "Hey." Laurel placed a hand on her arm. "Everything okay?"

Sarah gave a sideways nod. "Just the usual. Miles still doesn't have a job. Still waiting for his mother to die to get the inheritance."

"His mother is my age, early sixties," Joan interjected. "She's not going anywhere yet."

"Yeah, well, he's not in any hurry to get a job, *again*. It never occurred to me it was his mother's money he spent to sweep me off my feet. Kept it up for ten years until she cut him off." Sarah shook her head, and her long curls swayed over her shoulders. "Turning the house into the inn was the only way to support us after Morrison tanked."

"It's hard to support yourself when something like that happens." More steam hissed and drifted into the air with Joan's pass of the iron. "I went through that when my husband died. I was lucky Emily hired me at the bakery." She glanced at Laurel and Sarah. "The salary's not much, but at least, I can pay my bills."

Laurel endured the same. She and Pop lived with

constant financial insecurity. And she more than related to Sarah with the way Richard had swept her off her feet, sparing no expense on material things, but sorely lacking in the emotional and caring side of their relationship.

"Hey, enough of these depressing problems." Sarah lifted her lips and tossed a cheerful expression at Laurel and Joan. "This place will help all of us. We need to stay positive, people!"

"You're right. Before we get into it, I'd like to invite you and your families to Thanksgiving Sunday." Laurel rotated her gaze between the women. "Pop and I would love to have you both."

Joan's face shone a mischievous glow. "Frank already invited me—and I accepted."

"That's great!" Laurel cheered. "I'm sure he's just as excited as I am."

Joan raised her chin and beamed. "He was!"

"How about the Hoffmans?" Laurel turned to Sarah. "Do I add four more plates?"

Several reactions ran across Sarah's face, then she lowered her eyes and twisted her hands together.

"No pressure. It would be nice to have the manor crew celebrate the holiday together."

Sarah then set her gaze on Laurel with an expansive smile. "Set three plates. The boys and I would love to spend the holiday with all of you."

"That's wonderful!" Laurel leaned in to hug Sarah.

"I've gotta tell you"—Sarah hugged her back, then stepped away to pick up one of the drapery ties—"I'm glad you were gung-ho on this project. Since Morrison, it's been hard for the community to come together with all our financial problems. The manor bonded us again.

Thank you, Laurel."

"Stan's the one to thank." Laurel handed Sarah the matching tie. "This is filling a gap we desperately need."

"Speaking of gaps, what about the moth damage in the pink room draperies?" Sarah asked. "We need to move forward to fix those holes."

"Oh, right, I almost forgot the moth holes." Their discussion threw Laurel off track. Sarah said it was time to move forward. Something she'd been hearing from Pop and Jeanine regarding her own life. And holes...a hole still lodged in her heart because she refused to leave the past behind. Looked like she had more holes to fix than just moth holes.

Chapter 11

Adam came from the side of the manor to find Laurel stuffing a jumble of fabric into the back seat of her car. With the tail of the flowery, pink material dragging on the stone and dirt driveway, he sprinted toward the car. "Here, let me help."

"Thanks, but I've…got it." She pushed the drapery into the car with a forceful thrust.

"Are you always this stubborn, or are you just with me?"

"I'm *not* stubborn." She stretched her words through clenched teeth, shoved the last of the fabric onto the seat, and shut the car door. She stood and adjusted her jacket. "I'm used to doing things on my own."

"I can see that, but you can accept help once in a while."

She shivered with the whip of wind.

What had been nice when they arrived earlier, now grew cold with a wintery chill settling in for the night. "Here…" He tightened the collar of her puffer jacket. "You need to bundle up. We don't need my assistant coming down with the flu."

The simple task of adjusting her collar prompted Adam's instincts to wrap her in his arms, not just to warm her, but to take care of her…because he cared. "How about we go to The Acropolis to get you a bowl of chicken soup?"

"I'm not sick." She eased away.

Not the reaction I expected. "Doesn't warm soup sound good right now with this cold weather?"

She hesitated and bit her bottom lip. "Maybe."

"Good. It's a date." He looped an arm across her shoulders and guided her toward his muscle car. "I'll drive."

Leading forward, she stopped with her feet planted on the driveway surface. "Date? Umm…I've got my own car." She drew in her bottom lip again and lowered her chin.

He needed to reassure her that soup at the diner was not an actual date; although he liked the idea of a date. Hmm. Seeing her unsettling reaction, he withdrew his arm.

This time, both her lips pulled inward with a rise of her chest along with a huge intake of breath.

With a gentle rock of her shoulder, he guided his voice to a playful tone. "It's just soup. It will be more fun if we ride together."

Laurel's chin lifted, and her mouth quirked with the hint of a smile. "Will it now?"

Ahh…that challenge in her voice returned, but not wanting to pressure, he regrouped. "How about you drive, and I'll meet you there? Deal?"

"Deal," she replied with a brief nod.

Fifteen minutes later, they parked their cars side by side at the Acropolis. The drive usually took five minutes, but with the Harvest Festival's weekend traffic, Adam fought his frustration level from piquing as he inched his way two blocks to the diner.

"Hey, you two," Phyllis greeted. "Nice to see you

together." She nudged Adam in the arm. "What took you so long?"

Adam ignored her comment. "Traffic. Harvest Fest clogged the streets."

"Don't I know it. Look at this place. We're packed tight." She leaned close and lowered her voice. "It's great for my tips, though." She winked.

"I guess there aren't any tables left."

Laurel's sideways glance looked like she wanted to flee. "Nonsense. I can always find a place for you two. Give me a minute. I'll get one of the guys to clear a quiet table in the back."

Within minutes, they were seated as promised in a quiet, comfortable booth in the back of the main dining room.

He watched Laurel fidget with the utensils set on the paper place mat.

Since they weren't alone, he hoped she'd relax within the warmth of the crowded diner. "You okay?"

She nodded, but her eyes darted.

Where was the strong-minded woman he'd come to know? Her tenacity pushed him in directions he didn't want to go—but he found once he got there, her ideas worked, and her determination outweighed her stubbornness. Yeah, he'd been accused of being a little stubborn himself, too. Of course, he didn't see it, although Ma, Karen, and Parker pointed it out from time to time. But, with more time spent with Laurel, compromise became easier.

To relax her fear of the non-date, he directed the discussion to the upcoming holiday rush and its impact on her business, hoping the safe topic eased her anxiety. The subject of holidays at The Laurel Wreath morphed into the holidays themselves, and her relaxed smile replaced her frown.

Phyllis placed bowls of hot soup in front of them. "Thanks for donating those toys, Adam."

Adam shot his right hand up with a thumbs-up. "My pleasure."

"What toys?" Laurel looked up at the server.

"Church giving tree." Phyllis placed a soup spoon next to each of their bowls. "He brings a dozen every year."

Adam picked up his spoon and pointed. "No…only ten." He dove the spoon into his bowl.

"Okay, ten." Phyllis aimed her attention onto Laurel. "Most people give one." She glanced back at Adam. "Your bundle helps a lot of kids. We really appreciate it."

"No problem," he said with a mouthful.

As Phyllis left, Laurel tilted her chin and pursed her lips. "Why ten?"

Adam now fidgeted with his spoon and cleared his throat. Even though it happened decades ago, the subject still hurt. Taking another slurp of soup, he swallowed those feelings. *Here goes…* "When I was ten, there were no Christmas gifts."

Laurel opened her mouth but said nothing.

"There had been years when I got one gift, but that year…none." He shook his head and tapped the tabletop with a finger to make his point. "I don't want any kid to experience that kind of hurt. That even though things are tough, Santa didn't forget them."

Laurel took hold of his hand. "I'm sorry you had to deal with that, but you turned it into something sweet."

"Nope…not sweet." Even though her touch offered

warmth and comfort, he shook his head and inhaled deeply. "Necessary. Kids shouldn't be forced to deal with the garbage their parents impose on them." He withdrew his hand, re-lifted his spoon, and pointed his chin at her bowl. "Better eat up. It's gettin' cold." He realized his tone was short, but he didn't like dredging up the past. Taking a deep breath, he steered the conversation to the Rutledge house and parade.

By the time they were ready to leave, and he walked her to her car, not only had Laurel talked and joked like her old self, but he felt more relaxed. "Thanks for having soup with me. A nice warm meal did you good since you and the ladies worked hard today with all the inside house stuff. The bedrooms look great."

"Thanks." She opened the driver's side door of her sedan. "I didn't think you'd notice."

" 'Course I noticed." He held the door. "You're great with the inside frilly stuff. I'm good with the outside heavy stuff."

She lowered herself behind the steering wheel, narrowed her eyes, and raised her chin. "I think that was a compliment?"

"Sure was. I can't think of anyone else who could transform that old house better than you. I can't wait to see how it looks when you finish each room for Christmas. You're really talented."

"You sound like my father…and Jeanine. They're both biased."

"Well, I'm not biased. I call 'em like I see 'em."

"Thank you," Laurel whispered and bowed her head.

Hmm…not used to compliments? Her ex never

complimented her?

On impulse, he scooted to the opposite side of her car, opened the passenger door, and slid in. "When was the last time your ex told you how great you are, or how pretty you are?"

"P-p-pretty?" She shook her head, and a nervous laugh sputtered from her mouth. "…uhh…" She closed her door.

He saw her eyes grow the size of a pair of John Deere tractor tires. "Yeah, that's what I thought." He swiveled his body to face her. "What was the deal with you and him?"

"We…" She looked straight ahead, leaned her head back on the headrest, and heaved a sigh. "It was fun and exciting in the beginning. He took me to places and gave me gifts I *never* dreamed of." She rolled her head his way and scoffed. "Only the best money can buy. But never, never showed he cared. He was *nothing* like you. Not supportive…wasn't interested in what I liked. He knew better and always insisted on it."

"What a jerk."

She nodded while molding her lips in an upturned smirk. "When I told him I was moving back to help Pop, he said it was the biggest mistake of my life."

"No, the biggest mistake of your life was dating him."

She remained quiet for a moment. "We were both to blame."

He grasped her hand. "You deserve better. Someone who appreciates and takes care of you. Who treats you special and not with expensive gifts."

"I don't need a guy to take care of me. That's a little old fashioned, don't you think?"

He leaned in, and her intense vanilla-cinnamon scent tantalized him with longing, drawing him to act on his growing feelings. "Not if the guy is crazy about you." The impulse to kiss her grew stronger. Inching a smidge closer, he laid a hand on her arm.

And she leaned in, too.

"You need someone...who loves you," he whispered. He wanted to tell her he'd love her the way she deserved to be loved.

Whoa!

Love?

Too many thoughts rushed to his brain.

Earlier, she hesitated to have a simple bowl of soup with him, and an hour later, he wanted to profess his love?

None of this made sense. He could treat her how she needed to be treated, but his heart wasn't sure he'd be enough. And now he experienced the reality of how he cared, deeply cared about her.

So how did those feelings suddenly turn into love?

****

The next morning, Laurel arrived early at The Laurel Wreath since she'd been awake most of the night. The quiet of dawn gave her the opportunity to process some orders—a few floral arrangements and three keepsake boxes—but her mind kept drifting to the reason for the lack of sleep.

Adam's story of his gift-less Christmas had wrapped around her heart. She cared about him, even more after hearing about his toy donation. His surprising compliment of her decorating talent made her heart sing. Richard *never* complimented her.

But the shocker—the one responsible for her

restlessness—was that Adam almost kissed her. Almost kissed her! And she would have let him!

She shook her head, rattling sense into her hopelessly romantic brain. Last night she almost lost her head over a guy she had no business losing her head over. No matter how hard she tried to rationalize this unwanted yearning, it didn't make sense.

The stark comparison between Adam and Richard had her reasoning Adam's good qualities. Richard's narcissism trumpeted loud and clear when she told him she needed to help Pop. He said her irresponsible action would jeopardize their relationship, and he was the responsible one with his high-powered job and connections to the right people. He didn't understand Pop meant everything to her. Her priorities were more important than which restaurant to frequent or how to secure tickets for a golf tournament.

The minute she told him she gave up her apartment to move back with Pop, she was accused of being a child. Just thinking about it again made her blood boil. Such arrogance!

She had been forced into the adult world at age twelve, which made her an old soul. That tragedy also made it hard to find someone to relate to—someone to have a future with. To find *that* man meant she'd have the terrifying task of crumbling those impenetrable walls she depended on to shield her heart. So, in needing to protect her heart, she allowed Richard to fit well with the noncommitted relationship.

Adam was right, though. She deserved someone who loved and understood her. Was that man Adam?

The jingle of bells from the front door chimed. "Yoo-hoo? Laurel, are you here?"

Oh, no! Laurel closed her eyes and inhaled a long, deep breath. She rolled her neck, stretched it from one side to the other, squared her shoulders, and released her breath. "Coming, Clarice!" *What does she want so early in the day?* Stepping into the display room, she plastered on an insincere smile to face the woman ruining her day. "What brings you in this morning?"

"We have a meeting, don't we? Or did you forget?"

Clarice's usual, condescending tone graded on her nerves. "I've got a meeting with the Garden Club in another half hour." Laurel shot her gaze to the laurel-wreath-bordered wall clock and held in her patience. "I didn't realize you were a member."

"Well, actually, I'm not." With her chin raised, Clarice stood with her hands clasped over her heart. "It's my civic duty to utilize my talents when needed."

"That's kind of you." Laurel ran her gaze throughout the display room. "I haven't had a chance to set up chairs for the meeting." Lifting a shoulder, she forced her voice to a cheerful tone. "Guess I'll get started now. Be right back." She sprinted to the prep room, not to rush the set up, but to spend as little time as possible with the woman. Locating the folding chairs in the closet, she slow-walked them one by one, lingering with each trip. "Today is Wednesday. Don't you have a Ladies' Auxiliary meeting?"

"Why, yes, it is. Very perceptive." Clarice's lips folded into a frown, but then she shook her head. "It's urgent we make this grand opening a success. I postponed our meeting until tomorrow. I'm the president, you know. I have that power."

"Of course, you do," Laurel said over her shoulder,

and she retrieved Pop's worn, wooden chair from the prep room. She struggled with its weight through the doorway, dropping it with a thud, and then slid it across the tiled floor in front of the double-door cooler.

"Why are you moving those things? Isn't Frank here?"

Laurel hitched her shoulders. Why did Clarice *always* mention Pop? With the lack of sleep muddling her brain, Laurel didn't have the strength to bite her tongue at another demeaning comment about her father, but somehow, she managed to hold her temper. "He doesn't come in until a little later."

Ohhh...here it comes. Darn!

"Oh, my." Clarice raised her left eyebrow and crossed her arms. "Not many men have the luxury of showing up to work mid-morning. It must be nice."

"He's not sleeping," Laurel ground her words through gritted teeth and slid the stool from behind the counter. "He's at the food pantry distribution center, organizing meal deliveries."

Please, please, please, someone save me from this woman!

And just like that, the door opened to the beautiful bell chime when Adam's mother, Molly Carlson, appeared as her rescuer.

Of course, Clarice put on a show and embraced Molly like she hadn't seen her in decades.

"Good Lord, Clarice," Molly declared, "I just saw you yesterday." She rushed from Clarice's clutches to Laurel. "Let me help." She took the stool from Laurel's hands and placed it near the other chairs.

"Thanks." *Not only for taking the chair, but for saving me from your sister-in-law.*

184

The door bells jingled again with the arrival of Ellen Greene, Parker's mother, and Arlene Cavanaugh from The Bean & Brew. The ladies greeted one another with hugs and smiles, each one simply nodding at Clarice while giving Laurel extra-tight hugs.

She loved how the village moms treated her. While it broke her heart that Momma was gone, she cherished how these ladies always looked after her.

Clarice bolted to the chair situated at the head of the arrangement. She removed her jacket, placed it across the back of the chair, and sat ramrod straight with her eyebrows raised and her arms crisscrossed on her lap.

"Clarice, what are you doing?" Molly asked, her face molded in a scowl.

"The project. Naturally, you'll need my expertise in organization and execution."

"Execution?" Molly lowered her chin and glared at her sister-in-law. "I know what I'd like to—"

"Hold on there, girl," Arlene warned in hushed tones and took Molly by the arm to guide her to a chair opposite Clarice. "Tread lightly," she murmured.

"This is such a wonderful thing you're doing for the village, Laurel," Ellen Greene interjected.

"It sure is. You've got to see the work she's doing at the manor." Arlene put her arm around Laurel's shoulders. "Cleaning and decorating all those rooms is a part-time job. Plus, she's helping with the parade and running this place."

The admiration radiating from Arlene's eyes showed heartfelt approval.

She squeezed Laurel's shoulder and kissed her temple. "You're amazing."

"She sure is. I wish my Parker would stop seeing Heather and date someone like you." Ellen settled in a seat next to Molly.

With Arlene in the opposite chair, both women flanked Molly.

An empty chair and stool rested near Clarice, but Laurel opted for the stool and moved it near the cash register counter. "Ladies, I appreciate the kind words, but we need to get started."

"We're missing Joan," Molly said. "She couldn't get coverage for the bakery. But she said she'll do whatever you want."

"Speaking of coverage," Clarice broke in. "Who's covering The Cookie Cottage? Seems like that place can't survive without you."

Molly's eyes glittered like a twinkling gnome. "My Adam. He also told me to take a few hours since I never get a chance to just hang with the girls."

"Ohhh…" both Laurel and Arlene cooed at once.

And then Arlene motioned her chin to Molly. "He's such a great son." She placed a hand on Laurel's arm. "He'll make some girl a great husband."

"Don't think I haven't already thought of *that*." Molly directed her gaze at Laurel. "I can't think of anyone better to welcome into my family."

Laurel lowered her chin while an uncomfortable ribbon wove itself around her. Turning her attention from the group, she glanced at the red apples in the harvest arrangement sitting on the adjacent shelf, knowing the heat covering her face equaled their red hue.

"Don't worry, Laurel," Clarice began, "You'll find someone…someday. It's hard to find the right man when you aren't as sophisticated as my Annabelle. She and her husband are the perfect family with those two beautiful grandchildren of mine. I'm truly blessed."

"Yes, you are," Arlene said through her teeth. "As we all are." She focused on Laurel. "Family is most important." She softened her tone, "We're *all* fortunate to have family and *friends* who are like family." She leaned to hug Laurel again.

"Excuse me, ladies, but we're getting away from the reason for this meeting." Laurel veered from her non-existent love life and Clarice's snide comment.

"Okay, back on track," Ellen said. "We have an idea to get all the residents involved. We'd like to give out beautification awards to the best outdoor holiday decorations."

"It's exciting." Molly nearly jumped in her seat. "We decided on four categories—the best home, best farm, best historic building, and best business."

"I like it." Laurel took hold of her tablet from the register counter and entered the contest info. "Although, a lot of people already donated their lights for the parade. Would that stop some from entering the competition?"

"Is it possible to send out a post if anyone needs their lights for the competition to contact you to retrieve them? Maybe they can return them for the parade?" Molly asked.

"I guess we can." Laurel raised her gaze to focus on Molly. "I'll check with Adam about the return."

"That's what I like to hear," Molly prattled with a clap of her hands. "The more you and Adam work together, the better!"

"Molly…" Laurel's face grew warmer by the

second. "There's nothing between Adam and me. I recently ended a relationship—"

"That was two years ago," Ellen waved a dismissive hand. "Everyone knows that Richard person was *not* the one for you. Now, my Parker—"

"I appreciate all your concern about my love life, but it's a non-issue." Even though Laurel wanted to hide in the prep room, she stayed put. "Now the decorating competition, that's a great issue. If you ladies can handle it, then I'm sure the village council will be on board. I'll contact them ASAP and let you know as soon as I get a response."

"I already mentioned it to Adam, and he's okay with it," Molly said.

"Thank you." Laurel typed on her tablet, grateful they focused on the competition and not who she dated. "I'll contact Mayor Farley."

"What is my role?" Clarice demanded. "I can chair the contest. As you all know, I'm great at running things. I'm the president of the Ladies' Auxiliary—"

"We'll have Joan chair it since she's the Garden Club President." Arlene posed a sharp nod. "She'll contact you if something is needed. We're busy this time of year raising funds for our annual Planting Roots Project."

"That's a wonderful project!" Laurel loved how every year the ladies donated outdoor shrubs for several new homes built for veterans.

"All right, then." Clarice popped up from her seat. She thrust her shoulders back, elongated her neck, and twisted her chin toward the door. "I'll be on my way. Don't forget to keep me in the loop." Swinging her tapestry handbag, she flung her wool coat like a cape and headed for the door. "I have to run, busy, busy, busy!" Out the door, she went.

"Thank goodness!" Laurel slumped on the stool and released a heavy breath.

"Thank nothing," Arlene said. "That woman is a pain in the a—"

"Nope." Ellen raised a hand. "She's not worth it. And…you know she's not going to help."

Arlene glared at the door with her lips pursed in a tight line. "No, she'll show up when we present the awards and act like she personally picked the winners."

"She'll try, but we'll stop her." Ellen jerked her chin. "Be thankful she left. Now we can plan what we want."

"Yes, yes." Molly waved both hands and then clasped them together. "Laurel, we'd like to make a float for the parade and have the contest winners ride on it."

"That's an excellent idea, Molly." Laurel entered the float info into her tablet. "It might encourage more people to enter the contest if they know they'll be featured on a float."

"Laurel, we need your help." Ellen placed a hand on her arm. "The number of poinsettias we've grown isn't at all enough for the float."

"Yes." Molly's eyes glowed as she scooted to the edge of her seat. "We want to hire you to order the rest."

"The rest?" Laurel lifted her eyes from her screen, and her insides fluttered with anticipation of a little money coming her way. But in good conscience, she'd never try to make a profit from her friends. "How many do you need?"

"Oh, at least eight dozen, isn't that what we estimated?" Molly asked Arlene.

"Yep. Eight dozen."

"Ladies…" Laurel blew out a whistled sigh. "That's a lot of money. I can find out what my supplier's cost is and let you know. Maybe he can give me a break on such a large quantity."

"A break would be good. But we want to make sure you make money on it, too," Arlene said. "Our budget can handle it."

Laurel swiped the tablet to her supplier's page. "I'll supply them at my cost."

"Oh, no, you won't," Ellen barked a stern tone. "Arlene is our treasurer. If she says we can afford it, then we can."

Laurel smiled at Ellen's Mom voice. These three women were such a treasure. She'd never take advantage by charging the garden club for profit. They were instrumental in helping with the manor, and they had helped her with anything she needed all these years since Momma had passed.

"How about this…" she began. "I'll find out the wholesale cost and will add on a delivery charge. I think that's fair."

"I'm not comfortable with that," Molly tsked and shook her head. "You need the income."

"What I need most is having great friends like you."

"And we're thankful to have you in our lives. You're like another daughter to all of us." Molly leaned from her chair and squeezed Laurel's hand. "Thank you."

"Thank *you*, all of you." Laurel fought to keep her

voice steady for fear the emotions constricting her throat would surrender the urge to cry. She wanted to take all of them into a giant group hug. "Speaking of being thankful…Thanksgiving." She drew in a breath to compose herself. "I'd like to invite you and your families to Thanksgiving Sunday this year. Pop and I would love to have you."

"Last year was so special, Laurel. Thank you for that." Arlene held her hands upright in a tight steeple, then placed them to her chest. "Celebrating with everyone made our first holiday without Tom a little easier. We'd love to join you and Frank again this year."

"That's sweet of you to invite us," Ellen said. "Arlene always talks about last year's visit. I'll talk to Parker to see if he made plans, and I'll let you know."

Arlene and Ellen looked at Molly. "Molly?" Arlene asked.

The woman nearly bounced on her chair. "A family Thanksgiving with a houseful of people? How could I say *no*?" She jumped from her seat, wrapped Laurel in an embrace, and placed a kiss on her cheek. "Adam has always craved a big family Thanksgiving. We'd love to come. I accept! But I'll have to let you know if Karen is coming home. Is that okay?"

"That's fine. The more the merrier." Laurel's heart overflowed. She would share her favorite holiday with people she cared about with the added bonus of giving Adam the kind of Thanksgiving he always wanted. Perfect!

Chapter 12

With another intense rainstorm keeping Adam and Parker from completing their fall cleanup schedule, Adam took the opportunity to meet with Laurel to finalize parade plans. The perfect spot—a quiet booth at Lou's Luncheonette. Back in the day, high school seniors were allowed to leave campus during lunch. He, Parker, Tom, Evan, and Todd had eaten at the luncheonette almost every day of his last year.

"You two youngin's need refills on your drinks?" Lou's jovial voice added levity to the quiet luncheonette when he inched toward them, broom in hand.

Adam noticed the widower wasn't aging well, and that fact bothered him because Lou had welcomed him all those years ago the same way he had welcomed the guys who'd lived there all their lives. Adam had difficulties accepting the idea of Lou growing old especially since the luncheonette owner was alone now.

"Thanks, Lou. We're good," Laurel said.

"I want to thank you again for asking me to be Santa." The joy radiating from his eyes matched his smile. "Can't tell you what it means that you trust me to carry off such an important part of the Christmas parade."

"You're welcome," Laurel and Adam said together.

"There's no one else who could do Santa better than you." Pride circled Adam's chest that he brought happiness to Lou.

"And thanks for the invite to Thanksgiving Sunday." The man's grin stretched from ear to ear. "Yessiree, it's gonna feel like the holidays again. You need anything else for the parade—sandwiches and snacks—let me know. It's on the house."

"That'd be great, Lou. Thanks again for everything." Laurel organized a stack of parade papers.

"And thanks for letting this be headquarters on parade day." Adam used a pointer finger to salute the shop owner. "It's gonna help out big time."

"My pleasure. Made sense since the staging area is right next door." Lou swept under the table in the booth next to them. "Fingers crossed for good weather, not like today's storm. At least, you can keep your paperwork inside in case it's windy." He filled an old, metal dustpan. "You kids need anything else, give me a holler."

"Will do." Adam nodded to the man who was one of the father figures he most admired. He had a few examples of good fathers—Tom Cavanaugh who had worked along with Evan in the coffee shop; Ernie Donaldson who spoiled his daughter, Heather, with love; and Frank, Laurel's father—a great example of a loving father.

But Lou...well, without gettin' all mushy...Lou was special. Adam cherished all the times the man helped him over the years.

"He's a good man," Laurel said.

"He sure is. See...this is the reason I'm against changing Cedar Ridge." He scanned the luncheonette.

"It's two in the afternoon, and no one to bother us."

"You're right." Laurel tapped a pen to the side of her chin. "On the flip side, no customers for Lou. How sad is that?"

Adam's heart dropped. While he enjoyed the peace and quiet, he never considered how it affected Lou. Resting his arms on the table, he leaned in and lowered his voice. "You're right. He's handling it pretty well."

"Until when?" Dropping her pen to the table, she leaned to meet him halfway. "He's getting older. Has one employee. Years ago, there were five people working this place. You better brace yourself for the day he closes."

That reality smacked him as hard as a falling tree branch. Losing Lou sent a sudden panic coursing through him. "Hmm…maybe we need to ramp up promoting the parade and manor so more of those dreaded tourists show up." He winked to ease the panic in his chest.

"Finally! I knew you'd come around."

Leaning back against the seat booth, he squinted an eye. "Don't go gettin' all cocky on me. I'm still not comfortable with the *Historic Network* coming."

"You better get over it if it brings in revenue."

He drummed his fingers on the old laminate tabletop and considered it. The national exposure is what Lou and the village needed. "Yeah, I guess you're right."

"I'm right?" She tilted her head, raised her eyebrows, and placed a stack of papers in front of him.

He scanned the papers. "Why are you so surprised?"

"How do I put this without coming off snarky?"

Laurel tapped a fingertip in the air, casting a glance at the ceiling. "I didn't think you'd be as *cooperative* and…*flexible*?"

The playfulness in her eyes teased him. Adam slammed his right hand to his heart and pouted. "I come off as that stubborn?"

"A little." She shrugged a shoulder and curved her lips into a lopsided smile.

"Yeah…I guess I am. Been called hardheaded from time to time. But when the facts prove me wrong, I admit it." He noticed her facial expression change. "Why are you smiling like that?"

"You're a complex onion, Mr. Carlson."

"Me?" The surprising comment puzzled him.

"One minute you're all tough and macho," she said in a deep voice. She sat straighter, flexed her biceps, and took on a manly pose. Then she softened her tone, "But you've got a soft spot inside there." She pointed to his chest.

"Nah." He swiped a hand in the air.

"You can't deny it. I see how well you treat your mother and how your face lights up when you're with Lou. You're respectful to everyone."

He held up the same hand. "Ah, not so much—"

"Okay, your Aunt Clarice notwithstanding." She angled her head and raised two hands palm up.

He liked how she had the same opinion about his aunt.

"You *do* care about people." Her hands dropped to her lap, and she nodded.

He rested his gaze on the tabletop and tapped his pen while her words seeped into his mind. "I'm honored you said that."

She pointed to his chest. "You should be. You convinced me that everyone is important to you. The person you portray to the world isn't who you really are."

Now he wanted her opinion, and he looked up to press his eyes into a narrow glance. "And who am I?"

She squinted her gaze toward the ceiling and pursed her lips to one side. "I'm not sure yet." Her gaze then landed on him. "Need to peel more onion layers."

Adam laughed. "Layers, huh? This ought to be fun." He stretched a hand for hers across the table.

But she withdrew hers before he latched on.

"Okay…" oozed out of his mouth when he wanted to say *Ouch*. Retracting his hand, he scrubbed it over the back of his neck while recovering from the rejection. "If I have these layers—and according to you, most guys don't—what are you looking for in a guy?"

****

The skittish reflex that had Laurel pulling her hand away thirty seconds ago now shot off warning signals. She hesitated a moment before answering.

The other night, he almost kissed her. And, she had wanted him to.

What Molly and the other women said about her and Adam had monopolized her thoughts, forcing her to face the status of her love life. The Town Mothers agreed she and Adam were a good match, and so did the Town Fathers with their references of them as a couple.

Adam's question of what she wanted in a guy was too close to her heart. Hesitation kept her from admitting what she wanted. "He's got to be dependable, reliable, and in it for the long haul."

Adam leaned back in his seat and laughed out loud. "You're not buying a used car!"

She didn't expect *that* reaction! "No, I'm not. He has to be a family man who's flexible and trustworthy, and *never*, ever breaks a promise."

Everything Richard wasn't. Promises weren't his thing. But then again, she dated him because he wasn't the one for the long haul. Someday, she hoped she'd find a love like her parents had…but not now.

"Promises are important." Adam rested his right hand on the table top again while his four fingers tapped a rhythm on the surface. "I'm with you on that one. Karen, Mom, and me lived with broken promises."

Laurel considered his words. One of those layers peeled, slowly, very slowly. From what she'd seen, he was a man of substance, determination, and drive who lived with a deep sense of promises that accompanied his vow to trustworthiness.

"How was Richard with promises?"

The switch in the subject threw her off for a second. "Let's just say, he didn't fit that category too well. Another reason why I ended the relationship." A little disappointed that she hadn't ended things sooner.

"Got it…the promises and trust thing. I'm assuming you weren't in love with him."

She reared her head back and lowered her jaw. "Love?"

"Love." He lifted both shoulders and nodded. "Did you love him?"

"No." With a wag of her head, she grazed her teeth over her bottom lip. The muscles surrounding her heart tightened with the vision of loving someone only to lose them. "No, love was *never* a part of it." She inhaled a deep breath and collected her thoughts. "What about all the women you've dated? Was love part of that?"

His expression narrowed as parallel lines creased between his eyebrows. "Searching was the pursuit of love. When you realize after a few dates that there's no potential of a future with someone—where you can't see yourself loving that person—you break it off and continue until you find *the one*."

"What about Sophie? You were together for a while. Did you love her?" She watched his eyes widen and his lips mold into a straight line.

He fiddled with the straw, swirling it in his soda glass. "We wanted different things. Don't get me wrong—she's a nice person, just not for me."

Laurel suspected the problem. "She wanted to get married and you didn't?"

"Nope." His hand abandoned the straw, and he tapped his fingers tips on the tabletop again. "She wanted a life in the city. That's not my game."

"I didn't expect *that*."

His shoulders relaxed then. "You know when the relationship is right and when it's wrong."

A perfectly logical statement, but she needed more clarity. "So, you're okay with it?"

"Oh, yeah."

"I'm surprised you'd admit that."

His eyes sent a puzzled stare her way. "Don't know why I shared that. I'm not that open about who I date."

"Well, then I'm honored you feel comfortable enough to talk about it."

"Yeah, I am comfortable…talking to you."

And odd silence floated between them, as if he

wanted to say more, and then—

"Just remember, if a guy is serious about a girl, he'd be interested in what she does and care about the way she feels. Does stuff to make her happy like cook her a meal when she's had a hard day."

"You're right." She leaned back and let out a deep, gratifying sigh. "That's why I sent him packing."

"Good for you. I know Frank is proud of you for that."

Pop? Now she leaned forward. "Did he tell you that?"

Adam nodded. "Yeah, he still worries about you, even though you're quite capable of taking care of yourself. Keep looking." And then he winked. "I'm sure the right guy is closer than you think."

Laurel stayed quiet, not yet ready to admit to him of all people her fear of putting her heart out there.

"Think about this. You could up and move to Alaska, and if the guy isn't the right one, he wouldn't go because he doesn't care enough."

She rolled her eyes, folded her arms on the tabletop, and snorted. "I'd never move to Alaska, so that doesn't count."

"You get my point. Think about it. You deserve someone who will love and share things, laugh, and cry with you."

Just what Pop and Jeanine touted. This video replayed too many times for comfort. With her feelings for him intensifying, she needed everyone to stay out of her love life so she could sort things out.

Pop and Jeanine.

Ernie, Harold, and Winston.

Molly, Arlene, and Ellen.
And especially Adam.

Chapter 13

Laurel stood at the bottom of a Ferris wheel-like structure, staring up at the vertical spinning panels shaped like giant surfboards.

Momma stood on the opposite side of the wheel. "You can do this, honey."

"But I'm scared of heights."

Momma smiled the same smile she saved for whenever Laurel was afraid. But right now, they weren't in their comfy home, safe and secure. "It's okay," Momma called out. "I have faith in you."

Laurel inhaled a shaky breath and stood tall. Stepping toward the structure—watching the timing of the moving panels as they glided down toward her—she concentrated on how to catch onto one panel without slipping and falling.

"You can do this." Momma's soft voice floated to her ears.

Laurel jumped to grab the top of one moving panel, crawling over it as it rotated upward, careful not to lose her balance and grip. But her left foot slipped, and she lost concentration when she looked down seeing that she was far, far from the ground.

Panic soared in her chest, and she struggled to see Momma's loving face…but Momma was gone.

****

Last night's dream awakened Laurel in a cold,

trembling sweat. Still haunted from its effects, she made her way to Rutledge Manor in time to meet the reporters from *NJLocal News* television and *The Star Journal* newspaper. Tom had arranged their arrival for the same time, leaving Laurel grateful for the diversion to take her mind off that awful dream.

That dream more than likely meant a few things she needed to deal with—things she didn't want to face.

First, being out of control in both her business and nonexistent love life.

Second, by falling in love, she ran the risk of losing the love of her life who would leave her with the same anguish of losing her mother.

Sometimes fear is a good thing, Momma always said. *Don't let it stop you. It feels great when you conquer it. I'll always watch over you, I promise.*

Momma meant that promise. But that promise had been out of Momma's control.

Parked in front of the manor, a cameraman removed equipment from the news van's sliding door.

Laurel recognized the profile and long, black hair of the bubbly reporter she'd seen on TV countless times. She introduced herself.

Stanley bolted from the manor. "Good morning!!" He sprinted forward and shook their hands. "Thank you, thank you, thank you for coming."

Just then, an unfamiliar sedan slowed and parked behind the van. A middle-aged man approached and extended a hand to Stan and Laurel. "Hi, I'm from the *Journal*." He nodded to the TV cameraman and reporter. "Long time, no see."

"It's already been a long morning," the TV reporter said to Laurel and Stan. "Last night's storm damage kept us going all night. Roads closed and power lines down."

"Man…those transformer fires on Rt. 10 in Ledgewood were something," the newspaper reporter said. "Good thing no one got hurt." He pointed his cell phone to Stanley. "What have we got here?"

"This"—Stanley swept his arm toward the building—"is Rutledge Manor. Home to the spirits of young lovers whose lives ended abruptly."

"Spirits?" The young TV reporter motioned to her cameraman to roll, directing her microphone at Stanley. "Are you saying the manor is haunted?"

Laurel noticed the snicker from the *Journal* reporter.

"Haunted? No." Stanley confirmed. "Historic. The *Historic Network* is coming next week to film a segment. We're in negotiations for a series."

Negotiations? Viewership of the special segment determined if there'd be a series. Since Stanley counted on it, Laurel didn't want to clarify and dampen *his* spirit. A familiar car pulled in beside the news van, and Laurel pressed a hand to her mouth. "Oh, no!" *What is* she *doing here?*

"Yoo-hoo! I hope I'm not too late!" Clarice Carlson's hat flapped in the breeze, almost flying from her head. The wool fascinator—with its large, narrow bows—resembled a bird's nest, not appropriate for the cold, fall weather especially after last night's storm.

When she rushed toward them, the huffing breath from her buxom body strained the large buttons on her blue, popcorn-fabric coat. "I…need…to…tell you…about…Abigail."

Wow! Clarice went there? Laurel hurried to take

the woman by the elbow to guide her from the group. "Clarice, it's nice of you to come. You didn't have to rush over here. Catch your breath. Maybe grab a cup of coffee at The Bean & Brew. It's cold out with the windchill."

"Nonsense." She pulled away. "I was born and raised in this county. My blood is thick enough to handle any bothersome windchill." She sidestepped Laurel and moved closer to the group. "Now, I'm sure these nice reporters want to hear all about the times I've seen Abigail and Thomas. After all, they're the reason the manor is famous."

The TV reporter aimed her microphone at Clarice while nodding to her cameraman. "You've seen the ghost?"

"Oh, yes, several times. Both of them. They walk about the gardens...well...what were the gardens. I assume it's what they did when they were courting, you know, before their untimely demises."

"Can you tell me what you've seen?" the report asked, her cameraman zeroing in on Clarice while the *Journal* reported held his phone toward her to record.

"Abigail—that's the young woman who lived here—walks the gardens in her blue gown. To honor Abigail, I'm dressed in blue today."

Oh, brother! Laurel almost puked on the spot. Since ghosts weren't present—never had been, never will—evidently, Clarice didn't care that she clearly lied.

She hoped the woman wouldn't hurt chances for the *Historic Network* episode, let alone the series potential shattering the other plans of attracting tourists. No romance novel book signings, no garden parties, or tea luncheons, no reenactments…all their plans would vaporize like the supposed ghosts.

As much as it pained her, Laurel was forced to let Clarice run with the story. The camera was recording so stopping her would have been awkward with all of New Jersey watching.

But where did she discover the color blue? Laurel's research never gleaned blue being Abigail's favorite color.

"What about the crying?" the *Journal* reporter asked.

The cameraman zoomed in for another close-up.

Clarice preened with pride. "Up on the third floor." She pointed a white-gloved hand toward the manor. "At night, you can see Abigail's form walking across the windows. Her whimpers can be heard from here." Clarice elevated her hand to her heart. "It's so sad…she loved Thomas so much."

She explained the story, how Thomas was killed in a 1700s battle and how Abigail took her own life. With all the details she embellished, it appeared she had lived through the entire ordeal.

"She's a natural in front of the camera," Stanley whispered to Laurel. "She should be our spokesperson, don't you think?"

Laurel whipped her head to face Stan. "Have you lost your mind?" she whispered back. "None of that is true."

"Well, we don't know that." He pointed a finger straight in the air and tilted his chin. "Maybe she researched it. It might be true."

Oh…my…God! The village will be doomed if Clarice is our spokesperson.

Laurel and the entire village would be traumatized by Clarice's ego. Even though she didn't want to see Adam today, since she suspected her dream signaled her lack of control and her total attraction, she needed to get over it for the good of Cedar Ridge.

She needed to find Adam. She needed to find him now!

****

"There you are!" Laurel ran to Adam at Pembrooke Farm where he and Todd assembled one of the tents for the Harvest Festival. "We've…got…a problem!"

"Other than this place crawling with people tomorrow and a storm on the rise?"

Laurel pushed the hair from her face and tried to catch her breath. "Your aunt. She crashed the *NJLocal* and *Journal* interviews and will star on tomorrow's rolling news cast on TV!"

Adam pulled the tent rope taut and kneeled to anchor it to the stake in the ground. "How did she find out about it?"

"Who knows? The woman is the town crier. No offense."

Adam shook his head and rose. "None taken. She's family by marriage, not by blood."

"So, what do we do? She's going to be the face of Cedar Ridge and talked about seeing Abigail and Thomas' ghosts in the garden!"

He yanked on another tent rope. "What?"

Laurel gave several panicked nods. "Yep. Lied right to the reporters and looked straight at the camera and lied."

Adam froze and flung his gaze her way. "Oh, jeez."

"She's gone over the edge this time. You've got to do something," Laurel pleaded.

He scanned the width of Pembrooke Farm. "We've gotta find Tom. He's meeting with both reporters again in an hour to cover tomorrow's festival." He dropped the rope and withdrew his cell phone from his jacket pocket. "You go that way"—he pointed his phone to the west side of the property, and then to the east side— "I'll go this way. If we both circle the perimeter and meet at the Pumpkin Chunkin' area, maybe we can find him in between. If you find him, grab him, and call me." He held up his cell. "Got it?"

She nodded. "Got it. Cross your fingers."

"Nope. We're gonna fix this…together." He handed Todd the tent rope. "Sorry, man, I gotta go."

"No problem." Todd waved a hand salute. "Good luck."

Laurel shook her head. "Unfortunately, with Clarice, there is no such thing as good luck."

****

When they separated, Adam sowed an idea to keep Dear Old Aunt Clarice from becoming the face of Cedar Ridge. He scooted around a truck unloading hay bales and sidestepped the tent rental company's array of tents lying on the ground. He spotted Tom organizing the *Cedar Ridge Sentinel* table. Making his way, he tapped in Laurel's number with a text.

—Found him. Pumpkin Chunkin'. Meet me there—

Great. Maybe he could convince Tom to ask the reporters to cut the earlier footage including his aunt. With any luck, they'd replace the video with coverage on the large catapults used in the pumpkin chunkin' contest.

In the distance, he focused his attention on Laurel rushing from the opposite direction from the catapults.

Sprinting toward her and Tom, he hoped he could stop the reporters from plastering his aunt's face throughout the news cycle…even if he was about to tell a giant lie.

****

After Laurel left Adam to clean up the Clarice problem, she picked up the brocade draperies from the cleaners and headed to the manor to hang them before they wrinkled in the back seat of her car. She made her way to the manor's foyer stairs that were now covered with a new runner that cushioned each step. She mentally reminded herself to confirm her supplier's schedule for delivery of the five, pine Christmas swags to hang along the banister.

A step stool was left in the hallway, so she dragged it into what had been Abigail's room. She positioned the stool by the window for ease of reaching the curtain rod. Removing one rod from its perch, she struggled to slide the drapes onto the pole. The heavy weight of the silk made securing the material-laden rod back in place difficult. Standing on the stool, she stretched too far, felt the stool teeter and topple, landing her hands first on the mattress in a tangled mess of material on what had been Abigail's bed.

Righting herself, she slid the nightstand away from the wall to gain better window access. Positioning the step stool in the spot where the nightstand rested, she felt a small piece of floorboard toggle. The board loosened, causing a struggle to secure it. "That's odd." She lifted one corner of the small board.

"Whoa…" A spark of fear burned her nerves at the

sight of a dark box resting in the hole. Bending to inspect it, she couldn't stop her fingers from trembling for fear a mouse or spider would pop out. She jumped at the startled sound of her cell phone that added to her frazzled nerves over the contents of the box. Whooshing out a panic-stricken breath, she attempted to calm her voice. "H-Hi, Tom."

"Are you okay? Your voice is shaky."

"Yes, I'm-I'm fine. I f-found a box under a floorboard, and it's, it's kind of freaking me out."

"What's in it?"

"I don't know." Nerves rattled again that triggered quaking of the hand that held her cell phone. "I was trying to get the courage to open it when you called. Can you stay on the line? I'm afraid of what I'll find."

"Better than that, I'll come over. I want to take a few pictures for my next edition. Frank told me you were there, that's why I called."

"Okay, I'll wait to open it. Hurry!" An unnerved breath released with her shoulders relaxing, even though her insides still danced beneath her skin.

"I'm on my way."

For a good fifteen minutes, Laurel paced Abigail's room, speculating the contents of the box. Her imagination ran wild with possibilities. Some good, some not so good. Tom needed to get there soon to calm her pounding heart and ease her frazzled nerves.

Making her way downstairs to the parlor to wait, she couldn't keep her nerves from spiking again as the front door creaked.

"Laurel?"

She dashed to the foyer. "Thank God you're here. I'm freaking out. I've been in this place a few times by myself and was never bothered. Today…"

"It's okay." He placed his hands on her shoulders and rubbed them to her elbows. "Calm down, you're shaking so hard, you'll have a heart attack."

"I'm trying, but my mind keeps going to the dark side."

Tom squinted. "You're not making fun of me because I'm a *Galaxy Wars* fan, are you?"

"What? No! Let's get this over with so I can *calm* down." Grasping him by the arm, she tugged to guide him to the grand staircase. "Come on." She nearly tripped on several steps as she led Tom to the landing near Abigail's room. "It's in there." She stood near the door jamb pointing a jittery finger at the hole in the floor next to the bed, then balled her hands at her sides to steady them.

Tom bent and lifted the box from its hiding place, rested it on the nightstand, and blew a layer of dust from the lid. "I wonder how long it's been there?" His oversized smile boosted the curiosity visible in his eyes. "I love a good mystery."

Laurel noticed the small latch securing the box. "Don't just stare at it, open it!" Her heartbeat pounded against her ribs and pulsed in the hollow of her throat.

"Give me a minute." He swiveled the box, examining all sides, then fiddled with the latch. "Not very secure." The latch gave way, and he slowly, very slowly, lifted the lid a smidge.

"Are you purposely torturing me?" She needed this settled; her nerves were shot. "Open the darn thing!"

Tom chuckled. "Okay, okay. But you need to calm down first."

She took in a deep breath and whooshed it out.

"Nope, not good enough. Slow breath in, slow breath out."

She followed as instructed, steadying her breath to semi-normal.

Lowering his chin, he eyed her over the top of his glasses. "You good?"

With a sharp nod of her head, she convinced herself. "I'm good."

He opened the lid, exposing the contents. "*This* is what freaked you out?"

A leather-bound book in his hand—the edges revealed yellowed and browned pages inside—was extended. "I'll bet you're going to love what's in here."

Laurel crept into the room, took hold of the book, and rubbed her fingers over the cracked, leather cover. "It's so fragile. I'm afraid to open it."

"I understand *that* fear; but these are even more fragile. You're really going to *love* these." Tom passed her the stack of papers. "Looks like love letters…from Thomas."

She reverently took hold of the delicate letters tied with a faded, light-blue ribbon. "This is incredible!" Now her heart pumped a staccato rhythm.

These love letters—*real* love letters—from a romance ending with Abigail no longer wanting to live without Thomas, would now serve to satisfy Laurel's love-starved heart. Gently placing the letters on the nightstand next to the empty box, Laurel opened the book. "Abigail's diary," she whispered. Chills ran across her shoulders when she opened the book. Instead of reading the first entry, she gingerly thumbed toward the back, locating the last entry which wasn't difficult because a dried magnolia marked the page.

May 5, 1796

I can no longer bear the pain that my beloved was taken from this earth by the hand of my father. I shall join him, and we will be together for eternity.

"Oh, my God, Tom," she whispered again and flashed her gaze his way. "Thomas didn't die in battle?"

"Let me see." Tom read the entry over her shoulder. "'By the hand of my father.' Hmm. Addison Rutledge killed Thomas Baxter?"

She turned to face him. "That doesn't go along with the story."

"I know." Tom projected his gaze to the floor with the fingertips of his right hand to his forehead. "How about I do a little digging…see what I can find."

"Are you sure?" She skimmed a few pages. "Do you have the time?"

He looked up then. "I'll make the time. Uncovering the truth would make a good story for the *Sentinel*. The mystery will fit well with the *Historic Network*. Might lock in that series Stanley is banking on."

"Maybe the love letters will have more information." She inspected the dried parchment.

"How about I take the diary and hit the microfiche at the library? You read through the letters. See what we find."

"Got it."

So bittersweet…sadness filled her heart for the two young lovers. *I need to solve this mystery, not only for Abigail and Thomas, but for Cedar Ridge, too.*

****

The lonely quiet of Adam's apartment remained just as silent as when he had left this morning. The idea of another Friday night clicking the TV remote held little appeal. He wanted to share the outcome of the Clarice media chaos with Laurel.

Convincing the reporters to swap his aunt's interview with the Pumpkin Chunkin' Contest had worked well. Grateful they bought his explanation of how she was getting older and losing it, he wanted to tell Laurel all about his success. He had asked her to hang out to celebrate the small victory, but she had other plans. Now his celebratory warm and fuzzies were gone.

Did she have a date…a real date?

This unwarranted jealousy needed to be put aside to take advantage of his free time to focus on two problems he struggled to solve.

His promise to Stanley to get the manor heat repaired hung on his shoulders. He needed a way to pay Eddie from Eddie's Heating & Plumbing without being paid. Eddie always complained he never had enough time to take care of his own stuff at home since he and his wife were always running their three kids to the rec center. The last time Adam spoke to Eddie, the plumber said he was glad winter was coming so he wouldn't have to cut his grass, giving him more free time.

Grass! Oh, man! The solution had been right in front of him. If he offered to cut Eddie's grass for an entire season, maybe Eddie could fix the manor's heat. Bartering happened often in Cedar Ridge, so first thing in the morning, he'd give Eddie a call.

With that burden off his shoulders—and a promise kept—the tension in his shoulders subsided somewhat, but not enough. The second problem of finding jobs for more village citizens still hung on those shoulders, taunting him.

The Morrison building needed to play a big part—but how? The large building would be perfect to house a collection of businesses, but not a mall. Definitely, not a mall. The main purpose was to create jobs, not destroy the existing businesses.

Different possibilities sprouted in his mind, but nothing took root. Riffling through the papers on his desk, he huffed out a breath. Surveying his living room, he sighed, his loneliness growing heavier with only the TV to break the monotony. He didn't want to waste time having his brain switched off by watching the news or finding something interesting to stream.

Although, he wouldn't mind cuddling on the couch with Laurel, even if it meant watching a chick flick. She made his apartment feel like a home—gave it a life he didn't think possible.

After sending a few texts on his phone, he grabbed his coat, left the silence behind, and headed to meet Parker.

"Hey, bud. What's up?" Parker slid onto the empty bar stool beside him at The Ugly Goat. "It's Friday night. Isn't it date night?"

"You know I haven't dated in forever." Adam pointed his beer bottle at Parker. "Didn't feel like hangin' at home. Evan and Todd can't come…too busy getting their kids ready for tomorrow's pumpkin contest."

"Someday, it'll be nice to have kids…do dad stuff with them." Parker raised his beer bottle to his mouth. "But for right now, I guess this'll do."

"You and Heather any closer to gettin' married?"

Parker sputtered his beer. "What?" He shook his head and aimed glaring eyes at Adam. "Ah, nooo.

Nooo." Shaking his head a few times, Parker took a long swig of beer, followed by a smack of his lips. "We're good for now."

Adam turned and rested a bent hand and arm on the bar top as he eyed Parker. "Then how come you're free tonight?"

"She's on one of her day-long shopping trips with her mother. The outlets. Won't be back until late."

"Ouch." Relaxing on his stool, he now took a large chug of beer, swallowed hard, and snorted. "There goes your bank account."

"No way." Parker waved both hands in front of him. "That's *her* debt. I've got nothin' to do with it."

Adam wiped his upper lip with the back of his hand. "Smart man. So…this is good." He stared across the bar, focusing on nothing, his head bobbing up and down, and then he looked at Parker. "Gives us some guy time."

"Guy time?" Parker squinted a stare. "I just spent six and a half hours staring at your ugly mug on the job, then another two at the festival set up. What gives?"

"Nothin'." Adam hitched a shoulder as his stomach did an uncomfortable tumble. "I wanted to get out of the apartment, have a few beers…ya know, catch up." He scooped a handful of peanuts from the small dish on the bar top, popped them into his mouth, and just like that, Laurel's nut analogy repeated in his ears. *Hard on the outside, soft on the inside*. A quick glance at Parker to dislodge that comment from his memory only to be met by his buddy's sideways stare, causing him to nearly choke on the bits of salty nuts lodged in his throat.

"Okay…now I get it," Parker slowed his words.

"You're lonely."

"No, I'm good." He stared at the bar top afraid the loneliness might show in his eyes and rat him out. "Just wanted to go out."

The loud disruption from the bar's front door caught their attention. With a turn on the stool, he gritted his teeth, heated anger erupting inside, and he tensed his gut to suppress it.

Was no place safe from running into Russell Chapman? He turned and grabbed another handful of peanuts and chewed hard.

"Easy there, cowboy." Parker tapped on his forearm. "Your jaw looks like it's workin' overtime. Those peanuts didn't do anything to you."

Adam appreciated is friend's attempt at humor, but right now, he wasn't feelin' humorous. He'd withstood enough of Chapman and his threats.

"Gentlemen!"

The hard shove of a hand smacked him on the shoulder blade, and he jerked forward.

"Good night for having a few too many...maybe get those loose lips to spill where all your illegal campaign funds came from," the words slithered from the older man's mouth.

With a slight turn of his head, Adam spoke out of the side of his mouth without looking at Chapman. "Just trying to relax from a hard week of work."

"That's why we're here. Relax and keep an eye on you." Chapman motioned a pointed finger to Jack, the bartender. "Four shots of Jack, Jack." He laughed at his pathetic pun.

In an instant, Adam felt the pressure of Parker's grip on his arm. "Easy there, bud. He's not worth it," he murmured.

Adam kept his gaze on the liquor bottles lined up on the shelf across from him and worked his jaw while he squeezed his right fist. "Should you be drinking with all your medical problems?"

"That's none of your damn business. When I find out how you stole the council seat from my boy, I'll level charges." He then addressed Parker. "How can you be in business with such a snake?" He turned his attention back at Adam. "And you're dragging poor Laurel Eldridge into the manor and parade foolishness."

"Back off, Russell." Adam clenched his teeth, keeping his focus on the bottles to control the urge to deck the guy. "Leave Laurel out of this."

"Defending her honor. Very noble. How do you think she'll feel about you when you get hauled off to jail?"

"That's enough, Russell," Parker warned. "Take your drinks and go haunt someone else."

As Russell laughed, he grabbed his shots and walked away.

Flashbacks rushed from deep within Adam like a nightmare of all the times he'd seen his old man arrested, handcuffed, and swept away in a patrol car.

Laurel deserved better.

"This is worse than I thought." Parker snapped his gaze in Adam's direction.

"It's nothin' I can't handle." His face flushed as hot as one of his mowers on a summer day. "He thinks the constant threats will get me to resign from the council."

"That's not what I meant."

Adam shot a stare at Parker. "What?"

"The Laurel thing."

"There is no *Laurel* thing." *She's probably on a date right now.*

Parker swiveled on the stool to face him. "Ya know, being in a *real* relationship isn't such a bad thing."

The anger toward Chapman still had Adam's insides tumbling and tightening. "I never said it was."

"So, what's the deal? With Laurel?" Parker jutted a chin nod.

"No deal. We're…friends." Adam took a swig of beer, hoping the bitterness of the liquid would take his mind off of Parker's question."

"Did ya ever think if you settle down, you won't be lonely?"

He then glanced at Parker and scoffed. "I'm not some fifty-year-old who still lives at home with his mother."

"No, but you need someone. Maybe Laurel's the one?"

"When I do settle down"—Adam stared at his beer and rotated the bottle between his hands—"I want to get it right."

"Yeah, right," Parker said. "But you've gone through a whole lota choices to get it right. The perfect wife won't fix this." He tapped on the side of Adam's head. "You're looking for someone who doesn't exist."

"Yeah, well…maybe I am. It's that—"

"You need to stop that garbage about being like your old man—not knowing how to be a good husband so you need the perfect wife. You're *not* him." Parker elbowed a nudge on Adam's arm. "If you were, I wouldn't be in business with you."

Adam hesitated, appreciating Parker's honesty. "Thanks, man." He'd spent his life proving his honesty and trustworthiness. Deep in his heart, and in his life, he knew he wasn't like the old man. But even validation from others did little to convince him he wasn't living a lie.

"Okay, this is gonna sound a little weird, 'coz we don't get sappy, but you're a good guy. I'm not saying it because we've been friends for what, seventeen years? You proved that to everyone. That's why they voted you onto the village council."

"That's different." Adam shook his head and raised one shoulder.

"Bull. Even though you won't admit it, what you just did confirms it. You've got Laurel right in front of you—the kind of person who'd be good for you—and you're scared. Get your head out of your butt."

"My head's not—"

"Yeah, it is. There's something between you, everyone sees it. Everyone but *you*."

The shock of that statement bolted through him, and Adam dashed his gaze on Parker.

How can everyone see it? I haven't acted on it.

He stole a glance over his shoulder at Chapman's table where the former councilman sat with his friends like the godfather holding a meeting. The former councilman's comparison to his old man stung like hell. With that stigma hanging over him, he'd never be worthy of someone like Laurel.

"You need to get out of your own way."

Parker jarred him from self-doubt.

"Get rid of that stupid mental check list and go for it. Laurel isn't the kind of girl to lose. From the way she looks at you, she wants you just as much. You wanna give that up?"

Chapter 14

The next afternoon, Laurel strolled the Harvest Festival with warmth enveloping her, even though the quick weather change became cold and windy…a reminder winter was near.

She appreciated that the community worked together to make a huge undertaking like the festival better each year. And Tom's media blitz worked with more families at each stand than she'd ever seen—the Pembrooke Farms' parking field was packed with license plates not only from New Jersey, but Pennsylvania and New York, as well.

Tables lined under tents and canopies in a parade of new and homemade wares of every type—fall-themed tablecloths, candle arrangements, Christmas ornaments, and gift items. The festival gave a much-needed boost to all the local crafters who wouldn't have an outlet for their items.

She spied a Santa and Mrs. Claus cookie jar set, and her inner child kicked in. Their white-gloved hands positioned in a wave matched their cheerful grins drawing Laurel toward an impulse buy…until she read the price tag. *Maybe next year.*

While she brimmed with pleasure over the festival's success, the words from Thomas's love letters disrupted her thoughts over and over again. The love in his heart flowed in every phrase, and his honesty and heartfelt promise to Abigail proved that love was worth the risk and that fact reminded her of how crucial promises were to Adam. She wondered if he was capable of that kind of love. His openness and acceptance allowed her to be herself, and her longing for him emerged as a wake-up call—a call her heart needed to act on. Her mind…that was another story.

As she walked the fairgrounds greeting friends and residents, she noticed many people weren't from the area—just what Adam warned about.

But…

Cedar Ridge needs this…and so do I.

Glancing at one of the stands, she noticed a small boy crying.

His mother attempted to console him, and his body lurched with each, heavy sob. Adorable with black, curly hair and caramel-colored skin, the boy cried enough to cover his plump cheeks in a stream of tears.

Out of nowhere, Adam appeared—a large, Cedar Ridge volunteer button secured to his jacket—and he squatted to the boy's height. While Adam talked, the boy's cries slowed, calming the heaving of his little body. His tiny hand pointed to the balloon water gun game. Adam nodded, spoke to the mom, then took the boy by the hand with Mom on their heels.

Tugging in her collar to guard against the biting wind, Laurel realized she should have worn her puffer instead of the lightweight jacket. Ignoring the cold, she stepped within hearing range and wondered what Adam planned.

He plunked money on the game counter, then stood behind the boy. Placing the boy's hands on the water gun, they took aim. Adam nodded to the game operator, and in seconds, the gun sprayed water toward the clown's mouth as the balloon behind it grew larger and larger. When the balloon burst, bells sounded—game over.

"We have a winner!" the game operator yelled.

The child hopped and ran to the operator to accept a stuffed dinosaur prize. "Thank you, thank you!" he yelled with a huge smile exposing adorable dimples.

"See, I told you." Adam ruffled the boy's hair. "Nothing to it."

The mom thanked Adam with a grateful hug. "You're a good man."

The boy oozed cuteness and delight the way he looked up at Adam in clear admiration. "When I grow up, I wanna be just like you," he announced.

The mom talked with Adam for a few minutes, and then left, her son skipping away, stuffed dinosaur in one hand, Mom's hand secure in the other.

Laurel stepped closer. "That was a wonderful thing. Do you know that little boy?"

"Nope." Adam rocked back on his heels. "Never saw him in my life."

Laurel watched with the same admiration as that little boy. Now she understood why Pop preached about Adam's character. The more she got to know that side, the more attractive he became. She longed for Adam to take her by the hand and rescue her from herself. Everything she ever wanted, ever dreamed of, was the man who just took care of that small child. "What you did for him was selfless. You're amazing." She struggled not to gush about his actions.

"Hey…you okay?"

His eyes studied her with such concern it made her

heart flutter. She surveyed the fairgrounds to avoid declaring her feelings by wrapping her arms around him while wondering how to fit him into her life.

His hand rested on her shoulder, and he stared straight into her eyes, moving her hair from her face. He looked deep into her eyes a few seconds longer. "Let me know when you're ready to take the leap...ready to be treated the way you deserve."

Oh...how she wanted to shout, *Yes, I'm ready!* The gentle touch of his finger to her cheek and intensity of his gaze confirmed he understood the turmoil swirling in her mind. But the air grew thin, making breathing almost impossible with a heaviness constricting her chest. She needed to flee...she needed to flee now!

****

Adam stood alone by the balloon game after Laurel made a lame excuse for a quick exit. He'd been roaming the grounds, helping where needed, talking to everyone...friends and even strangers since the village council members served as festival ambassadors to aid visitors.

Even with all these people, without Laurel beside him, the surrounding loneliness had him worried he scared her by declaring he'd be there when she was ready to take the leap. Wandering the fairgrounds, he looked upward to see the gloom of clouds and biting winds darken the sky. He found his friend near the face painting tent that swayed with each strong gust.

"Hey, Adam, how ya doing?" Todd Ellison pressed a soft fist to Adam's shoulder.

"Hey." Adam pretended his arm hurt since Todd was so fit from his two jobs—volunteer firefighter and handyman business. Adam returned the punch, and they laughed like kids. He considered himself lucky to have friends who were more like brothers. "Where are your kids?"

"Mom's got 'em. They're heading for the candy apple stand. Gonna cost me a week's pay in dental bills if one of them breaks a tooth on those things."

Adam pushed a tuft of windblown hair from his forehead. "How do you afford something like that?"

"Believe me, it's hard. I kind of spoil them though…they're all I have left of Kristie." Todd nodded his chin toward Adam. "You should try it. Kids give you a different perspective on life."

"I've always wanted kids, you know, in the future. But…I don't know." He glanced toward the sky again, noticing a train of drifting heavy clouds almost resembling a family of five. "Been thinking about it more and more."

"You'd be a great father." Todd motioned a hand for Adam to follow. "You care about people, and you treat them right."

Adam traversed the crowds along the aisle of tents with Todd as Laurel became his focus. "Yeah, when someone's important, you do everything you can for them, like keep promises." The idea of caring about Laurel might have scared him a few weeks ago…but now, he wanted to spend as much time with her as possible.

"If you don't want to lose that important *someone*, you might want to jump on that."

Had Todd read his mind, or…"You been talkin' to Parker?"

Todd dodged a flying balloon from hitting his head as it sailed untethered with the wind. "Nope. Did he tell you the same thing?"

"Basically." Adam also ducked as they arrived near the candy apple tent.

"You know we wouldn't steer you wrong. You gotta go for it. It's scary, but I don't regret a minute of it. Being married to Kristie was the best part of my life, besides my kids."

"Hey, man, I'm sorry." Adam clamped a hand on Todd's solid shoulder. "It's gotta be hard without her."

"It is. The kids help, and Mom's been great. Every day gets a little easier, and then, boom!" He smacked his hands together. "The memories come back and knock my feet out from under me."

"Anything I can do?"

"Nah, just being around helps. You and the guys have been great."

"It's the least we can do."

"So, hey, what about you?" Another gust of wind barreled through the fairgrounds almost knocking him and Todd off balance. "You better get movin' before Laurel does something like marry the next guy who comes along."

"Marry?" Adam's heartbeat halted in his chest, and he steadied his footing. The image of Laurel with another guy cut into his gut. From the way Laurel had stared at *him* a few minutes ago, he was sure the attraction between them grew stronger each day. Although, when he had confessed his intentions about moving on, she became skittish and bolted. Maybe he's not the one, maybe…"Have you heard something I haven't?"

"Nah, nothin' like that. But a woman like Laurel wants a family and needs one since her mom and all."

When did Todd become a Laurel expert? "How do you know that?"

"We talk. She's been helpful since…ya know."

Adam nodded, imagining the pain Todd and his family had suffered.

"You *don't* want to lose her," Todd continued. "It would be the biggest regret of your life. Don't blow this. I know what it's like to lose someone you love."

Whoa…even though he felt it, he never mentioned love to anyone.

How do they all know?

****

"Come on, spill it!" The next day at her flower shop, Laurel unpacked the last flower vase from an order as anticipation flashed quicker than the lightning strikes from last night's storm.

Tom squinted. "Interesting facts surrounded Thomas' death." His expression intensified, and his eyebrows knit. "They didn't keep thorough records back then. The death record read, '*succumbed to gunshot in battle,*' as cause of death. It was in the *Soldier Battle Losses* headline in the local paper."

"Not so compassionate." She stopped removing the packing from the vase order and focused on Tom. How sad that they merely listed Abigail's beloved as a number rather than a person. "He was a hero."

"Not really." Tom shook his head. "Back then, unless you were a high-ranking officer, you weren't considered a hero. Just another casualty for the greater good."

"That's terrible." *But wait…* "If that's the case, why does Abigail's diary say he died at the hand of her father?"

"Addison Rutledge was a man of extreme wealth and power. He was the original newspaper owner and publisher of the *Morrison Mill Gazette* back when Cedar Ridge was named Morrison Mill."

"I remember hearing that." She placed a vase on the shelf next to the others. "Isn't that why they named Morrison Shoes, because the factory was built on the mill property?"

"Yep. It was a perfect place for the mill next to the river. With all our cedar trees, the mill did well. The shoe company thought the name would give it the same good luck the mill had."

"Both closed." Laurel lowered her gaze to the countertop. "Maybe it wasn't such good luck." Pop and their friends who had lost their jobs were victims of that bad luck. "But that has nothing to do with Thomas's death."

"You're right. I read through old papers from the surrounding counties. What I found wouldn't have been printed in the *Morrison Mill Gazette.*"

Laurel used a box cutter to break down the shipping box. "What did you find?"

Tom glanced at his phone, and then looked up. "Addison didn't like Abigail keeping company with a blacksmith's son. Gossip buried in the society pages stated the two were courting. When Addison was interviewed about being the first newspaper to make deliveries to surrounding counties, they asked if Thomas Baxter would run the paper in the future because of Addison's advanced age."

She stopped collapsing the box and glanced on Tom. "What was his answer?"

"He said"—Tom read from his phone—"*There is*

no truth to the rumor that my lovely daughter would keep company with the likes of a blacksmith's son. The Morrison Mill Gazette *will be run by me and me alone.*" Tom swiped his cell phone screen. "When pushed for a comment on Thomas Baxter, Addison simply answered, '*the boy is no longer an issue.*'"

"Meaning what?"

"Several issues later, one paper reported Thomas Baxter died under suspicious circumstances because he was shot in the back, his body found a few miles out of Morrison's Mill instead of on the battlefield. Unfortunately, there was no follow-up."

Laurel exhaled a heavy breath. "So, Abigail was right."

"It's possible. Let me know if you find anything in the love letters. Maybe Addison was threatening Thomas or forbidding Abigail from seeing him. I'll do more digging. Maybe it will add to the history of the Rutledge family to give Stanley another marketing angle." Tom's eyelids stretched along with his massive grin. "It's a great puzzle. I love digging into this stuff."

Knowing Tom enjoyed the story's intrigue didn't stop Laurel from being swallowed in sorrow as if she personally knew Abigail and Thomas. Her heart broke for them. She longed that someday she'd find her special person to love and cherish. Abigail had found that person…but he was taken away.

People you love die. Laurel didn't want to open her heart, but sometimes, the heart didn't give you a choice. She protected herself from loss, but Adam broke that protective barrier, wearing her down and forced her heart to do what her mind feared…and she didn't know how to stop it.

****

When Adam entered The Bean & Brew, he glanced around as the entire coffee shop buzzed with chatter about last night's storm. Some of the damage that hit the village left large, downed branches and piles of scattered leaves.

"Did you see it?" George Statler swirled his cane in the air like a tornado. "Knocked down everything in its path."

"Oh, there you go again," Howard Waldorf admonished. "It wasn't *that* bad. The brunt of it was by the manor."

"The manor?" Adam stopped short before nearing the counter, hoping the storm wouldn't delay the project. Too many people depended on the opening. "What kind of damage, Howard?"

"All those trees falling this way and that." The old man shook his head full of white hair. "It's a shame. Don't know how Frank is going to clear it all."

"Frank? What's Frank got to do with clearing the manor property?"

"Oh, no, son. Not the manor. It's Frank's property next door. The place looks like a bomb exploded. Strange how everything around it is untouched, but Frank's lot is a total mess."

Phew, Adam thought, grateful the storm spared the mansion; but it stunk that Frank's property took the hit. Even though Frank didn't have plans for the grounds right now, the property was important to both Laurel and Frank.

And just like that, the urge to protect Laurel and make everything right for Frank hit him like last night's storm. He had an idea.

****

When her alarm sounded at 5:45 a.m., Laurel covered her head with a pillow, she searched and smacked the snooze button. After additional alarms ten minutes later, she groaned and dragged herself from the warmth of her favorite down comforter.

Big mistake reading Thomas' love letters when she should have slept. Each night, the letters tempted her ever since finding them in Abigail's room. Last night again, the letters summoned her to find the truth about their love story.

Just like Tom's research had gleaned, Laurel read the anguish in Thomas' response to Addison's disapproval. Even though he was a blacksmith's son—and wasn't educated as those in the Rutledge society circle—the eloquence of his simple words of love and adoration for Abigail caused Laurel's emotions to swell.

'I will show your father I am a man of integrity, worthy of your love. I will put my life on the line to protect and care for you, my love.'

The letters indicated when Thomas returned from war, the two would elope. He must have asked for Abigail's hand because he had written,

'Your acceptance of marriage has touched my soul and will guide me back to you once my duty to God and Country are fulfilled.'

Poor Thomas, Laurel thought, after reading and re-reading letter after letter. She had searched the responses for an answer, but none had surfaced. Just evidence of a deep, powerful love—gratified with the hope of a long, shared life together—that nothing, not even war, interfered with their happiness.

Reading each letter, Laurel couldn't keep heartbreaking tears from streaming her face because with all the optimism and anticipation of spending their lives together, their fate was different. Eternal love would be forced to prevail when reality stripped these young people of a happily ever after just like it had done to her parents. Laurel knew her heart couldn't withstand that kind of pain.

****

"Parker told me you were here."

Adam tugged on a broken tree branch at Frank's vacant lot and glanced over his shoulder at his sister, Karen, when she arrived in Ma's car. "Parker again?" He clenched his teeth, and with a wrenching tug, the branch gave way in a snap. He stumbled but maintained his balance. "What's with you two?" He tossed the released branch onto a chaotic stack of already piled branches.

"Nothing. Why?"

With a wipe of his brow on his sweatshirt sleeve, he ignored a shiver of cold from the near-freezing temperatures and faced his sister. "You two are a little too cozy."

"Cozy? A little old fashioned, don't you think?" Exhibiting a shiver, she wrapped her arms around her waist and shot a narrow-eyed glare.

"That little sweater you're wearing isn't gonna cut it. Don't evade the question."

"You can stop the big brother interrogation. Mom told me you were at the jobsite. Parker was there; you weren't. He said I'd find you here."

"Hmm."

"Don't hmm me." She pulled her sweater to her

neck. "Drop the overprotective brother act. It's getting old. I'm only home for a few days—don't ruin it."

"I'm worried you're not still hangin' onto that old crush you had on Parker. He's dating Heather. You still crushin' on him is gonna end with you gettin' hurt."

"I'm fine. That crush is *long* gone. I can't believe he's dating her. She's such an airhead."

Adam stared at his sister. She almost sounded like she convinced herself her crush was gone, but he wasn't buyin' it. And he still wasn't used to her red hair. "Heather's a little out there, but she's a nice person. She's been through a lot."

"She wasn't nice in high school."

"You were a freshman. We were seniors. You can't blame her because I wouldn't let you hang with us. You were a little kid."

"Laurel wasn't like that, and she was older than me."

Images of Laurel back then surfaced memories of how cute she was. "That's because she's closer to your age. Besides, Laurel is nice to everyone. She's a good person. She's caring and smart and—"

Karen knotted her arms across her chest and shot him one of those *uh-huh* glares. "That brings me back to what you're doing here, at Laurel's father's property? You're not crushin' on that good, caring, smart girl, are you?"

"She's all right."

"All right?" Karen sputtered a laugh. "Your eyes just glowed when you mentioned her."

"She's been a big help with the parade."

"The parade, huh? By the way, how did *you* become the parade chair? Had to be alcohol involved."

"No." Thoughts of the beer he had nursed during the meeting at the diner rushed to his mind when the whole parade thing went down. Laurel had deadened his senses and had his brain spinning off his game when he had unknowingly volunteered.

"So, what gives?" Karen waited for an answer.

"The storm blew through the other night. Did a number on Frank's lot. I'm helping him. He's been a good friend. I'm paying him back for everything he's done for me."

"You and Mr. Eldridge?"

"You haven't been home much. Things aren't the same. With all the people coming into town, it's more important than ever to appreciate the friends we've got. Frank treats me more like a son than Ned ever did."

Karen threw a quizzical glance. "Has Dad gotten any better?"

Adam dropped his head. A *Dad* was a man who loved and protected his kids—not a lowlife who stole money from them to gamble away. Ned never stole from Karen. He called her *Kitten* in an attempt to make her believe he was a real Dad. Luckily, she never bought the act, but she didn't know the whole story.

Adam's old frustration of keeping the ugliness from Karen resurfaced and settled in his neck, tightening his shoulders. "Look, there's a lot you weren't aware of growing up. Let's just say, Ned is no Mike Brady."

"I'm fully aware of what happened. Stop evading the question. What's with you and Laurel?"

After he scared her with his intentions, he wasn't sure anything remained between him and Laurel, and he didn't know how to convince her they belonged together.

****

"What are you doing?" Jeanine shouted from her car window when she pulled along the curb of Frank Eldridge's property.

"What does it look like?" Adam yelled back. "I'm helping Frank."

"Does Frank know?"

"No." Adam struggled with more twisted, intertwined branches. "He's…got…enough to worry about. This…is the least I can do." With one last yank, the main branch snapped, almost knocking him off his feet for the second time today.

"Him? Or Laurel?"

Adam ignored that comment. *What's with the women around here?* He'd just gotten Karen off his back, and now he didn't intend to waste time dodging questions from Laurel's friend. Jeanine was fishing, and he wasn't takin' the bait. *Change the subject.* "Where are you off to?"

"Joan's. A drapery finishing party. You know, lady stuff. Tea and tiny desserts. The only hard thing she'll be serving are cookies. Don't get me wrong, it's a little too early for drinking spirits, but I'm not into all the village gossip that goes along with these gatherings."

"Didn't think you were the drapery type."

"Laurel roped me in."

Adam bobbed his head, knowing his co-chair had a knack for getting people to help. But he didn't have time for this small talk, although it did involve Laurel. "Laurel's not much of a drinker. I'm sure you'll both survive." Lifting his chain saw, he waited for Jeanine to leave before felling the large trunk since the lower branches were now free.

"Laurel bailed. Said she had a problem with one of her accounts." Jeanine wagged her eyebrows. "She gets to deal with that hunky bank guy."

He bristled at the idea of Laurel and that guy. Yeah, he was good-looking, if you were into someone who resembled a wrestler turned action-hero actor with all those muscles and the charisma to charm women into signing all kinds of bank offers. Adam shouldn't be jealous, but he was. Face it, he and Laurel were just *friends*, and that fact made him bristle even more.

His friends were right. He needed to let her know how much he cared. But her bank problem was a concern. He didn't need the whole town hearing their conversation, so he placed the chain saw on the ground and ambled toward Jeanine's car. "What's going on with the bank?"

"She didn't say. That's private stuff. It doesn't take a brain surgeon to realize she's treading water."

"Right." He dipped a single nod and hoped Laurel's financial problems weren't worse than she let on. Or… "You don't think she's interested in that bank guy, do you?"

She cocked her head and narrowed her eyes. "You know, for a really smart guy in business, you're kind of dense when it comes to women."

"How do you figure?"

"Anyone who knows Laurel knows how deep the loss of her mother affected her. She protects herself. She won't even get a dog because she can't bear another loss. That's why she's—"

"—overbearing with her father and needs to protect him, too."

"There you go, Skippy. Now you're catching on."

Was it possible the same way he had denied his feelings for Laurel that she might be doing the same? Another thing they had in common. That list grew longer each day.

"So?" Jeanine asked. "What are you going to do about it?"

That question brought him out of his own head. "Me?"

"Yes, Romeo. You. You've obviously got it bad for her. Are you wasting time, or are you sweeping her off her feet?"

He'd love nothing more than to gather Laurel in his arms and spend the rest of his life making her happy. But how in the world could he convince her he was what she wanted? And was he enough?

Chapter 15

Another dinner at Adam's apartment, and Laurel reciprocated with a corned beef—the perfect size for two. She had set the meat in the slow cooker before work, added potatoes and carrots, and then delivered it to Adam's after she closed the shop.

During the day, she had convinced herself getting together was a working dinner. But the anticipation of sharing another meal in his apartment kept her mind from concentrating on all the orders she processed for the manor's different Christmas tree themes.

But what honestly distracted her—throwing her off balance—was Adam's declaration to let him know when she stood ready to take their relationship to the next level. Ready for that leap like her dream where Momma had confidence she could handle the change and urged her to jump.

Laurel wasn't so sure.

As she sat across from Adam at his small, kitchen table, Laurel distanced the sentiments of Thomas' love letters from the affection she now held for Adam. Putting those emotions aside, she decided to rapid-fire read the parade units from her tablet to keep her mind on track. "Okay, we've got the high school and middle school bands. Bag pipes, the equine students from the university in Warren County—I asked them to decorate the horses. The garden club has a poinsettia float with the winners of the house decorating contest. The fire trucks will be decora—"

"Whoa, take a breath." Adam laid a hand on hers. "We eat first, then work. It's been a long time since I've been able to enjoy a homecooked meal with company in my house."

A heated excitement caught her off guard, and she lifted her gaze. "You cooked for me two weeks ago." That night had yielded so much pleasure, she looked forward to repeating it again.

"Yes, but *I* cooked. Even though you had a busy day, *you* cooked for me today." Grabbing her hand, he stroked it with his thumb. "I hope you know how special you are."

A current darted through her arm straight to her heart. She tilted her chin downward, her gaze casting on her tablet. Images of Thomas' love letters nestled back in her mind. "I'm no different than anyone else." She curled her lips inward, uncomfortable with the compliment. She finally peeked and saw sincerity laced in his eyes. "And you…you've proven how open and giving you are. That's pretty special."

Adam chuckled, and his eyes grew the size of Gerber Daisies. "Now, that's something! Guess I'm not as stubborn—and what was the other word you used— pigheaded, as you thought?"

"Point taken." She giggled and relaxed, enjoying the security of her hand in his. "I did warn you that once I cracked that shell of yours, I'd find a softy. Just saying…" The flirty banter between them added to the anticipation she experienced all day—anticipation laced with angst.

Tightening his hold with a squeeze, he then

released her hand. "You found me out. Don't go tellin' anyone. If you do, I'll deny it." He passed her a wine glass of lime-flavored seltzer.

Tipping her head to the side, she examined the glass. "You served this the last time. How did you know I like it?"

"Jeanine."

"Hmm." She drew her eyebrows together and twisted her drink in her hand. "You too are getting pretty chummy."

With arms resting on the table, he leaned in. "Are you jealous?"

"No reason to be." She watched him over the rim.

"Damn." He tapped the table with one hand. "I thought I was making progress."

"I'm not looking for a relationship, remember?" Even though she wanted him more and more each day.

"Yep, you've made that perfectly clear." He stretched an arm across the table and tweaked her nose. "Now, my dear princess, it's time to eat."

"Princess? Hmm?" She plated their meal while Adam tossed the salad. "You've called me that before. I'm *not* a princess."

"No, you're not, but you should be treated like one. You're always doing for everyone. More of us need to do for you."

"I do for others because I'm grateful they're in my life. It's my way of taking care of them…keeping them happy."

Adam's face rumpled in a downturned frown, and then his eyebrows creased in the middle. "What makes *you* happy?"

You make me happy! Laurel hesitated. "A lot of

people want stuff to make them happy. I don't need *stuff*. People I care about make me happy."

"Well, I hope I'm one of those people." He raised his glass. "To being happy. Hopefully, our working relationship brings happiness to everyone in Cedar Ridge, but to us, too. Cheers!"

Laurel took another sip of the tart, effervescent liquid and acknowledged the anxiety bubbling her insides that she found herself falling…falling hard. Whirling in her own emotions, she suspected those feelings intensified because of the love letters and the comparison she had done between Adam and Richard.

Those factors ping-ponged in her brain during the entire time she and Adam enjoyed their meal while she savored how they talked and ate and talked and ate. "Favorite season?" She crossed one leg over the other, rocking her ankle and tried to stop fear from taking over.

"Fall. The colors and cooler weather get my blood pumping. You?"

"Spring. Everything comes alive in spring!" She took a bite of corned beef and thought of another topic. "Okay, Christmas carols…classics or new?"

"Classics." He stopped midair and scooped potatoes and carrots from the crock to add to his plate.

"Really? I would have bet you'd be a fan of Jersey's famous rock star's song."

"Nope." He shook his head. "The ones about sleigh rides and being home for Christmas."

"Wow!" She leaned forward and folded her arms on the table. "Explain please."

Adam became quiet, and a serious shadow cloaked his eyes. "It's about wanting to be home with family where everything is safe. Isn't that what the holiday is all about?"

"Yes, definitely…family." For the guy she initially thought didn't have a serious side, she had been totally wrong.

"Okay, your turn. Classic or new?" he volleyed.

Laurel took another bite of savory meat and mumbled with a mouthful, "New."

"No way." He tilted his chin and widened his eyes. "You…the traditionalist?"

She swallowed hard, suppressing the memories of Christmases past. "The holidays are still hard, especially Christmas. A lot of the classics are solemn and sad."

"I get it," he said in between mouthfuls. "So, your favorite is?"

Thoughts of the song brightened her mood. "The original 1989 version of what to wish for Christmas."

"Hmm. I'm sensing a hidden meaning."

She toggled her head. "No hidden anything. It's a happy song with an upbeat melody."

"And it's wishing for a guy to spend Christmas with. Is that your Christmas wish?"

"No. It's just happy."

"Mm…mmh." He studied her like he was reading her mind.

Warmth tingled across her face. Okay, maybe she wanted to share Christmas with someone special…

Adam stood and lifted the slow cooker crock into the sink while she followed with the dishes.

"Italian"—they cleared the table together, standing side by side in his small kitchen—"or Chinese?"

She angled her head, waiting to see his reaction.

"Neither. Indian."

"Really?" He stopped loading the dishwasher midair with a plate. "I wouldn't have taken you as an exotic eater."

"There's a lot you don't know about me." *Like my fetish for pretty colored underwear!* Holding in *that* secret, she handed him a serving bowl with another question. "Cats or dogs?"

"Dogs. I'm allergic to cats."

"Ooooh…There was a commercial with an adorable Bernese Mountain Dog." Yes, she sounded like a little kid on Christmas, but she'd been so taken with the dog, she couldn't contain her excitement. "It was sooo adorable!"

****

Adam leaned his head back and laughed. He loved how Laurel's eyes danced when she got excited. Loved how relaxed she was in his home. Like she belonged there. "Adorable used twice in the same sentence. Tell me how you *really* feel about the dog."

"Oh, it's nothing." Swiping her hand in the air, she lowered her chin with her lips bowing downward. "I've always wanted one, but they're really, really expensive."

He noticed her excitement wither. "Yeah, they are. But if you really, really want one"—he lifted her chin with his finger, flashing her a smile to help improve her mood—"you could save for one. Might take a few years, but then you'd have the adorable, adorable dog you've always, always wanted."

The conversation stopped. The air between them grew heavy with a longing he found hard to resist. Seeing her step away, he wanted to draw her toward him and wrap her in his arms in comfort. She clearly wanted a dog.

Laurel pushed a strand of hair away from her face and handed him the two wine glasses. "Not the right time for a dog, what with my shop and my father, the manor, the parade."

"Timing, huh?" He conveyed an expectant eye.

"You wouldn't understand." She bit her bottom lip.

"I might. Try me."

She cocked her head and remained silent.

He noticed her studying him, but he didn't utter a word. Jeanine had said Laurel didn't have a dog because she didn't want to love it and lose it. Given dog years…an eventual outcome. Such a shame not to open her heart to people, or in this case, a four-legged companion. She had so much love to give someone…er, a dog. Time for a gentle nudge for her to open up. "What is it?"

"Dogs are great, but…they don't last very long, you know?"

He nodded without saying a word.

"Maybe someday, but not now."

"Someday," he encouraged. "And when someday comes, that little ball of fur is going to be one lucky pup to have you to love it."

Anyone who has the good fortune to be loved by you is lucky.

****

A few days after her dinner with Adam, Laurel arrived early to a meeting at Rutledge Manor. Dinner had gone well. Better than well. Spending time at his home made it easier to sort her confused feelings, even though fear kept getting in the way. A few weeks ago,

Adam Carlson didn't fit her idea of a life partner. But the more time she spent with him…

As she got out of her car, she noticed the damage on her parents' property from last week's wind and rainstorm was gone. The downed trees and branches had been cleared. She scurried toward the hedges bordering the properties when the crunch of tires sounded from the manor's gravel driveway.

"Hey, princess," Adam yelled from his car. "What are you doing?"

Turning toward him, she pursed her lips and shook her head a few times. "I'm not sure. The property was a disaster"—she pointed over the hedges and then at Adam—"and now it's cleaned up."

He approached and surveyed the lot. "Looks pretty good."

"Yeah, but…" She quirked her gaze toward him, suspecting he was involved.

He leveled a sideways glance. "What's wrong?"

"How did it…uh…who did it?"

"Maybe it was the ghosts?" He cleared his throat and sputtered a laugh. Then he let loose a heavy laugh. "From what I've heard from my dear old aunt, Abigail and Thomas walk these grounds all the time. Maybe they didn't like living next to the mess."

"Oh, come on—get real." Her focus pivoted between Adam and the property. "Wait a minute." She pointed an index finger. "It was you!"

"Me?" Adam slapped a hand to his heart, feigning surprise. "What makes you think I'm the guilty one?"

"Call it woman's intuition." She puckered her lips and squinted her eyes to pin him in place. "Did Parker help you with this?"

"Parker? I'm not sure. You better ask him." He rocked back and forth on his heels, an odd smirk on his face. "Hey, ya know, it's getting' kind of cold out here. Better get inside, we have a lot of work to do."

"Nice change of subject, Carlson. You're still not off the hook."

Adam laughed and took her by the hand, guiding her toward the manor.

She didn't know what to make of this situation but loved the security of her hand in his…natural, like they'd been doing it forever. Her heart told her he cleared the land because he cared. They climbed the stairs, and she noticed the solid feel beneath her feet, and then again on the porch. "Wow, these are fixed. They look great!"

"Yep, and all the wood trim has been scraped and prepped around the windows and doors. Painting should start soon."

Laurel dug through her purse for the manor key, and a frigid gust surrounded her in a bitter bite. She struggled to open the door, and Adam put his arms on either side of her from behind, and together they pushed the heavy wood. With a weighty thrust, she shut the door, and shivered when a chill shot deep to her bones.

"Here." Adam nestled her in his arms. "I'll keep you warm."

Snuggling her in a cocoon, his body heat slowed the chattering of her teeth. She lifted her chin to his breath warming her face. The reassurance in his eyes made her feel safe and secure. "You cleared my parent's property, didn't you?"

"And what if I did?"

His selfless act was not only a gift to her, but to

Pop, as well. Adam's many good qualities and sincerity provided a trust she longed to hold onto. "That's a wonderful thing you did, taking care of us. Thank you."

"I'll always take care of you. I promise." Lowering his head, the touch of a gentle kiss pressed her lips surrounding her heart with love.

Yes, it was love. She couldn't deny love no matter how hard she tried.

He was a good man who didn't make false promises. They were as important to him as they were to her. His promise to always be there for her would never be broken...something Laurel counted on.

****

With the commotion of a freight train, Stanley Palmer, Mayor Winston Farley, and Ernie Donaldson from Donaldson's Hardware barreled through the manor door like a storm of their own.

"Getting mighty brisk out there." Mayor Farley rubbed his gloved hands together.

"Laurel, Adam, we didn't interrupt anything, did we?" Ernie asked, removing his hat.

Adam cleared his throat while stepping from Laurel. "Nah, we were just commenting on how cold it is outside."

Laurel licked her lips while a pink blush ran across her cheeks.

"I knew you were going to put the trees up and get the decorating going," Stanley said. "I wanted to make sure the heat was working since Eddie fixed it."

Heat? Oh, yeah. The heat was stronger than ever between him and Laurel that he didn't notice the manor's temperature.

Mayor Farley pressed a hand on Adam's shoulder.

"Nice work clearing Frank's lot. You did a good job. Bet you could park a few semis in there and still have room to build a house."

Winston's comment instantly replaced the memory of their kiss, and Adam dashed his gaze to Laurel whose eyes opened wide. "Are you thinking what I'm thinking?"

Her mouth popped open then. "Can we do that?"

Adam raised his eyebrows, and he lifted his shoulders. "Don't see why not. Have to go to the Planning Board for approval."

"But that takes time," she said.

"I know. But since it's for the town, maybe they can rush it. How about I come over tonight and we talk to Frank about it?"

"Okay." She lowered her voice and whispered, "It's going to cost money. Money, we don't have."

Adam took hold of her hand. "Don't worry. I'll call in a few favors and get the materials at cost. It'll work. I promise."

He wasn't sure about covering any unforeseen expenses, but he'd figure it out. This project was a priority now since it was the answer to Laurel and Frank's financial problems. And…it would be the answer to his long-time question of where to park everyone.

Calling in a few favors wouldn't be a problem since his work connections were always willing to help.

And then a solution popped into his head. One he didn't want to entertain, but if he did, it would be worth it. But in doing so…he'd be letting go of a piece of his past.

****

Laurel tossed and turned and flipped and flopped on her bed. The feel of Adam's lips and the taste of his kiss kept her awake. Sleep, the one thing she needed to keep her engine going this time of year, was near impossible. The sincerity and promise in that one little kiss had her heart screaming that what she needed to do scared the Dickens out of her.

Adam loved her; even though he hadn't said so. Everything he did proved his love.

Her brain struggled to keep her protective iron shield in place because more and more, she fell deeply in love. He satisfied a void in her heart, and she couldn't deny her feelings any longer. Even though it terrified her, she realized what she needed to do.

****

With the energy of the flower shop running a marathon, two students from the vocational school horticulture class helped re-create all the sample arrangements Laurel had designed.

Glancing at her phone, she rolled her eyes with an exasperated sigh. She didn't have time to engage in another voice message from Richard. His ego wouldn't accept that she—a nobody in his social circle—wasn't clamoring to get back together since he was so important.

Not interested in meeting for drinks to rehash their finished relationship, she ignored the message just like the last few. But when the bells jingled over The Laurel Wreath door, he was the last person she expected.

Pop lugged cases of supplies from the basement and stopped dead when he entered the display room. He directed a gaze her way that was colder than the icicles that formed after last night's storm.

"What are you doing here?" She glared at Richard.

"You haven't answered my calls." Dressed with perfectly cleaned shoes, his 100-watt smile, and trendy styled head of light-brown hair gave him the appearance of being picked out of a movie's central casting. "One would think you're avoiding me."

"One would be right." *What a pompous jerk.* Now she was mad. Mad she hadn't blocked his number. Mad for all the foolish time she had wasted with him. She should have ended it long before Pop needed her.

"Think about that answer, Laurel," he said in his usual condescending manor, arching a judgmental eyebrow. "We were good together—have a history."

"The only thing we had was me dealing with your ego and *your* life. There's no room for you in *my* life. Didn't I make that clear?"

He shook his head. "You don't belong here, working in this store with flowers. Your talents should be utilized elsewhere—somewhere much more important. I can—"

"This isn't working," she interrupted through her teeth. She grabbed his arm and forced him through the door.

They stepped outside into the cold.

"You're right, this isn't working." He suddenly halted. "These worthless flowers are a waste of time."

She skidded to a slippery stop. The cold had settled on the sidewalk and just her luck, she hit a small, icy patch.

He stood, watching without aiding her from nearly falling.

How foolish she had been for putting up with him all those years. He didn't value her or her business.

"No, not the flowers." She pointed a finger at herself, and then at him. "Us. *We're* not working. It's time you leave. Don't come back again and don't contact me."

His posture straightened and with a slight turn of his head, his eyes popped open. "After all we've been through—"

"Goodbye!" She pointed toward the sidewalk. She hoped the shock on his face meant he finally got it, but she knew him well enough that the wheels in his head were plotting how to save his dignity. Seconds later, a smug expression spanned his face that she'd seen whenever he encountered someone he didn't deem worthy.

"Your loss." And with that, he sauntered away, head held high as if she didn't matter.

Good Lord. Her fear had forced her to settle for a guy who didn't respect her.

Pop, Jeanine, and Adam were right. She deserved better.

Wrapping her arms at her waist when the weather sliced a raw bite, she stared at the back of Richard's head while he strutted along the sidewalk.

He climbed into his high-end sports car, then the car peeled away.

She finally put an end to that chapter in her life. Richard was gone forever.

Chapter 16

"Okay, what gives?" Jeanine bounded into The Laurel Wreath just before opening.

Laurel's insides jumped at the interruption. "About what?"

"You. You were all happy on the phone this morning. And this…" Jeanine pointed to Laurel's head. "Your…your hair is…nice. It's brushed. Did you lose your hair scrunchy thing?"

"Felt like keeping it down today." A light giggle bubbled in her throat. She enjoyed experimenting with the large barrette holding the hair from both sides of her temples secured to the top of her head with the rest cascading onto her shoulders.

"That"—Jeanine pointed again—"that smile. You always grump around in the morning like you have the weight of the world on your shoulders."

"I do *not*." Laurel stifled that giggle, but it escaped anyway. The exhausting heaviness she carried with Richard's constant resurfacing became a toll on her life. Now she'd never have to hear another *Richard* lecture from Jeanine again.

She wasn't sure when to come clean to Jeanine about her newfound happiness since a definite *I told you so* was in order; and yes, she deserved it. But she didn't want it to ruin her good mood, so she'd keep the secret a little longer.

With her world feeling lighter and brighter, even the colors of the flowers in her shop were more vibrant. The Christmas decorations lining Main and Elm seemed more festive. She ignored the interrogating frown from Jeanine. Nothing bothered her today. Last night, she'd slept the best as in a long, long time. "You can look at me like that all you want," she said to her bestie. "I'm happy because everything is going great. Is that a crime?"

"I'm not buying it." Jeanine crossed her arms over her chest.

Her raised-eyebrow glare bore through Laurel.

"Not buying what?" Pop asked when he returned from a delivery.

"Your daughter is holdin' out on me."

Pop stopped. "Oh, you mean the reason she was up early dancing in the kitchen, singing along with a country song blaring from her phone? And why she spent three hours in the bathroom fixin' her hair? Nope…nothing strange going on today, is there, sweetie?"

"I did *not* spend three hours on my hair. Can't a girl just be happy for once?"

"No!" they said together.

"Wow"—Laurel pouted—"tough crowd." They stood staring, as if their stares could make her crack. Okay, maybe they could. They were the people she loved the most and trusted most.

"Wait a minute!" Jeanine yelled and hit her forehead with the butt of her hand. "You did it! You gave Richard the final heave-ho!"

Laurel didn't say a word, just bit her bottom lip.

"She did!" Jeanine said to Pop.

Pop's gaze was on Laurel in a flash. "Is it true?" Instant happiness flooded his face, and his eyes glowed like Fourth of July sparklers.

She had to come clean. Telling the truth would make them both very, very happy, so holding out seemed cruel. But a little teasing would be fun. "I'm not sure…" She purposely dragged out her announcement.

"Not sure about what?" Jeanine asked in a rush.

"That you're going to—"

"Laurel Marie?"

Uh-oh. When Pop used her full name, it was time to declare Uncle. "—to lecture me about Richard anymore." She closed her eyes for a second and grimaced, waiting for the explosion.

"Thank God!" Jeannine jumped up and down.

"Hallelujah!" Pop looked toward the ceiling. "Did you hear that, Belinda? Our little girl finally came to her senses."

With that, they both wrapped her in a group hug.

"It's about time." Pop pressed a kiss to the top of her head. "Welcome to the real world."

Jeanine and Pop stepped away, all happiness and joy. Then Pop took hold of her hands, his gaze laser-focused solidifying the serious straight line of his lips. "So…what are you doing about Adam?"

Her heart knew exactly what to do about Adam. Now the impossible task of convincing her brain had her cemented in fear.

****

A few days had gone by, snatching Laurel and Adam's free time together. She needed to give serious thought to move forward since she loved Adam. Their schedules finally meshed for them to meet at her house to review the list of parade participants.

Settling on the worn, comfy couch, she set two mugs of hot chocolate on the old maple coffee table and placed them next to the pumpkin, caramel cookies Molly sent from The Cookie Cottage. Laurel lit a cinnamon-scented candle hoping to add a snuggly warmth to the season.

"Nice and cozy in here." Adam rubbed his hands together, looking relaxed and comfortable in her home. "They're talkin' snow flurries for tomorrow night, but it sure feels like it tonight. I'll take snow over ice any day."

Laurel remembered the ice that almost had her butt-sliding on the sidewalk the other day—the day she finally put Richard in the review mirror. *Maybe this is a good time to let Adam know I might be ready.* "Funny thing happened with the ice." She rapid-fired her words, and a chuckle slipped out of her mouth. "I was running after Richard to tell him he was no longer part of my life, and I hit a patch of ice. I didn't fall, but it was pretty close."

"Glad you didn't fa—wait, what did you say?" His mouth quirked to one side accompanied by a slanted stare.

"Ice patch—"

"Oh, no you don't." He shook his head several times, scooched closer, and slid an arm along the back of the sofa. "You did? For real?"

"Yep." Cocking her head, she inhaled, her nerves settling, and simultaneously, she raised both eyebrows and lifted both shoulders. "He won't be back."

"No more text messages?"

"Nope. I blocked him." A small task that yielded so

much satisfaction. "When he realizes it, he'll be offended that I'm not groveling to get him back."

Adam snorted. "That guy's more of a jerk than I thought."

Laurel sniffed a soft laugh. "Well, there's that. I can't blame him. I should have been firmer a long time ago."

"True. But, a long time ago"—he fingered a strand of her hair—"you didn't have me to make you see the light."

"Really?" She sent him a teasing glance. "So now that I've seen the light, what do you suggest I do?"

Adam's arm floated across her shoulders and pulled her closer. "I suggest you cuddle up on a cold winter's night right next to me."

"Do you?"

"Yes. Maybe you can turn out the lights. Candlelight and hot chocolate…very sexy."

She curled her lips in a slow smile and followed the urge to finger his shirt collar. "I'd have a lot of explaining to do if Pop walked in."

"No problem." He raised two cross fingers. "Frank and I are like this. Betcha we'd have his blessing."

Laurel hesitated. While she'd love the idea of getting cozy with Adam, she wanted to take it slow. After all, even though she loved him, she needed to ease into a relationship. "I'm sure Pop would be happy, but would it be okay if we take it slow? My relationship experience isn't great."

"My track record isn't either." He nodded. "Slow and steady is the way to go…wait, no," he stammered. "Not steady as in *going steady* like they did in the old days…you know, spend more time together. Get to know each other's quirks." He winked.

"I'm sure we've gotten to know each other pretty well these past few weeks."

"Yes, we have."

Adam removed his arm from her shoulders.

Her heart begged for it to return, but that didn't go along with taking it slow.

"What were we talking about before you dropped the good news?" He scratched the side of his head. "Oh, now I remember. Snow."

"A little snow might be nice, make things feel more festive." She handed him a mug of hot chocolate, wishing she was ready to jump head first. *Baby steps*. "We don't need another surprise ice storm ruining the parade and opening."

"I'm with you. A dusting of snow would work." Adam sipped the hot chocolate with a moan. "Mmm…this is great. What'd you put in it?"

"Can't you tell?" She lifted a smile to her lips, knowing the ingredient she *always* put in hot chocolate would make him happy.

He shook his head and took another sip. He smacked his lips like a child.

Visions of a little Adam swirled in her head. He must have been an adorable kid with that impish grin. Laurel couldn't resist that same grin that now drew everyone to him. "It's one of your favorites. Vanilla."

He flashed a round-eyed expression. "For me? That's really nice."

"Sorry." She lifted a little hop of one shoulder and grinned. "Momma always added vanilla."

"Your mom must have been a great lady."

"She was. Pop and I continue her traditions as

much as we can." She ran a finger over the edge of the mug, and a familiar sadness weighed on her. "It's hard, but we keep trudging along."

He laid a hand on her arm. "Your mother would be proud."

Laurel shook off the emotions that repeatedly swelled when memories of Momma emerged, but she needed to focus on the present. "Speaking of traditions, I understand you and Molly will be joining us for Thanksgiving Sunday."

"Yeah, we are." He plucked a cookie from the platter and examined it from side to side. "Ma and I are looking forward to coming. Karen won't be home"—he bit and said while chewing—"but she will for Christmas."

"I'm glad." A gentle laugh tickled her throat and her insides. "The house will be packed with lots of people, a little bit of chaos, but a lot of fun."

Adam swirled his fingertip on her shoulder. "Sounds perfect."

"We have another tradition you might like. Pop goes crazy with outside Christmas decorations."

"I've seen it every year." He held up his hot cocoa mug and pointed it. "Pretty impressive."

"Thanks. He's hanging the outside lights this weekend. Takes a few weeks to get everything wired and in place for the big reveal."

"Big reveal? Like those home renovation shows?"

Laurel's memories of long-ago reveals played at her heart. "Between dinner and dessert, we assemble across the street. Pop does a countdown, and he turns on all the lights at once. We "ooh" and "ahh" and laugh, and then run back in because it's always freezing." *Oh, when will the memories get easier?*

"Hey…" Adam rubbed her arm. "What's wrong?"

Thoughts of Momma flooded her mind, and Laurel focused on the mug in her hands. She sucked in a deep breath. "When I was little, Momma rushed me in the house, leaving Pop outside to fix the light strings that wouldn't light." Again, the image of Pop made her chuckle…a sad chuckle, but a happy one, too. "He was like a madman running from spot to spot, figuring out which light was the culprit. Momma and I watched from the window, and we would laugh and laugh." She viewed Adam through water-brimmed eyes as the melancholy memory took over.

He stroked her cheek with the back of his fingers and wiped away a loose tear.

How he knew just what to do to give her comfort amazed her. But, on the bright side, this year she and Adam would share the holiday together.

"You know"—he took hold of her hand—"that sounds like that holiday vacation movie."

Laurel snickered, grateful for the levity Adam offered. "Oh, the Griswolds have nothing on us. Pop's been doing it way before that movie. And speaking of Pop, he's happy with our parking lot idea. He's talked about it every day since we presented it."

"Good. It's a win-win for everyone. I already talked to Stanley. He and Frank agreed on the rent. As soon—"

This time, Laurel placed her hand on Adam's arm. "Yes, it *is* great." She hedged before continuing, hoping he didn't think she was complaining. "The monthly income is generous. But we've been crunching numbers to convert the property into a parking lot." She bit her bottom lip. "We don't have that kind of money."

"I know. But like I said, I know a guy who can help with the gravel. You have the hard part taken care of because your parents got the driveway opening approval years ago. I spoke to Ron Whitmore from the planning board. Since Hemlock is already a residential-commercial zone, you're good. Frank and I finished the paperwork yesterday. Ron's got it on the agenda for approval at their next meeting."

Laurel inhaled a significant amount of air, then released it through puffed cheeks. "We still don't have the money for the excavation. It's kind of you and Parker to donate your time clearing more land, but that's not fair to both of you."

"Don't worry, it will work out. I promise." He placed his mug on the coffee table, pulled her into his arms, and placed a gentle kiss on her temple.

She snuggled close and believed he'd stand by his promise. But she also believed, a Christmas miracle was needed for that promise to be kept unless Santa had a bundle of cash in his bag.

****

This is where Adam wanted to be, right here, on the sofa, with Laurel by his side and contentment in his life. He'd do everything in his power to make her happy…make a good life with her. Their ability to share all the good and the bad was something he'd been missing with all the other women he auditioned for life partner. And maybe that was the problem. No audition was necessary with Laurel. Their natural transformation from working together, to becoming friends, now led to love.

Even though she didn't need it, he wanted to take

care of her. Someone needed to—to show that she was important and valued and special. She showed everyone in her life how important they were; she needed to have the same. "Hey, I've been thinking."

"Is this an old habit, or did you recently realize thinking is a good thing?" She tickled his side, giggling like a teenager.

He loved that about her—the ability to be serious when needed and switch to teasing without warning. "Recently." He played along. "Takes a lot of energy, but seems to be worth it."

"So, what have you been thinking about, Einstein?" She snuggled closer into his shoulder.

"The Morrison Building."

She sat up from his embrace, staring with her eyes wide, mouth open in a perfect oval. "You have an idea about opening Morrison?"

"Sort of." He shrugged one shoulder and hoped she like the idea. "I'm thinking it has to house a few businesses, but not like a mall."

Laurel nodded. "Agreed. We don't need a mall closing all our stores on Main and Elm."

"Exactly. A vendor rental space. You know how Ellen, Parker's mom, and her quilting club make all their quilts?"

"Yes, but what does that have to do with rentals?"

"One section of the building can be for craft vendors. Like an indoor flea market with new, handmade things. Each crafter can rent a small space for as long as they want, making it their own little store."

"I like it." She bent one leg to sit on, positioning her body to face him. "But what about the other part of the building?"

"Same concept, except it would be antique shops."

"Like the Dusty Closet?"

"Yeah." Adam took hold of her hand. "Myra just closed because the rent was too high. She might reopen if the rental is affordable. We could probably fit a good fifty businesses in there, which would keep the rent down."

"That's a great idea." She squeezed his hand in return. "It would be another place for people to visit when they come to the village."

"Yep. Maybe a food court, too. Start with the food businesses in town setting up small stands to make it convenient for customers to eat while shopping."

"I like it. What does the rest of the council and planning board think?"

"I haven't told them yet. I wanted to get your opinion first. Do you think it would work?"

"Yes." Laurel squeezed his hand again, bouncing on the sofa like an excited butterfly. Then she froze like her excitement butterflies fizzled. "Wait…who's going to buy the building and run things?"

"That's one of those *minor details* I have to work out."

"Minor details?" Laurel's eyes popped open again. "You were upset with Ernie for brushing off the minor parade details. Now who's not being illogical about business?"

"Hey"—he held up a staying hand—"he's proving me wrong. The manor and parade are somehow working. I'm hoping with a little faith, things will work out."

****

"You're quiet. What's going on?" Jeanine sat in the passenger side of Laurel's sedan.

"Nothing." Laurel pulled into Donaldson's Hardware parking lot and didn't glance at Jeanine for fear her bestie would see right through her. "I'm going through the decorations' order in my head...to make sure Ernie ordered the right items."

"Ahhh...no." Jeanine shifted her body to face Laurel. "Something's bothering you."

Laurel hit the ignition button to stop the engine, took in a deep breath, and stared through the windshield. *I can't face the I-told-you-so glare in Jeanine's eyes.* She grimaced, closed her eyes tight, and attempted to contain everything she'd suppressed until a small implosion formed in her gut. "Adam's been doing things that have me thinking about him in a different way." Sucking a breath between her teeth, she opened one eye and waited for the celebration.

"It's about time!" Jeanine's voice pealed inside the car's interior. "That means you're giving him a chance!"

"Yes, but...I've got to."

"Oh, please. Just go with it and see where it lands." Then Jeanine quieted. "He's not going to die on you. Take that leap of faith."

Leap. Just like Momma said in that dream. Laurel needed to jump, hang on, and trust everything would be all right. Many tried to convince her to put her fear aside, but doing so wasn't easy. Fear caused the sound of her heartbeat to drum in her ears.

She wanted Adam—needed him in her life. His kindness almost had her in tears when he had helped that little boy at the Harvest Festival. His love for

263

Molly reminded her of her love for Pop—the love she still had for Momma. Adam had cooked her a meal when he learned she'd had a hard day. And…most of all, he vowed to stand by all his promises…paramount in her heart.

Right there in front of her stood a potential love like her parents, and she'd been too scared to trust it. If she admitted her feelings out loud, then she'd have to act on them. She hesitated, then willed her courage to guide her. "I'm falling for him," she said in a quick breath.

Jeanine threw her hands in the air. "It's about time."

Carrying fear and suppressing her feelings for Adam posed an emotional tug of war. A lightness now surrounded her, releasing that cumbersome pressure. Within seconds, optimism washed over her that maybe her fear wouldn't control her anymore. "Wow, that feels *really* good." She whooshed out a breath.

"I'll bet it does." Jeanine struck a thoughtful pose with her hand perched on her chin. She squinted at Laurel.

"What's going on in that head of yours," Laurel asked, afraid because when Jeanine formulated an idea, no one could stop her.

A deliberate, excited upward curve of her lips energized Jeanine's already happy mood. "A makeover!"

"A what?"

"You heard me. I'll make an appointment with my hairdresser. She'll make you look like a new woman."

The ridiculous idea had Laurel coughing. "I don't need a makeover." Reaching for the door lever, she eased out of the car. "Let's get those decorations. Ernie is expecting us." She shut the door to end the conversation and hurried toward the safety of the store.

A makeover? Jeanine watched too many of those self-help, online videos.

Jeanine slammed the door, keeping pace through the parking lot. "You can change the subject all you want, Laurel Marie, but you still need a makeover."

"No, I don't." A few steps more and she'd be in the safety of Donaldson's Hardware to retrieve her order.

"Yes, you, do." Jeanine stopped walking. "When was the last time you cut your hair?"

A few seconds clicked by while Laurel contemplated the answer, keeping her from entering the sanctuary of the store.

Jeanine stood with her hands on her hips that looked awkward given the bulk of her winter jacket. "Hmmm"—a few more seconds of silence—"exactly. You look like you were pulled through the back end of a hedge."

"Excuse me?"

Jeanine charged toward her, taking her by the arm. "I'm your best friend, and I love you, but you're not showing what you've got. You're gorgeous, but no one knows it because you dress like an old lady with Mom jeans and T-shirts under flannel."

Laurel looked at her feet, hiking boots were comfortable and functional for her job. "I work with plants and dirt, how am I supposed to dress?"

"Like a lady when you're not working with plants and dirt." She grabbed Laurel's arm hard and spun her around, ripping the knit hat from her head, revealing static electricity sticking hair to her face. "After we tame your hair, we're going shopping. You need a new outfit for the church fund-raiser this Sunday."

Laurel tried in vain to swipe the electrified hairs out of her eyes. "What's wrong with my church clothes?"

"Let's just say the 80s called—they want their wardrobe back."

"That's cruel."

"Cruel, but true." She took hold of Laurel's two, gloved hands. "This is the plan. We're going to shift you into the 21st century—"

"But I don't—"

"And when we do, both you and Adam won't be able to deny your feelings for each other, because you, my dear, will knock his socks off!"

How in the world will I do that?

Chapter 17

Eight days before Thanksgiving and the flower shop bustled with holiday preparations. Two students from the vocational school were back to help Laurel and Frank complete orders for Christmas arrangements that a few customers wanted for their Thanksgiving celebrations.

While Laurel loved Christmas, she wished more people focused on giving thanks and appreciating their loved ones instead of using Thanksgiving as a kickoff for the year's most popular holiday. But Christmas remained a wonderful moneymaker for The Laurel Wreath, so she'd indulge their wishes.

"Okay, we also need to make the centerpieces for Sunday's church fund-raiser." She relocated a case of plastic pumpkins and acorns and placed the case on the floor in front of the workstation. "At least, these will be Thanksgiving themed."

Utility knife in hand, Pop sliced open a box of foam blocks and another of fall-colored, silk leaf picks.

Laurel took hold of two, giant, gold-and-orange ribbon spools to show the girls a sample centerpiece and relaxed when both caught on by creating exact replicas.

Things seemed under control, so she took the opportunity to order more boxes of mistletoe and flowers for the manor. With fresh magnolias impossible to get, she substituted silk versions and mixed in gardenias. With that chore completed, she joined Pop in the display room.

"I'm looking forward to digging into that turkey." Pop slid the old, metal, tea cart from under the window to make room for the new, wooden shelves he made. "My mouth is watering just thinking about it."

Pop believed the holidays were special because they had a lot to be thankful for.

And keeping Momma's holiday traditions helped Laurel feel closer, as if gaining Momma's approval from heaven.

"What size turkey do I need to get this year?" he asked. "How many people did you invite?"

"A few more than usual. Evan and Arlene. Todd's family. Lou. The guys and their wives…although, I think Howard said something about visiting his daughter in Vermont, so the Waldorfs won't be joining us. I also invite Sarah and her sons. And the Carlsons, too."

"Well, then, looks like we'll have a full house!" A heartwarming smile drew a curve on his lips. "So much to be thankful for." A broad, full-mouth grin then spanned like a little boy opening a shiny, new bike on Christmas morning. That smile never wavered as Pop grabbed the full trash bag and headed outside to the trash container.

Laurel shared his happiness that a full house was something to be thankful. Sweeping the empty spot under the window—readying it for the new shelves—she let her thoughts drift to how fortunate she and Pop were to be surrounded by friends who were more like family.

With Pop's return, he pointed to the old, tea cart. "This still going to Dusty Closet Antiques?"

Laurel nodded. "Myra said to deliver it to her house, even though she closed the store. She's hoping to reopen someday." She grabbed the dustpan, and Adam's idea for the Morrison building came to mind. She wished it a reality for people like Myra to restart their businesses.

"Okay, I'll load it into the van now and drive it over later."

"Thanks. Oh, I forgot to tell you. Sarah said she'll make green bean casserole for Thanksgiving Sunday. Molly's making stuffing and candied yams."

"Hmm." Pop posed a thoughtful expression. "We need pies. Sure hope Walter's wife, Dolores, brings sweet potato pie again this year. Since we'll have a full house, can we add mincemeat, too?"

Laurel chuckled at the request. "Well…" she teased, "since it's your favorite—and there will be enough people to help you eat it—we can have mincemeat. I'll have to find a recipe."

"Ahhh…that might not be necessary."

"You have one?" She glanced at Pop over her shoulder as she bent to sweep the floor under the window of dust and dried flower petals into the dustpan.

"No, not really." His sheepish grin gave it away. "I happen to know someone who has access to all kinds of pies."

"Anyone I know?" She hoped Pop would admit he already invited Joan.

"Would it be okay if I asked Joan to join us?"

"More than okay. I asked her, too." Laurel stood,

balancing the dustpan to avoid a mess. "Joan's lovely. I'm glad to see you're taking the chance. You deserve to be happy."

"Might be good for you to take a chance, too."

She shifted past Pop in search of the trash can. "I'm getting there."

"He's a good guy, you know. Give him a chance."

"You're just saying that because he brought you lottery tickets when you hurt your ankle and chicken wings when you watched football together."

"They were *really* good wings." He snorted. "But seriously, underneath that armor, he's considerate. Takes care of everyone…same as you do."

"I've seen it." She remembered how he changed the light bulb for Molly at The Cookie Cottage. Witnessed his concern when Molly's car was in the shop. "He thanked me for driving Molly home from Joan's a few nights ago. I guess he didn't care I drove home alone, but then again, I'm not his mother or sister."

"Yes, he did." He motioned a chin toward the new shelf unit. "He asked me to text him when you got home. That really impressed me."

"He did?" Laurel took hold of one end of the unit, raising it enough to follow Pop's lead. "Why didn't you tell me?"

He tilted his head and scrunched his lips to one side. "Wasn't necessary."

They rested the unit under the window.

"Maybe not, but letting me know he cared would have been nice." Laurel eyed the location of the shelves. Yep, they would allow her to display more holiday items.

"You're right. I should have told you," Pop said. "Then you would have known how much he cares."

"Okay. Uncle." She raised her palms into the air. "I give up."

"So, you admit he's a great guy?"

"Yes. Adam is a great guy."

"Good. What are you gonna do about him?"

Her conversation with Jeanine about a makeover screamed to become a reality, even though the change terrified her. But it probably was a good idea.

Taking a deep breath, she summoned every ounce of courage. "I'm going to knock his socks off."

****

After Sunday's church service, the pancake breakfast fund-raiser in the church fellowship hall was in full swing. The congregation bustled with discussions of the Rutledge Manor Grand Opening and the Christmas parade in two weeks.

Laurel made the rounds, talking to everyone she invited to Thanksgiving Sunday. Molly's comment that she was all '*gussied up*' had her feeling a little self-conscious, but she did love the feminine, updated hair style, tight-fitting leggings, and trendy sweater.

The golden highlights that brightened her brown hair would take slightly longer to get used to…but she loved how the cut flowed on her shoulders. The soft, wispy bangs framed her face and kept them from falling in her eyes. Her usual ponytail was no longer necessary and was only be needed during work or cleaning the house. The makeup applied during the makeover was a bit much, so she used half the amount; and Jeanine approved.

So how would Adam react to her transformation?

271

Wondering where he was, she headed straight to the table where Howard, George, Walter, and their wives sat. Walter's wife, Dolores, had an adorable, old-fashioned Thanksgiving pin on the lapel of her tweed jacket.

"Laurel!" Dolores waved her over, then wrapped her mocha-toned hands around Laurel's. "Would it be okay if I bring sweet potato pie to Thanksgiving Sunday again?"

"Absolutely. Pop's counting on it."

"Great." Dolores squeezed Laurel's hands before releasing them.

"Laurel." Howard waved from across the table. "The wife and I were just saying it won't be the same not spending Thanksgiving with you and Frank."

"Thanks Howard." She leaned her hands on the back of an empty metal folding chair across from him. "Visiting your daughter and grandchildren will be special."

Howard's wife pointed to the center of the table. "Your centerpieces are beautiful. You always make it feel like the holiday."

"Thank you." The woman's compliment filled her with pride. "The decorations do feel festive, don't they?"

"Speaking of festive," George said. "Me and the guys brought in all those Christmas trees into the manor. Do you need help decorating?"

"I've got a small crew coming in, but thanks for the offer."

"Not a problem." George fashioned his usual salute. "We're always here for you."

She gave his arm an affectionate squeeze, told

everyone to enjoy themselves, and made her way to Sarah who stood alone near the coffee and pastry table. "How are things going?" she asked. "With Miles?"

"They're going." Sarah blew out what sounded like a weighted breath. "The boys keep asking questions. They're confused about Miles not working like other dads. I don't have the heart to tell them their father's not exactly a go-getter."

Laurel placed a hand on Sarah's shoulder. "That must be hard on you?"

"It is. I'm glad he stayed home today. The boys are happier when he's not around."

"Well, well, well. Whatever do we have here?" Clarice Carlson interrupted. "Good morning, ladies."

"Good morning," Laurel and Sarah said together, forcing their voices to a pleasant tone.

"I see your two boys are growing like weeds," Clarice addressed Sarah.

"Yes, they are." Sarah nodded and rolled her eyes. "Keeping up with their clothes is difficult."

"I can't help but notice the absence of their father." Clarice raised an eyebrow with a knowing nod. "Is your husband not joining us?"

"He's working on a project at the inn." Sarah's hand clutched her neck. "Making sure everything is ready for our busy grand opening weekend." She eyed Laurel. "Thanks to you, Adam, and Stanley, the inn is booked just about every day until New Year's."

"That's wonderful!" Laurel followed the lead to deflect from Sarah's apparent lie about Miles. "It wouldn't be possible without everyone working together."

Clarice crossed her arms over her chest.

"Hmm…everyone but *your* husband," she said to Sarah. "Is there trouble brewing?"

"Clarice, everything is fine." Laurel took the woman by the arm and guided her away from Sarah toward the dessert table. "Did you try the new scones Joan brought from Muffins 'n More? The cranberry is perfect for this time of year." She shoved one into the woman's hand. "Make sure you have some tea with it. Delicious!"

Sarah mouthed *thank you.*

Laurel scampered away—and without looking—pivoted, bumped, and tripped into the security of strong arms. "H-hello." The greeting fell out of her mouth in a whisper, and her heart raced while her hands found their way to rest on his solid chest to gain balance.

"Wow! You look great." With a lingering hold on her, approval shown in Adam's eyes. "I'm likin' those bangs. And your hair"—he fingered a few strands—"soft, the color matches your freckles."

Seconds clicked by in breathless moments as they stared into each other's eyes, almost as if bonded by magic.

"Thank you." *The makeover…totally worth it. I should have done it long ago.*

"Uh, um…" Adam cleared his throat and dropped his arms. "The, uh, parade plans are coming along."

Yes, they've already done most of the work. But she liked how he needed to make small talk since they were in a crowded room. Once again, Jeanine was right. She did knock his socks off. "It's getting done sooner than expected. I'll be—"

"Putting together the final spreadsheet soon," Adam finished her sentence.

She dropped her right shoulder and expelled a breath. "That's what I was going to say." She loved how he anticipated her thoughts. "But I am concerned there won't be enough room to coordinate the parade units at the staging area."

"No worries. I've talked to Lou about using his parking lot and the grassy area of his luncheonette. It'll work." He tweaked her nose, giving her a reassuring smile. "Everything will go off without a hitch, I promise."

"I'll hold you to that." Oh…how she needed these projects to work.

With Adam not comfortable with all the extra people coming to town, she appreciated him setting his feelings aside for everyone's sake. Not only did she depend on their success, Adam's friends, and his mother, Molly, did, too.

He gathered her into his arms again, looking straight into her eyes. "You can hold me to it. I'll do whatever is needed to make it all work." He inhaled deeply, and a questioning squint spanned across his eyes. "I love the way you smell."

"Excuse me?"

"Vanilla, cinnamon, sugar cookies. You always smell like them."

She smoothed the waterfall of hair cascading over her right shoulder. "It's the cheap stuff. Tames my curls."

"Whatever it is"—he released her, and his gaze traveled the length of her hair—"it reminds me of special memories."

"You never said why vanilla and cinnamon are special."

He motioned a hand to sit at a table away from the crowd, held a chair, and waited for her to get settled before he sat. "When I was a kid—and another of the old man's scams blew up—which they always did—Ma baked her vanilla, cinnamon, sugar cookies. A treat to take our minds off the mess we just survived. Money had been nonexistent. With a bottle of imitation, vanilla extract and a shaker of pre-ground cinnamon, Ma got a lot of practice making those cookies. That's how she perfected the now-famous recipe."

His eyes lit with a pensive twinkle. "Those cookies meant a lot. Meant we survived. The smell of warm vanilla and cinnamon lulled me to dream of a happy life where money wasn't tight and bill collectors weren't circling like vultures."

"Oh, Adam." She laid a soft touch on his arm. "I didn't realize your childhood was that bad."

"Yeah, well, that wasn't the worst of it." He sucked in a steadying breath. "I did everything to save money to buy myself a car. Cut lawns, shoveled snow, worked at a few stores emptying garbage and cleaning toilets from the time I was twelve. Saved enough to get a car that *wasn't* a piece of junk."

"Something practical and reliable." Laurel nodded, noting the two traits important to him.

"Yep." Looking deep into her eyes, he wrapped his hands around hers. "You know how it feels when you've worked hard for something and you've lost it."

Laurel lowered her chin and squeezed his hand. Momma had been taken, and if the manor project didn't succeed, her business would be lost, too.

"Before I bought the muscle car, I found a 1991 SUV. A little rusted, but in good condition. Ran well.

Ma and I went to the bank to withdraw the money"—he paused, focused on the floor, and clenched his jaw—"but the money was gone."

"Gone?" Laurel felt her mouth gape open.

Closing his eyes, he finally opened them and nodded. "Ned wiped me out clean. Stole everything."

"Oh…my…God." Laurel's lungs ran out of breath, and a gulp let loose in her throat. "Your father?"

"Yep. Took me another three years working my butt off to save half the amount stolen. That's when I bought the muscle car. It was in poor shape, but it was all I could afford."

"And now it's your pride and joy. I'm so sorry—"

"Nope." He horizontally wagged his pointer finger. "No apologies. No sympathy. Just wanted you to know why I have no use for the old man and why trust and promises are important."

"You poor thing." She tightened her hold on his arm when she wanted to wrap him in a hug. "And all that constant moving from place to place."

"Yeah…my dreams were always of me, Ma, and Karen being safe without the old man sucking the life blood out of us. My dream came true when he went to jail and we came to Cedar Ridge."

"So, that's why it's important for the village to stay quiet and safe."

He just nodded.

And right then, Laurel understood why he didn't want Cedar Ridge to change. Another layer unpeeled. Now she had a mission to slow the village's growth, while easing Adam's fears and ensuring the village safety. She didn't know how she'd do it, but Adam was worth the challenge.

Christmas was a time for miracles. Maybe tapping into some holiday magic would help her maintain Adam's dream.

****

Ever since Adam shared his story on Sunday at the pancake breakfast, Laurel imagined the distrust of growing up with a father like Ned Carlson...an untrustworthy father. Her heart ached for the little boy who didn't have his father's unconditional love.

She valued that Adam trusted her enough to share that horrible memory and how Molly turned difficult situations into a celebration with a simple cookie. Her actions made perfect sense because that's what Molly Carlson would do.

Learning more about Adam's past, Laurel wanted to experience the symbol that represented his independence and freedom. She arrived at his apartment on Tuesday afternoon and found him descending the exterior stairs with a box in hand. "Hi." She glanced at his mother's car in his driveway. "Is Molly here?"

Adam placed the box in the backseat and came close. Touching her arm, he placed a kiss on her cheek and then guided her toward the stairs to his apartment. "No. Karen's here to get an end table."

"How will she fit it on the plane?" She glanced over her shoulder when they climbed the steps and entered his living room.

"On the wing." He spread both arms resembling an airplane. "A few bungee cords should hold it."

Laurel raised an eyebrow. "Or...just buy an extra seat, buckle it up next to her all cozy and safe."

"Hmm. Touché." He slid the end table away from the wall. "I'm glad you came by. It was a nice surprise when you called."

She folded her hands behind her back and swayed from side to side. "Well, I do have an ulterior motive."

"Yeah, I hope it involves makin' out on the couch." He wagged his eyebrows with mischief gleaming in his eyes.

"While that sounds tempting, I thought you could give me a ride in your muscle car."

His eyes clouded; the mischief gone. "Yyyeah…" He scrubbed a hand over the back of his neck. "That's…not happening."

"If you're busy, I can come another day."

"No. Not busy." Turning his back, he leaned both hands on the end table top, and his shoulders rose with a heavy, inhaled breath. "The car doesn't do well in the cold. The tires." An awkward pause. "Yeah, the tires. Ice. Doesn't do well on ice. Slides all over the road."

"Okay, maybe another time."

"Another time for what?" Karen stepped into the room and munched a cookie in one hand, a backup cookie in the other.

"Time to get this piece to Atlanta."

"Thanks," Karen mumbled with the rest of the cookie in her mouth. "Just get it down those stairs and into Mom's car. The delivery company will handle the rest."

Adam hefted the wooden piece. "Be back in a few." And he dashed out the apartment door.

With Adam gone, Karen moved her gaze from the empty space where the end table stood and placed it on Laurel. "Good to see you, Laurel. What brings you here?"

"I wanted a ride in Adam's car, but I guess it

doesn't do well in the cold."

"Car?" Karen sniffed a chuckle. "Um…that can't happen since he doesn't have it anymore."

"What do you mean?" Laurel declined the cookie Karen offered with a head shake.

"He sold it."

"What?" She stepped back and leveled her full attention to Karen. "Why? He *loves* that car."

"Guess he got tired of having three cars. It's a bit much, what with the cost of New Jersey car insurance."

Laurel inhaled, her chest muscles clenching in response. They talked about how hard he worked to get that car. Just the other day, he had driven it because the sun had shown bright after a string of gloomy, pre-winter days. She had witnessed him give the black, vinyl roof a gentle stroke after closing the door. He treated the car better than most people treat their pets. "What made him do it?"

"Price, I guess. Got fifty-three hundred for it. He said he had plans for the money."

"No money can replace something you love." Heaviness weighed on Laurel's heart.

Karen shrugged both shoulders. "Knowing Adam, if he sold that car, the money is going to something or someone he loves. Guaranteed."

Something or someone he loves…what or who could that be?

****

Two days later, the order of fresh mistletoe arrived, and Laurel headed to the manor to add their final touch to the empty doorways.

Driving through the village, holiday excitement flourished with every inch decorated for Christmas with

Thanksgiving's arrival in four days. Everyone's jovial mood added to the stress and tension settling inside Laurel. Life was about to blossom into holiday hectic with the manor and parade kick-off plans added on her to-do list. The future of her financial life rested on the success of the next two weeks, which increased the mounting stress already tightening the muscles in her neck and shoulders. Her bones ached as if they'd crack with just a simple, wrong move.

When she rounded the corner onto Hemlock Road, she slammed the brakes and skidded to a stop in front of her parents' property. With the car still running, she bolted, left the door wide open on the street, and ran onto the makeshift driveway entrance, nearly tripping on large formations of mud and small boulders. "STOP!" She waved her arms in a frantic panic.

The massive bulldozer stopped mid-run in an already dug-out row. The operator climbed from the machine, removed his protective head gear, and clomped through the mud. "What's wrong?"

"What are you doing?" she nearly screamed. There was no way she nor Pop could afford this.

He spread both hands wide. "I'm leveling the parking lot."

"How? Why? We didn't hire you." She shook her head several times. "We can't pay you!"

"Relax." He held up a hand. "It's paid in full."

"Paid?" *What?* Had Pop secured a loan? Even if he used the house as collateral, his income was too low to qualify. Besides, Pop shared everything, including that he hadn't raised the money. She hoped he didn't do something foolish like borrow against his pension. "Who paid you?"

"Adam," he said with a nod. "Paid fifty-three hundred." He shielded his mouth with a grungy-gloved hand and lowered his voice. "I didn't charge sales tax since he paid in cash. Saved you a bundle."

"Fifty-three—" Laurel's heart instantly palpitated against her ribs, and her breath left her lungs.

No! No way!

Then…Karen's words echoed in her ears.

'The money was going to something or someone he loves. Guaranteed.'

Chapter 18

The day before Thanksgiving, Adam drove Laurel to Frank's property, counting on the surprise to make up for her being upset about the excavation.

When she learned he had sold his car, she called him out big time. Said something about being indebted to him for the rest of her life. He could deal with that.

Yeah, he loved his car; but he loved Laurel more and hoped the surprise proved just that. Transforming Frank's property into a graveled parking lot turned out better than he thought. It would work out perfect for all the manor's visitors while providing an income for Frank.

He glanced her way as she sat in the passenger seat of his SUV. "You're cute with that scarf over your eyes." Out of the corner of his eye, he noticed she lifted a hand to her face, and he tugged her hand to rest on her thigh. "Uh, uh. Nope. No peeking."

"This is ridiculous. I feel like a stalker or a bank robber with this thing."

Almost there, he turned onto Hemlock Road. "You don't want to ruin the surprise, do you?"

"No." She hesitated. "Can you give me a hint?"

"That would be cheating."

She lifted her head. "How much longer?"

A chuckle left his throat as he noticed her trying to peek from under the scarf. "Another minute."

He drove onto the bumpy surface just at the edge of the driveway. Cutting the engine and sprinting to his SUV's passenger side, he opened the door and took Laurel by the hand to guide her to step onto the gravel. His insides quivered, and he hoped she liked the results. Taking her by the shoulders, he pivoted her toward the property entrance. "Okay, you can lower your scarf."

"Oh…my…goodness," she whispered and glanced one way, then the other. Her gaze perused the split rail fence flanking the driveway entrance leading to a gravel parking lot.

"Do you like it?" His insides crashed to a halt as he watched Laurel's mouth open wide without a word. "Oh, no." His breath hitched. "I can fix whatever you don't like. Just say it, and it's done."

Her eyes filled with unshed tears. "I love it," she whispered again. "How? How did you do all this?"

"A promise is a promise."

"I know, but you did this in such a short time." And then, "Oh…the trees!" She cupped her hands to her cheeks.

Yep. Planting two magnolia trees behind the two fences flanking the entrance was the right decision. "I figured they belonged here since Thomas Baxter picked Abigail's flowers from the magnolias trees on this property."

She pointed a finger. "And the sign…"

The sign had been a nice touch, if he did say so himself. The wooden sign with the words *Eldridge Acres* bracketed by two magnolia flowers took several days to make. "The flowers are a symbol for your parents and for Abigail and Thomas. Two love stories torn apart too soon."

Her tears flowed now, her hands hanging onto his arm while her head rested on his shoulder. "Looks like I'm not the only romantic one," she choked out between tears. "You're a closet romantic." She gave his arm an extra squeeze.

"If you tell anyone, I'll deny it." He kissed the top of her head covered by a knit hat. "Come on, there's more." Taking her hand, he led her to the back of the property. A three-foot tall, picket fence outlined a square formation of tilled dirt. Waiting for her reaction, he held his breath.

"Oh!" A small cry left her throat. "You...you..."

And there it was...

With a flood of tears streaming her face, she flung her arms around his neck.

He struggled to keep them both from falling. When a droplet of tears flew from her wet cheeks and landed on his hand, Adam laughed. "You like?"

"Yes. Yes." She bobbed her head up and down about a million times, releasing more tears. "I love it. And I love you." She stood on tiptoes and kissed him.

Any misgivings he had about selling his beloved car evaporated into the chilly air. Her lips were warm, mixed with cold, salty tears. She hooked her hands behind his neck and drew him close, proving all the doubts he had about Laurel not being his *right one* had been far off the mark. She didn't fit his checklist, but she was the perfect person he needed in his life. His friends, his family, all recognized he and Laurel were a perfect fit. He'd been too stubborn to realize they were right, and he was so wrong.

When the kiss ended, he stole a quick peck and then smiled for good measure. "I love you, too."

"I can see that." She stole away and ran her fingertips over the second wooden sign—another he made. "Belinda's Garden!"

Her gaze on him again, it looked like her wet cheeks would freeze in the bitter cold.

"Momma would have loved this." She came closer and held onto his arms. "This is perfect. You're perfect."

"Not bad for a stubborn nut." He winked while seeing her happiness. Hearing her declaration of love filled the void in his life and in his heart.

She cast a playful smile. "I knew I'd un-shell that softy inside."

And he was glad she did.

****

Laurel finished weaving the wide, pale-pink and gold ribbon on the branches of the Christmas tree in the manor's 1920s sitting room. The sound of an engine and tires crunching on the stone drive drew her attention to peek out the window at the *NJLocal News* van and out popped the same reporter who had covered the first interview.

Laurel opened the window halfway to hear the voices below, watching the interaction with Stanley.

"Well, folks, a miracle seemed to happen in Cedar Ridge," the perky reporter stated into her microphone, her cameraman focusing on the old building. "Owner and funeral director, Stanley Palmer, is at Rutledge Manor where the renovations are almost complete. To be honest, Stanley, I didn't think your tiny village could accomplish such an impossible task."

"Never underestimate the determination and fortitude of our residents!" Stanley exclaimed into the microphone. "We're going to make our deadline. The grand opening will be kicked off with a village parade with Cedar Ridge's own Trevor Lawrence from the *Homegrown Superstar Competition.* It will end right here for a spectacular celebration!"

"Is it true the *Historic Network* will film the event?" the reporter asked.

"No, not the event." Stanley shook his head. "They're coming the weekend after when things are calmer and nothing is disturbed."

"*Things*…as in spirits?" The reporter chuckled. "Are the rumors true this old manor is haunted?"

A few snickers from the small crowd of teens standing across the street drew the reporter's attention. Within seconds, both she and her cameraman moved from Stanley to the group. "Why the snickers?" she asked, pointing the mic toward one of the young men. "Is the manor haunted?"

The teen took a step back like he'd been busted and sent to the principal's office.

Stanley stood at the foot of the driveway, shaking his head and making a frantic slicing motion at his neck to signal the teen to stop commenting.

"Um…I've never seen the ghost," the teen stammered while his friends chuckled.

"Wait! Wait!!" A bellow sounded from a car approaching the small crowd—a woman's head leaned out the open, driver's side window. "I'm here. I'm here!"

"Oh, no!" Panic and anxiety bolted through Laurel's chest. "Not again!" By the time she grabbed her coat, dashed down the stairs, out the door, and across the street, she'd been too late.

Clarice already positioned herself next to the reporter.

"You mentioned the last time we were here, that you've seen Abigail Rutledge walking the gardens, crying at night," the reporter stated with the mic positioned toward Clarice.

"That's right," Clarice Carlson confirmed as if gospel truth. She stood ramrod straight, all decked out once again in her light-blue, popcorn-fabric coat, flowered handbag hooked across her arm, the pillar of 1950s society.

"And you frequently walk here…in front of the manor…that has been abandoned for at least a decade…by yourself…at night?"

"Well…" Clarice hesitated. "I don't *walk* by myself. I usually drive, you know, when I'm on my way to my Ladies' Auxiliary meetings. I'm the president, you know."

Laurel rolled her eyes. The Ladies' meetings were during the day. And from the way the reporter eyed Clarice, Laurel realized she wasn't buying the story. Clarice's insistence she had seen ghosts validated the fib Adam had told the reporter about his aunt losing it.

The reporter motioned her chin toward the cameraman whose hand relaxed the camera from his shoulder, obviously no longer recording. But that didn't stop Clarice from droning on.

"We're presenting a play about Abigail and Thomas' love story. I'll be portraying Abigail's mother, of course. And we're…"

The reporter glanced at Laurel.

Laurel drew her lips into a straight line, shaking her head several times.

Stanley then stood next to her and did the same.

With an acknowledged nod, the reporter dropped the mic to her side. "Okay. We're done here."

"But I'm not finished," Clarice demanded.

"We are. We have time to take one more shot inside the manor, and then we're heading to Middlesex County. They're holding the annual Christmas Channel Event next month at the convention center, and we have to interview the organizer." She stepped away from Clarice and motioned to Stanley. "Let's take a few shots inside with *you,* Stan. No crowds in the shot. We want to spotlight all the work that's been done."

"Sure thing." Stanley guided the crew into the house.

Laurel lagged behind, even though she hadn't finished her task. If she followed Stanley, guaranteed Clarice was sure to do so.

"Can you believe that?" Clarice huffed. "She dismissed me. How rude!"

"I'm sure she didn't dismiss you." Laurel reserved a smile because, *yes*, the reporter had. "She's on a deadline. They have to go wherever their producer wants. Part of the job."

"I'll have to contact her producer. I'm sure he'll want her to cover the production of our play."

Laurel whooshed out a pent-up breath between her teeth. "Clarice, we never agreed to the play. There's no time and no money. We've got enough happening for the opening."

"I'm sure there's room for improvement. You and Adam don't have the experience to handle something of this magnitude." She puffed out her chest and raised her chin. "I'll talk to the mayor to see where my expertise can be utilized. Then I'm sure the media will have time for another interview."

"You do that, Clarice." Laurel drew in a huge breath. While she wanted to tell Clarice what she really thought of her *expertise*, she wouldn't waste her time. "You'll have to excuse me. I've got a few things to get done before I head home. Have a nice evening." Not wanting to engage in more of Clarice's nonsense, Laurel stepped away and meandered across the street toward the manor, hoping Clarice wouldn't follow. By now, Stanley and the reporter should be done, enabling her to finish the 1920s room, and she arrived halfway up the stairs.

Stanley stuck his head over the wooden banister from the second floor. "Laurel, there you are! We were just talking about you." He waved her up. "Come, come!"

When she reached the landing, she was asked to be interviewed about decorating the old house. She wasn't at all dressed for a TV debut, but she didn't have a choice. Explaining how she decorated each room in a different time period, she also mentioned how she and the ladies had refreshed and mended what was already in the manor, making sure to give the names of all who volunteered their time.

The cameraman zeroed in on few of the special ornaments placed in the different rooms.

"Each room has a magnolia arrangement," the reporter stated. "What's their significance to the manor?"

"Thomas Baxter picked magnolia flowers from the property next door and gave them to Abigail each day before he went off to war. Supposedly, she dried and pressed those blooms in her Bible, but the Bible was never found. To honor Abigail and Thomas' love story, I've included silk magnolias throughout the manor."

"And the angels? What significance are those?"

Laurel grinned. "Those are mine," she confessed. "A selfish tribute to my mother. She always said whenever I saw an angel, it meant she'd be watching over me."

"Like a protective spirit...goes along with spirits of the manor?"

"No." Laurel chuckled. "Momma's a happy spirit. From what I've heard from Clarice, Abigail is a sorrowful spirit."

The reporter let out a whisper of a laugh. "Well done." She pointed to the doorway of the 1800s room. "Each doorway has mistletoe...another of your trademark secrets?"

"It's a Christmas tradition. Kissing under the mistletoe is a promise to one another and a prediction of happiness and a long life. Since Abigail and Thomas were committed to each other, it's fitting each doorway brings the same magic to those who visit here."

"So, there you have it, folks," the reporter said to the camera. "Romanticism and holiday spirit in one place. When you come visit Rutledge Manor, stop by The Laurel Wreath, say hello to Laurel, and pick up a magnolia and an angel. But make sure to look up...there might be mistletoe looming overhead!"

Laurel thanked her lucky stars for her good fortune. The reporter promoted her flower shop! But...everyone would see she's a hopeless romantic, which might be a little embarrassing. Or...maybe it wasn't a big deal...since happiness surrounded her after she and

Adam both said the *L* word.

****

Frank's 1930s Craftsman-style house brimmed with warm hugs as chattering friends gathered in the living and dining rooms with a few crammed into the kitchen. With just enough space to open the oven door to check on the Thanksgiving turkey, satisfaction overcame him as his home hummed with laughter.

Thanksgiving Sunday.

The day he looked forward to all year.

Covered dishes of heavenly smelling food laid on the kitchen table in a makeshift buffet.

He opened the back door and poked his head out after opening the screen door, and he studied the vibrant blue sky and white puffy clouds. A contented smile widened his lips, and his heart swelled with both happiness and a little heartache, picturing Belinda elegantly sitting peacefully atop one of those clouds. "I'm trying my best, but no one can cook a turkey like you," he declared to the heavens with tears clouding his eyes. "Happy Thanksgiving, my love."

He blinked away the moisture, blew a kiss upward, and released the screen door, leaving the wood and windowed-kitchen door open. The heat of the oven intensified with the crowd of ladies congregating in the kitchen to make sure he didn't ruin the bird. He did love a perfectly cooked turkey—wings his favorite—but nothing got his taste buds popping like the creaminess of sweet potato pie and the sugary goodness of mincemeat pie.

As if on cue, the holiday just got sweeter when Joan arrived, mincemeat pie in hand made special from Muffins 'n More. Such an extra special Thanksgiving with much to be thankful for. The adrenaline soaring through his body had him on a holiday high with the knowledge of surprises in store for the guests. He opened the oven door to check on the star of the meal.

"Frank Eldridge! Get your nose out of that oven," Molly scolded. "How do you expect that turkey to cook if you keep peeking at it?" Standing no taller than five-foot, hands on her hips, she tried to sound commanding, but a tiny smile inching its way to her lips gave her away.

"Molly, my girl. That bird is almost done." He raised his nose and sniffed as his chest swelled with the scrumptious poultry aroma. "I can smell it."

"Move your sniffer into the living room. We're short a few chairs." The wink she threw him sent her message loud and clear.

He and Molly were in on the surprise planned for after dinner; but no one was in on the surprise he had planned after they all said, *Grace*. Again, his adrenaline pumped and sputtered like a teenager at the impending night to remember. And he knew in his heart that his beloved Belinda would approve.

Chapter 19

"Aren't you exhausted?"

Laurel admired all their friends enjoying the holiday, and she nodded in response to Ellen Greene's question.

"Nah." Sarah scoffed and laid her arm across Laurel's shoulders. "She's tough. Laurel doesn't let a little thing like a major holiday, a mansion renovation, and a parade slow her down, right, kid?"

Laurel laughed out loud. "I'm exhausted just hearing that list!"

"Did the *NJLocal News* segment provide more holiday orders for The Laurel Wreath?" Ellen asked.

"Yes, it did. Guess a little holiday magic sprinkled on us. I'm grateful the girls from the voc school helped with all the extras orders. And Jeanine was a huge help delivering with Pop." She turned her attention to Sarah. "They took turns with Ben. He ran the deliveries to the customers while they drove. They were fighting over who was getting Ben yesterday, our busiest day."

"Run he did," Sarah added. "That kid came home all three days and hit the bed facedown."

"Oh, no." Laurel rushed her hand to her mouth. "I'm sorry we overworked him."

"No way. It taught him responsibility. He loved that you paid him. He's hoping you'll hire him for Christmas."

"Definitely." Laurel gave her a thumbs-up. "Pop and Jeanine already requested him."

"Laurel!" Pop yelled from the archway between the living and dining rooms. "Timer went off, turkey's done!" He sprinted into the kitchen like a kid rushing to open presents on Christmas morning.

She followed, weaving between their guests, catching up to Pop and Molly who transferred the bird to a platter.

Pop reverently carried the majestic bird to the dining room table for presentation.

Everyone "oohed" and "aahed." From the wide smile and gleaming eyes radiating from Pop's face, Laurel held the same contentment. She hadn't seen Pop this happy in a long time.

Love also tickled the edges of her heart that this was the first holiday she and Adam celebrated together. She noticed him standing next to Pop, large utensils in hand as Pop's carving assistant. The delight on his face equaled Pop's while they mastered the art of slicing the bird.

Loading their plates at the buffet table in the kitchen, everyone bumped into and sidestepped each other. But no one cared that they were crammed tight into seats throughout the dining and living rooms. The closeness bolstered the love of family and camaraderie of friends.

Before the first forkful, Pop tapped the side of his wine glass, gaining attention for his annual reciting of *Grace*. With a collective "Amen," the group launched into the ritual of abundant eating, and Pop tapped his wine glass again. "Before you all partake in this delicious meal, I have an announcement to make." He moved to stand in the center of the room that quieted the chatter. "I'm sure you all heard the rumor."

"Which rumor are you talking about?" Adam chimed in. "Clarice has a bunch of them floating around."

Pop tried to continue among the communal laughter, but the boisterous speculations made it hard to compete.

"Hey, everyone, give Frank a minute," George Statler hollered and tapped his cane on the floor a few times. "He's about to confirm a rumor. Let's see if we're right about which one."

"Thanks, George." Pop's face beamed. "This rumor is true. Joan and I are officially keeping company. Joan"—Pop outstretched his hand for Joan to join him—"You can all begin wishing us well."

With more "oohs" and "aahs" and congratulatory greetings, Pop's announcement gave Laurel a Thanksgiving gift—her father's happiness.

"There was never a more deserving couple than you both," George declared and then said, "You can get Mayor Farley to make an honest couple out of you."

Adam laid an arm on Laurel's shoulders and kissed her temple. "I'm glad your father took the leap with Joan."

Leap? Yes, in this case, a good leap. Momma would approve. "Joan's a wonderful person. Perfect for Pop."

Tightening his hold, his hand cupped her shoulder. "And you're a wonderful person. Perfect for me. When you're ready to jump-start that leap, I'll be here to catch you."

The honesty in his words touched her heart. "I

know you will. Be patient. I'm getting there."

"I'll nudge you along."

"Not too much nudging, I hope."

"Only what you can handle."

Lou eased upon them. "Looks like the romance bug bit another Eldridge. It's about time you two got together."

"Thanks, Lou." Adam tipped his head forward and the edges of his lips relaxed into a slow smile. "She was a hard one to catch, but I'm stubborn and wouldn't take *no* for an answer."

"Stubborn is good." Lou winked at Adam. "Gets you what you want."

"Adam?" Molly called. "Come here a minute."

"Be right back," he whispered to Laurel, leaving another kiss on her temple.

The man she loved stood across the room, conferring with Molly and Pop—the three turning their backs to everyone. She had a feeling Pop had been hiding something, but after his surprise announcement about Joan, she didn't think there was anything else. But the three acted suspicious by glancing her way, then at the door.

Laurel scanned the rooms. All the guests had arrived. No one else was expected, although most of their friends knew Thanksgiving Sunday was an open-door policy. She hoped Molly and Pop didn't get wind that Clarice planned to crash their celebration. That would send everyone heading home before the pies were served—before Pop's Christmas lights' reveal.

The conspiring group ended their little meeting.

Before Laurel had a chance to ask Adam about it, she had to answer Arlene about which song the Ugly

Sweater Singers were performing for the manor opening. Answering Arlene, she lost sight of Adam.

"Looks like Adam is saving the town again." Evan snuck up on Laurel. "That Morrison idea sounds like a good one. I'm thinking of setting up a small coffee bar there."

"That's great." She searched the room for the new village hero.

"I think it's wonderful," Molly chimed in. "I'll set up a cookie booth in the food court. Maybe I can get Karen to give me ideas about branching out into cakes."

"Is Karen a cake baker?" Laurel asked.

"No. But when she was younger, she baked cakes all the time. She was addicted to those cable, cake-baking shows."

"I'd buy one of your cakes if they're as good as your cookies." Evan licked his lips. "They'll go great with my coffees."

"Cakes?" Ellen asked, passing the breadbasket loaded with dinner rolls. "Who's buying cakes?"

"I am." Evan plucked a roll from the basket. "When Molly sells them at Morrison."

"Isn't the Morrison Project a wonderful idea!" Ellen offered the basket of warm rolls to everyone standing with their full plates. "I'd love to open a quilt corner. I've got a lot of handmade quilts…it would be a perfect place to sell them."

Yes. The Morrison Project, as Ellen called it, was a hit with the villagers. Now all they had to do was find a buyer. Maybe Adam had a direct link to the North Pole to ask Santa to sprinkle some Christmas magic over Cedar Ridge to make that happen. But in the meantime, where in the world was Adam?

****

Laurel glanced at the clock while clearing empty drink glasses from the living room. No one seemed to care Adam was MIA, each one blowing her off with outrageous explanations of his whereabouts.

"Abducted by aliens," Todd joked.

"Betcha he broke into The Bean & Brew and set off the alarm system. *My* coffee is worth getting arrested for," Evan said as if a viable reason.

"Joined the National Commandos." George placed a hand on his heart.

"There are no National Commandos anymore," his friend, Walter Buchanan, counterd.

George looked up at the ceiling for an answer. "Well, then, maybe he joined the Peace Platoon."

"Hope he'll be back for Frank's lights' reveal," Sarah interrupted their *Where's Adam* game.

"Do we have to go out there?" George asked. "It's so cold you can freeze your giblets off."

Molly smacked George on the arm. "Your giblets will be fine. Put a coat on."

While they were having fun at Adam's absence, Laurel grew wary. This was supposed to be their first holiday together—but they weren't together. Where was he? That leap everyone kept telling her to jump into seemed higher than Mount Rushmore so that if she fell, she'd lose everything.

As she worried her bottom lip and bit her thumb cuticle almost to the point of bleeding, a commotion at the front door caused her to stop.

More "oohs" and "aahs" erupted from her guests than had sounded at the last July Fourth fireworks.

Emerging from the backs of heads and bodies,

Adam stood with a huge grin.

But a large, red ribbon drew her attention to the bundle in his arms. "What is this…what…what are you doing?" She stepped closer.

"Happy Thanksgiving, Laurel."

"Who's this little guy?" Laurel sighed, her insides melting at the sight of the furry bundle. She stroked the soft fur of the puppy's head.

"He doesn't have a name yet, but I'm sure you'll come up with a good one."

"Me." Her hand stilled, and her insides froze. "Why?"

"Because people name their dogs. Having one makes it easier to call them so they'll come."

"No." She yanked her hand away. "I mean…why is he *here*?"

"Because you're always doing for everyone else, and never do for you."

She took a minute to process his words, confusion clouding her brain. "But he costs so much."

"All taken care of, shots and everything. Although, you'll have to license him. I hear people have been arrested for not licensing their dogs." He winked.

The adorable black-brown-and-white puppy mirrored the Bernese Mountain Dog she's seen in the commercial.

As Adam put the dog in her arms, Laurel nuzzled the little creature. When she felt his tiny, pink tongue lick her cheek, she immediately fell in love. And then adrenaline rushed through her chest in a heaving panic. No. She couldn't. This little guy was perfect in every way. Except—"No." She pushed the puppy toward Adam, and he nearly dropped the puppy. "I can't." She took a step back. "No. No time." She continued to back away and bumped into a chair.

Jeanine leaned forward to steady her and took hold of Laurel's shoulders. "It's okay. You can do this."

"No." A veil of tears clouded her vision, and she wagged her head several times. "No, I can't."

"Yes, you can." Jeanine squeezed her shoulders. "This is the best gift anyone's ever given you. You need him—this puppy needs you. You need each other."

Frank stood beside her. "Jeanine's right. It's time, Laurel. Time to open your heart. This little guy's already stolen mine and everyone else's."

She swiped her eyes with her shirt sleeve. "But what happens—"

"It won't happen for a long time. Think about it. From this moment, your life will be filled with buckets of love from this little guy—who, from the looks of those paws—will not be little for long."

Adam inched before her, and the wiggling puppy climbed up his chest and licked the side of his neck. "Laurel, I didn't mean to upset you. You bring so much joy to everyone. I thought you needed a little dose yourself. You can handle this."

Laurel focused on the floor, squeezing her eyes tight. She wanted to take hold of the little bundle and love him for the rest of time. But her research showed their time together would be a few years, maybe ten if she was lucky. She opened her eyes and stared into the pair of pleading eyes so full of promise and hope…and love.

Jeanine was right. Adam had given her the best gift. Because *he* loved her.

She glanced at Pop who nodded. Yes, she had to do this. Needed to if she wanted to fully open her heart.

She raised her hands toward Adam and, with a nod, took hold of the puppy. She rubbed her cheek across the top of his soft head, knowing that from this point forward, her life would never be the same.

Chapter 20

Cooper rested in his crate, exhausted after the run he and Laurel took at Wilkinsen's Pond. In a few days, the little fur ball became part of the family with him hanging at The Laurel Wreath. Laurel had named him Sunday night.

Pop gave her a bear hug with a kiss on her forehead. "That's a fine name," he had said, pride shown on his face. "Momma is smiling on you and that little pup."

Yes, her mother's family name would live on a little longer because of this bundle of energy. And just then, Cooper sprang into a full bark, dancing inside his crate.

"You're not keeping him locked in the cage all the time, are you?" Pop asked when he entered from the back door.

"That's the safest place for him now." Laurel scanned the spreadsheet on her laptop. "When he's older—and won't be under foot—he'll have free rein of the shop."

"Under foot?" Pop bent to talk to the pup. "You're gonna be plenty under foot, under the table, in the doorways, and ruling this place in a few months, right, little guy?" Pop then squatted and put his hand through the crate's wire wall.

Cooper slobbered his little, pink tongue all over

Pop's fingers.

Pop glanced at Laurel. "Can I take him for a walk?"

"Sorry, we just got back from a run around Wilkinsen's. Maybe after dinner."

Pop rose, heading toward the workbench in the corner of the prep room. "That'll work. Going to Joan's tonight. Maybe after dinner when it's dark, I can take Coop to see the Christmas lights on Main and Elm."

A chuckled cough left Laurel's throat, and she lifted her gaze from the spreadsheet again to watch Pop with Cooper. "I doubt he knows what Christmas lights are, but I'm sure he'll enjoy them." It was heartwarming how Pop took to Cooper. She imagined how attentive and caring he'd be with grandchildren.

Grandchildren. *Wow. That's the second time the idea of having kids surprised me.*

Immersing herself into The Laurel Wreath—and taking care of Pop—she had pushed kids to the back of her mind. She wanted a houseful, but other priorities kept her from thinking far into the future. She also never had anyone she'd consider having kids with…until now.

"Can you put some flowers in this box?"

Seeing the box distracted her newfound thoughts. She spied the keepsake box. "Where did it come from?"

Pop shrugged a shoulder. "I made it. Like I made all the rest."

"I know that." She rolled her eyes at the obvious. Walk-in orders rarely came in. The box orders usually came from online. *Hmmm? What's he hiding?* "When did the order come in?"

Pop reached to the workstation and fiddled with a

spool of craft wire. "It…it was a walk-in."

Sure, it was. "Do you know what *they* want? What kind of flowers?"

Pop hesitated "No. They…uh…didn't say. Just wanted something pretty." He replaced the spool and picked up the box to open and close the lid. "Why don't you put one of your silk magnolias in it? In honor of the opening."

Laurel eyed him. *Why won't he admit the box is for Joan?* The entire village knew he and Joan were together—why the secrecy? "You know, it's the season for giving. It's okay if you're giving it to Joan. I approve."

Pop shook his head and waved a hand. "Nooo, no. It's *not* for Joan."

Right. And I'm Santa Claus. His rushed denial was a dead giveaway. "So, who is the *customer* who ordered it?"

"Um, I, uh, don't remember their name. But, if they come in, I'll recognize them."

"Really?" *Come on, Pop, how vague can you get?* "You don't know their name… I'm guessing you have no cell number or email address. How do we let them know it's ready?"

"Uh…they're gonna pick it up in a few days." He nodded like he believed his own lie.

"Okay." Laurel raised both hands in surrender. "Who am I to question? I just hope this mystery person pays with real money and not board-game money."

****

The day before the parade when former councilman Russell Chapman heard the chime of his cell phone, he summoned his act of surprise, even though he anticipated the call for the past hour. He answered the call from his long-time friend and village chief financial officer.

"Russell, it's Arthur."

"Hello, Art." Chapman leaned back and rocked in his office chair, satisfaction flowing through his veins. "How are you today?"

"We have a problem."

"Oh." He suppressed a chuckle and wet his lips. "What kind of problem?"

"You were right not to trust Carlson," the CFO confirmed. "The parade money is gone."

"Gone? Are you sure?" His muscles quivered as he clamped down his jaw to suppress his excitement. "Maybe it's misplaced. Did you check with the admin?"

"Yes, she wasn't in yesterday…has the flu."

"How do you know it was Carlson?"

"Security code at 11:32 p.m. has him entering the building."

Yes. Knowing security codes were the first four digits of elected officials and employees' last names made it easy to enter the building under the code 2275 for Carlson. "His code, huh? So, what are you going to do?" Keeping his voice steady became difficult with the adrenaline rush surging through his veins.

"I don't have a choice. I'm calling next door."

"Well, Art, you're in a tight spot…I guess it's necessary to call PD. Carlson has to pay for what he's done."

As Russell ended the call, he didn't conceal his happiness, even when he noticed his son staring.

"What's going on?" Keith asked.

He steeped his fingers and smirked at his son. "Carlson is finally getting what he deserves."

****

Adam sprinted out of his apartment, looking forward to fulfilling a promise with today's parade and manor opening. Both had seemed impossible with such a short deadline, but the long hours were worth the effort to see Laurel's vibrant smile and excitement over their plans becoming a reality.

When an unfamiliar sedan blocked his driveway, he recognized the driver, Keith Chapman, his election opponent—a kid a good five years younger than him.

"Hey, is everything all right?" the younger Chapman asked through the open driver's side window.

Adam approached. "Fine. Why'd you ask?" *Why is this kid so jittery?*

"I don't know. Something's"—Keith shook his head several times—"something's not right. I'm sorry for everything my father's putting you through."

Adam studied him a minute, trying to make sense of the apology. He simply lifted his shoulder and shrugged. "Nothin' I can't handle."

"Just want you to know I have nothing to do with it. Nothing against you. *He's* the one who pushed me to run."

Why the overdue confession? "You didn't want it?"

"No way. I'm going back to art school in January. He threatened not to pay for it unless I ran."

Adam stepped back on that one and hooked his hands under his armpits, thumbs pointing up. "He blackmailed you?"

"Not exactly. More like pressured me to conform."

Adam nodded. He lived with a less-than-perfect

old man. "Guess we got the short end with fathers?"

"Not really. Your father didn't want you to be a political puppet so he could control things from behind the scenes."

Maybe, but the kid didn't have a clue what living with Ned was like. "If you had won, how could you serve while you were at school?"

"Manhattan," Keith answered. "Deal was, I'd come home every two weeks for the meetings."

Adam relaxed and spread his feet apart. "Guess I ruined your plans."

"Not mine...no way." He held a staying hand. "Dad on the other hand..."

"Yeah, I get it."

"No hard feelings?" the younger Chapman asked.

"Nah. We're good. I appreciate your honesty." He unhooked his arms and extended a hand to the kid. "Good luck dealing with your old man."

Keith shook Adam's hand. "Thanks. You, too."

Watching Chapman's son backed out of the driveway, Adam yelled, "Hey...good luck in art school," but thought—

What the hell is Chapman planning now?
****

Laurel's nerves overshadowed the thrill of parade day. In a few hours, everything they worked for would become a reality. As she drove to the staging area later in the afternoon, she noticed the village bustled with people placing lawn chairs along the parade route to secure the best viewing spots.

A few groups of teen and tween girls already gathered to stake their claim while cheering and holding signs that read, *We love you, Trevor Lawrence!*

Butterflies fluttered in Laurel's belly. Their decision to have the *Homegrown Superstar* contestant as Grand Marshal produced people from all over New Jersey. She bet from neighboring Pennsylvania and New York, too.

As she pulled into the crowded parking lot at Lou's Luncheonette, she noted the absence of Adam's SUV. She entered the eatery, and Lou—all decked out in his Santa suit—extended a cup of steaming coffee.

"There's hot pork roll and egg sandwiches on the counter. I gotta run." He grabbed the Santa hat resting on the counter. "If Adam doesn't get here soon, those sandwiches will be cold."

"Thanks, Lou. I'm sure he's on his way. This parade is important."

"Sure is. It's all he's been talking about. That…and you."

An instant sense of pride rippled through her that Adam let everyone know how much he loved her. "Don't worry. He'll be here. Now, you get going. Don't want Santa to be late."

After the older man acknowledged with a "Ho Ho Ho" he left the luncheonette with a spring in his step.

Warm satisfaction wove through her that asking Lou to be Santa provided pleasure to his holiday. Adding cream to her coffee, she left the building and walked the street blocked to traffic that served as the staging area.

All appeared to be in place. The public works department placed barriers in the exact spots where Adam had instructed. A few flag team members from the high school marching band assembled to practice their routine. The university equine students placed water troughs for the horses in their section.

When two of Cedar Ridge's finest approached, she met them halfway. "Thanks for being here. This couldn't happen if it weren't for all of you on the force."

"It's our pleasure," one officer said while his partner gave her a thumbs-up.

"There's coffee and sandwiches on the counter inside." She pointed her chin to the luncheonette. "Go help yourselves."

"Lou's pork roll?" one asked.

"Yeah. Made special. Get 'em while they're hot!"

Watching the uniformed officers headed for the luncheonette door, Laurel glanced to see any sign of Adam. She opened her tablet and perused the order of the units needed to check in, but her mind wasn't on units.

Where on earth is Adam?

****

The hairs on the back of Adam's neck pinched like steel wool penetrating his skin when he noticed the police cruiser in his rearview mirror, following him with lights flashing. Pulling over, he patted the steering wheel several times, needing to get to the parade staging area. When he opened his window, he saw Patrolman McDonald step near his car. "Hey, Mac, what's up?"

"Not such good news. Step out of your vehicle please?"

The acid in his stomach threatened to rise into his throat. "What? Why?"

"This is hard enough, Adam. Just step out."

Doing as told, Adam got out and stood next to

Mac. Flashbacks rushed from deep within his brain of the times his old man had been arrested and swept away in a patrol car. This couldn't be happening, not when he spent countless years towing the line determined not to trace his father's footsteps. "What's this all about?"

"I gotta bring you in for questioning. I'd appreciate if you'd comply and get in my cruiser."

"Questioning for what?"

"Grand theft."

Flashing is gaze at McDonald, Adam slammed his hand to his chest. *This can't be happening.* Thoughts of Laurel raced to his brain. This now proved his fear of not being enough, No matter how he struggled to fight it, the tainted blood that ran through his veins could never be changed.

****

"I don't understand, he was supposed to be here over an hour ago." Seated at the registration table, Laurel glanced at the list of marchers. "The parade is set to begin in thirty minutes."

"I know he's coming," Molly said. "When he picked up the trays of cookies for the post-parade reception, he said he'd meet me at the staging area in a few minutes. Gosh, I know he was looking forward to it. I haven't seen him this happy in a long time." She tapped her cell phone and then put it to her ear. "I'll see if I can track him down." She walked closer to the starting point.

"We have a situation!" Clarice flew in like a tornado of trouble. "Where is our parade chair? The mayor's car should follow the flag colors. He *is* the highest-ranking village official."

Laurel squeezed the bridge of her nose and looked

up at Adam's aunt. She bit her bottom lip before answering. "He's…not here."

"Not here? How irresponsible!" She plunged her hands to her hips and scowled. "It shouldn't surprise us now, should it? He said this parade was a waste of time. That's just like Adam to say he'll do something with no follow-through—just like his father."

Sharpening her focus, she couldn't believe Clarice just made that comparison. "That's not fair. I'm sure he'll be here. He's probably sorting out some kind of parade problem." Laurel stopped. *Wait.* "Did you say Adam thought the parade was a waste of time?"

"I certainly did. I can't believe he kept up the charade this long."

"I don't think it was a charade."

"Oh, my dear…" Clarice bent to pat Laurel's arm. "That's generous of you to think the best of him, but believe me, his branch of the family is always in trouble for one reason or another. Don't put too much faith in them." The woman snapped her head right, then left. "Well, then, I'll just have to take charge and get the mayor into the proper position. This parade is scheduled to step off in a few minutes. Good thing I'm here to see it through!" She spun and charged toward the starting point.

Laurel swiveled in her seat when Pop approached, she couldn't stop her mind from reeling. "He never planned to be here? He pretended all along?"

"Don't listen to that quack," Pop warned. "Adam knows how important this is to you."

"He promised," Laurel whispered and stared at the papers in front of her while the heaviness in her chest skewed her breathing. What a fool for believing Adam.

"You're wrong, Pop," she replied. "This has nothing to do with me. He never wanted the project from the beginning."

"All right now, you listen up. It's time you get out of your own head, listen to the facts, and don't be sucked in by that egotistical gossip." Pop grabbed her by the shoulders, a stern warning in his eyes. "Adam wasn't pretending. This *is* important to him because it's important to *you*. And he understands how it will help the village." Lowering his hands, he took hold of Laurel's with a reassuring squeeze. "He'll show. And, if he doesn't, something is wrong."

Laurel stopped a moment...disappointed that she questioned Adam's intentions by listening to his blabbermouth, lying aunt. Adam proved time after time he always honored his promises. She needed to ignore all the white noise Clarice caused to fog her mind, clouding her judgment.

Time to think with her heart.

Adam loved her and would *never* do anything to hurt her. Pop was right. Something was wrong...very wrong. Laurel hopped to her feet and pivoted, yelling over her shoulder, "I'll be right back." Rushing to Lou's, she found the officers munching on their pork roll sandwiches. "Did either of you see Adam on your way over here?"

With a mouthful of pork roll, one motioned to the other who answered after he swallowed a gulp of coffee. "He's at headquarters."

"Headquarters?" She rubbed the fingertips of one hand over her forehead. "Why?"

"Something about missing money. If you ask me, Adam's getting' a raw deal."

"What money?" Laurel's heart palpitated hard. Becoming lightheaded, she grabbed onto a nearby chair to keep from swaying.

"Not sure," the officer said. "If you ask me, Adam's a stand-up guy. Gotta be a mistake."

Laurel inhaled a deep, steadying breath to control her heart rhythm. She remembered all the times when Russell Chapman complained that Adam couldn't be trusted since Ned Carlson had served time for racketeering. Like father, like son, he had touted. Nothing was farther from the truth. "Is he there for questioning?"

One officer nodded while the other stuffed his face. "Yeah." He shrugged. "They have to figure out where the money is."

Laurel took in several deep breaths again. *Think, think.* Adam helped her countless times; now was time to do the same. Several options popped up in a flash and then—"Can one of you move the barricades so I can get my car out of the lot?"

"Sure. You need help?"

"I don't know. I gotta hurry."

"No problem." The officer put his sandwich on the plate. "Watch this for me, buddy," he said to the other. "Be right back." He turned to Laurel. "Let's go."

Laurel rushed out of the luncheonette and yelled across the street to Pop and Molly as she sprinted to her car. "I have an idea. Be right back."

"Where are you going?" they both yelled.

"I'm saving Adam!"

Chapter 21

"I'm telling you I dropped the money off yesterday afternoon and gave it to Arthur." Adam sat in the small interrogation room at the police station and stared at Patrolman Randazzo, a new guy who acted more like FBI instead of a rookie.

"Yeah," Randazzo said. "Arthur, the CFO, corroborates that."

"After that, I went to the rec center, got the bullhorns, and went home. Did a favor for my landlord, then went to bed by ten since there was a lot to do today…stuff I'm not getting done because I'm here."

"Your code was entered in the alarm system at 11:32 p.m. The electronic key code was punched into the Finance Department door at 11:33 p.m., one minute after you entered the building."

"I wasn't here!" he bellowed and tried to contain the panic coursing through him. "Contact Eleanor, my landlord. She'll verify I was home. I fixed her kitchen faucet before I went to bed." His greatest fear choked him, tightening his chest as his heartbeat battered his ribs. All his energy to stay on the straight and narrow now blew up in his face in a cruel joke. No matter what he did, or who he was on the inside, he'd forever be judged as a criminal—no better than his father. Sweat beaded on his forehead, and his body trembled.

"Hey…what's going on here?" Chief Gavin

D'Angelo entered the interrogation room. Viewing the paperwork Randazzo handed him, D'Angelo shook his head. "Are you kidding me?" He looked at Adam, then back at Randazzo. "Anyone connected with this town knows the passcode system. I've been trying to get the council to amend the policy to correct it, but it's fallen on deaf ears. Did you check the cameras?"

Randazzo stood ramrod straight. He shook his head.

"Yeah, that's what I thought. MacDonald!" Chief yelled into the Patrol Room. "Check cameras eleven, fifteen, and sixteen from last night. 2330 to 2340. Let me know what we've got."

Adam knew he wasn't the one on those cameras, but all Russell Chapman's threats came back to haunt him. *Was he the one who set me up?*

****

Laurel faced the bulletproof window at Cedar Ridge Police Department, her hands shaking and her throat holding a wail of a cry. "Have you charged him yet?" she asked the patrolman at the window and saw Chief D'Angelo standing nearby. "He's innocent!"

D'Angelo waved her on.

When the door lock buzzed, she entered the patrol room and rushed toward the chief. "There's got to be a mistake. Adam would never steal money."

Chief nodded. "I know—"

"I mean, just because of his family history, you can't assume he'll be the same."

"I know—"

"He's the most trustworthy, honest person I know, well…except for Pop and Jeanine and well, a lot of people."

"I know—"

"I'll get a lawyer. What's the bail?" She took a breath. "Oh…I don't have the money, but…I'll raise the money."

"You don't have—"

She took hold of the chief's arm with both hands. "Please you've got to believe he's not guilty of…what was it he's charged with?"

D'Angelo snorted. "Are you done yet?"

"This is not funny! The man I love is locked away in a jail cell. I need to get him out!"

Now he laughed. "This isn't *Rule & Order*. We don't have a jail"—he pointed across the room—"just a bench where we handcuff perps."

Nerves shook Laurel's entire body, but she didn't care. She'd battle an army if they were harming Adam. "Where is he?"

"In the bathroom. Be out in a minute."

"Thank goodness." She'd be crushed if Adam had been put in a cell. Luckily, Cedar Ridge was small with little crime to warrant jail cells. But that was no consolation that the man she loved had suffered. *Wait?* "The bathroom?"

Chief nodded. "Was a setup. We checked the video. Sent MacDonald to get the alleged criminal. Adam's free to go."

"Who was it?"

"Russell Chapman."

****

Adam couldn't believe his ears when he walked out of the police department bathroom. The woman he loved moved heaven and earth to save him. Fearless and determined and relentless—all rolled into one tiny package of courage and bravery. His very own personal warrior of love. Her actions convinced him being held was worth witnessing her faith in him. After a few seconds, he made his way into the patrol room.

Laurel flung herself into his arms. "I love you," she yelled.

He kissed her right there in front of the officers. "I love you, too. I can't believe you're here."

She threw an evil glare at Randazzo. "I came to save you."

"I hate to break this up, but you two have a parade to get to," the Chief reminded them. "Roads are jammed. I'll give you an escort."

Laurel glanced at the large clock on the wall. "The parade is almost over. Oh, my God!"

"What?" Adam asked.

"Without us there, that means Clarice took charge!"

"Quick!" Adam warned. "We better get to the manor before she ruins the opening!"

****

With lights flashing and sirens sounding, Adam and Laurel made an impressive entrance to Rutledge Manor minutes before the parade's arrival.

The middle school chorus stood in place on the lawn, practicing their songs. The fireworks' company, set up in the back gardens, double-checked everything ready to go. In the distance, the melodies of Christmas songs from the high school marching band announced the parade's appearance in a few minutes.

Inside the manor, they separated.

Laurel rushed to every window to turn on the battery-operated candles.

Adam sprinted to each room to turn on the LED lights on the Christmas trees.

When they met back in the foyer, Adam breathed a sigh of relief that enough time remained to finish his plan. Walking to the credenza that rested alongside the staircase wall, he retrieved the box he'd hidden in the bottom drawer. "Laurel."

She tilted her chin with a sideways glance. "What have you got there?"

He held out the keepsake box.

"Wait a minute…" She took hold of the box. "I decorated this. Pop said to put a magnolia in it."

"Frank kept my secret."

"This wasn't for Joan?" Her eyebrows squished together.

"Nope." He chuckled, even though his nerves were still hot-wired from his arrest, but even more now about her reaction. With the sound of the parade closing in, Adam stilled, his anxiety amping. "Open it."

She lifted the lid, and looking inside, she gasped. "Oh…there's a gold-and-crystal angel."

He stood behind her and looked over her shoulder while his nerves sped like a race car. "An ornament. To hang on your tree, or maybe on our tree?"

"Our tree?"

"Your mom always said when you see an angel, she's watching over you. Maybe watch over both of us. Together." He motioned his chin. "Pick up the angel."

Laurel did, and with the angel in hand, she gasped again when she noticed what it covered. "Oh, Adam!"

Adam's heart jumped in his chest. "If you'll have me. I'd follow you to Alaska or wherever you want. Just give me the chance."

"Alaska is a little too cold," she teased. "How about we stay right here, in Cedar Ridge, where we belong?"

"Sounds good." Adam's heart soared. He found the girl of his dreams, and she wasn't anything like his stupid checklist. She was everything he wanted...and more.

Placing the square-cut emerald ring flanked by two diamond chips on Laurel's trembling fingers, he couldn't stop his hands from shaking. "I'll do everything I can to make you happy. I promise."

They laughed while tears streamed her cheeks.

He looked up at the mistletoe dangling above, daring them to seal their promise. He winked at it and kissed her. Her lips had him soaring along with his heart, high above the sky, mimicking the pending fireworks display planned. Laurel was all the fireworks he needed to be a happy, happy man.

****

The sounds of the middle school chorus signaled the grand opening about to begin. Even though Laurel wanted to stay inside—alone with her new fiancé—they needed to finish what they started. Concentration on the rest of the festivities would be difficult because her open heart almost burst surrounded by love and happiness.

They stepped outside, noticing the sun had already set.

Even though the damp air smelled of snow and winter's early arrival, Laurel wasn't cold, not with Adam by her side and in her heart.

The school chorus' version of "Golden Bells" was drowned out by the marching band's rendition of

"Santa Claus is Watching."

Holding onto one another, Laurel and Adam walked to the end of the driveway to wait for the first unit to appear.

Coming closer, the grand marshal's car wasn't the first car.

"Oh, no!" The sight caused her to shudder, and she shot her gaze to Adam.

"What the h—" Adam stopped himself. "How did she pull that off?"

There, sitting atop the back seat of a convertible, Clarice posed, dressed in what appeared to be a vintage 1700s costume, waving to the crowd. Signs that read, *Cora Rutledge, Abigail's Mother*, were affixed to the car's two front doors.

"She is *unbelievable*." Laurel hung onto Adam's arm with one hand and slapped the other to her thigh. "Do we have to invite her to the wedding?"

"Nah." He plowed his fingers through his hair and slid them to the back of his neck. "We'll have a small, private wedding. Fifty of our closest friends and relatives. We can have it in Pembrook's barn. Tell everyone to keep it a secret."

"In this town?" Laurel scoffed. "I don't think anything goes on that she doesn't know about."

"Hey, there's Trevor Lawrence, our *Homegrown Superstar* in the second car." Adam pointed in that direction. "At least, she didn't rip the Grand Marshal sign off his car."

The parade stopped just at the manor's driveway, and the Ugly Sweater Singers and First Holy Church Choir joined the middle school chorus.

Mayor Winston Farley made his way toward the

podium where a mic was ready for the countdown. Visibly catching his breath, he gave a thumbs-up to Laurel and Adam with an approving nod.

After the marching band assembled at the back of the driveway, an SUV pulled alongside the drive entrance. With pride, Walter, Howard, and George carefully lowered themselves out of the vehicle decorated with signs that read, *Greatest Generation.*

Laurel and Adam guided them to the seats behind the podium toward the best viewing spot for the celebration.

George saluted. "It's an honor to see this opening through. Our mission is accomplished."

When the three gentlemen saluted her and Adam in unison, Adam returned the salute.

Laurel graced each with a smile and warm hug. "It's been our pleasure working with all of you. Thank you. We couldn't have done it without you."

Marching units, spectators, and friends passed, greeting and shaking hands in a grand-opening receiving line. And then the arrival of the man himself—Santa!

Donned in the traditional red suite, Lou's exceptional performance closed the holiday event riding atop the last firetruck where Todd and his fellow volunteer firefighters had affixed a bench to the roof decorated with greenery and lights. Lou rang a large, brass bell announcing his arrival followed by a boisterous "Ho Ho Ho!"

Everyone's efforts gratified Laurel with pride that, by pitching in, Cedar Ridge had a successful endeavor. The Laurel Wreath's business bloomed, and even though the village buzzed with tourists, Adam never looked happier.

Just then Pop and Joan joined them, bundled up with winter wear.

"It's cold, but not that cold." Laurel chuckled at the two, her own happiness increased because of the happiness Joan gave her father.

"Guess you didn't get the weather alert on your phone. Should be snowflakes coming any minute."

Laurel glanced toward the sky. The clouds were heavy except for a small patch where the night stars peeked down. *I know you're up there, Momma. I wish you were here. I've got so much to tell you.* She bet Momma knew before Laurel did that Adam was her one true love. She leaned her head on Adam's shoulder.

He placed a kiss at her temple. "You okay?"

"Yes." Her throat narrowed and her eyes prickled. Fate had her heart filled with so much joy and heaviness at the same time. "Just looking at the sky."

"She's in here, you know." He pointed to her heart. "She'll always be with you. Just like I will."

Wrapping both arms around his waist, she nuzzled her cheek against his chest. "How did I get so lucky to find you?"

"No." He pulled her in tight and kissed the top of her head. "I found you."

"Ah, no—" Backing her head from his chest, she gazed up at him. "I'm the one who approached you to convince you the manor was a good idea."

"But, *I'm* the one who opposed everything so you'd pursue me." He tapped his temple twice. "All part of my master plan."

She raised her eyebrows and threw a sideways smile. "Did I check all the boxes in your checklist?"

His eyes opened wide. "You knew about that?"

"Mmm, mm." She nodded. "Jeanine told me."

"That checklist was garbage. Once I got to know you, that list was history."

"What was history?" Jeanine greeted Laurel with a hug.

Laurel pointed to Adam. "His—"

"Oh…my…God!" She grabbed Laurel's hand. "Is that an engagement ring?"

With that, Pop, Joan, and Molly appeared, chattering, congratulating, and hugging her and Adam.

Mayor Farley approached. "Congratulations! This is wonderful news. But I have to break up this celebration. We have a countdown to get underway."

With that, the countdown began. Everyone cheered from ten to one, and then the mayor pushed the toggle switch. The lights on the darkened manor suddenly sparkled and glowed in concert with the fireworks shooting into the sky. The school chorus, the Ugly Sweater Singers, and the First Holy Church Choir were accompanied by the marching band with the song "Joy to Everyone." And on cue, festive snowflakes fell—the perfect addition to the celebration.

Laurel and Adam had done it. They worked together, butted heads together, and would now spend their lives together.

Adam's arm tightened across her shoulders, and watching the sky light up with bursts of color, they were serenaded by the sounds of Christmas. He guided Laurel's chin with a fingertip to gaze into her eyes. "I'll hold you for the rest of your life; and I won't let go. I promise."

And Laurel knew, with Adam, a promise was a promise. She'd found her Christmas miracle.

A word about the author…

Leigh Raffaele's life mirrors Goldilocks. Growing up in the suburbs was a little too soft. A short stint in the city, a little too hard. But a move to the country proved just right.

Married to her college sweetheart, she lives on a farm in a small town in the mountains of north-west New Jersey. With acres of ponds, pastures, and woodlands, 20+ goats and 50+ chickens, she juggles writing between a full-time job in municipal government, and plans and hosts events, weddings, and parties on her farm for guests who rent her Circa 1787 barn.

She experienced the adventure of her lifetime raising her three sons who grew up to be the models for the heroes in her books. Biased, as all grandmothers are, the adventure continues with her two beautiful granddaughters and two energetic grandsons who call her Farm Mama.

Leigh loves jigsaw puzzles, coloring, and is addicted to Hallmark movies and home rehab shows while struggling to become a better Italian cook.

To "talk" to Leigh about her books, small-town life, The Goats, her crazy obsession with her TV shows, or anything and everything (she's Italian…she loves to talk!), contact her at LeighRaffaele@aol.com or visit LeighRaffaele.com.

Thank you for purchasing
this publication of The Wild Rose Press, Inc.

For questions or more information
contact us at
info@thewildrosepress.com.

The Wild Rose Press, Inc.
www.thewildrosepress.com